Glass Tower

Glass Tower

by

Sarah Isaacs

www.hhousebooks.com

For my family
Inge, Colin, and Pedro

Paperback ISBN: 978-1-7391047-4-0

Cover design by Ken Dawson

Typeset by Julia B. Lloyd

Published in the UK

Holland House Books

Holland House

47 Greenham Road

Newbury, Berkshire RG14 7HY

United Kingdom

www.hhousebooks.com

Leilah

Sarah Isaacs

Chapter 1

The first time Leilah saw her, she thought Frankie was a boy in a skirt. Her legs ran in straight lines, into a straight waist and a long, straight neck. She looked like nothing scared her. Frankie was different to the other Grade 7 girls, twelve- and thirteen-years-olds who stood in clusters, untying and retying their ponytails, with a moment in between to let their hair fall loose about their shoulders while they glanced at a passing boy. Frankie didn't seem to notice boys.

She did notice Leilah, though, standing alone against a pillar at the edge of the schoolyard, her arms wrapped around the cold concrete as if hugging a tree. Frankie walked past with an amused smile and, with a click of her tongue and a cock of her head, invited Leilah to follow her. Leilah obeyed, because she had no one else to follow, and because she wanted some of Frankie's confidence, which she wore like a crown. The two girls went to their empty homeroom class and sat down, Frankie at the first table she passed, Leilah at the very back, next to a fig tree that was dying slowly in its pot.

"Do I stink?" Frankie asked. "Or is it because I'm new here?"

"No," Leilah said, her body lurching forward. "I'm new too. I just don't want to sit so close to the front." She dipped her head and started fiddling with her hands in her lap.

"Oh, I get it," Frankie said. "You're a scaredy cat. That's okay, I'll come to you." She walked back and sat down next to Leilah, her hips slipping easily into the narrow gap between the chair back and the edge of the desk. Her wrists

3

were fine as chicken bones and she was wearing Ingram's cream, a smell Leilah had always associated with her mother's cracked heels and weathered elbows. On Frankie, though, the camphor smelt different, musty-spicy like a cologne.

"Let's see what we've got here," Frankie said, opening the desk lid and peering in. "At my last school, I found a pack of highlighters, and the school before that an unopened bag of Chappies. Can you believe that! Took me two weeks to get through it all. I'll chew gum for ages, you know, even when the sugar's all out. And when it loses its juice, I'll stick another piece in, without taking the old one out. You can build a gobstopper of bubble-gum like that you know? So big your teeth – your whole mouth! – hurts." She smacked her lips and stuck out her hand. "I'm Frankie. Francesca actually, but I've never liked the full version. Don't know why my ma decided to give me an Italian name when she's the most Afrikaans person you'll ever meet. I hate that, you know, South Africans pretending to be international." Frankie turned her nose to the ceiling to denote an international person and Leilah giggled. "So, what's your name, scaredy cat?"

"I'm Leilah." She lowered her eyes again. There were a bunch of names and dates carved into the wood of their table, and Leilah ran her finger across them, trying to imagine herself there, for everyone to see. "Have you changed schools a lot?"

"Yes."

"Maybe...maybe you can teach me how to do it?"

"Sure," said Frankie, but she didn't sound so sure, and Leilah wondered if change was something she could learn to do, or if she'd have to get good at pretending.

The bell sounded and kids started filtering into class,

boys tucking white shirts into grey shorts, girls smoothing pale blue pinafores and straightening each other's name badges. The first few to enter went straight for a desk, knowing where and with whom they wanted to be for the rest of the year. No one seemed to notice Leilah and Frankie at the back, their blue jerseys blending into the blue wall, the slow overhead fan casting long shadows across their faces.

As the second bell rang, a barrel-shaped teacher with red hair and green eyes arrived in the doorway and, without looking at her class, walked over to the blackboard, her floating skirt at odds with her stoutness.

"Miss Caxton," she said as she wrote her name in oversized letters, filling the board the same way she filled the room. She turned to survey her class of 1997, scanning each face and stopping at Frankie and Leilah. "You must be the newcomers," she barked, squinting at them. "Didn't take long to find each other I see. What's wrong with our Kingston girls, not good enough for you?"

"I'm sure Kingston girls are very good!" Frankie said, scraping the floor with her chair as she stood up. Leilah's hand shot out to grab Frankie's finger, which was long and surprisingly cool. Miss Caxton didn't look like the kind of grown-up who would appreciate Frankie's confidence, but the skinny boy-girl didn't back down. She let Leilah hang onto her finger for a moment longer before shaking her loose and raising her hand to wave at the class, slow and deliberate, like the Queen. "I'm Francesca," she said. "But everyone calls me Frankie. It's so nice to meet you all." She did a slight bow and winked at Leilah, whose face had turned red under the spotlight of the class's stare.

The room was quiet. Sounds from the neighbouring classroom filtered in, soft laughter, pens rearranging in

Space Cases, chairs shuffling as students settled. Frankie kept turning her face slowly from one side of the room to the other, smiling at everyone before landing on Miss Caxton, whose short red hair made her look as though she'd been set alight.

"That's quite enough!" Miss Caxton said as their eyes met. "Stop that right now and sit down. Girl next to you, get up and introduce yourself."

Frankie kept standing, seemingly undeterred by Miss Caxton's sharp teeth and voice, and pulled Leilah up by the elbow. They stood side by side, close, so the hems of their uniforms touched. "It's okay," Frankie whispered. "Don't be scared."

Leilah took a breath, focusing on Miss Caxton and letting the rest of the faces in the room soften and melt to the edges of her eyeline. "Leilah. My name is Leilah. I moved here from Cape Town. This is the first school uniform I've ever had to wear." Two girls at the front started laughing, then two boys somewhere in the row she shared with Frankie, then two more, and two more, until the whole room was laughing. Leilah sat down. Her feet felt too big for her shoes.

Frankie sat down too. "Why did you tell them *that*?" she asked.

"I don't know, it just came out."

"Don't tell anyone anything you don't want them to know. That's the first rule of surviving somewhere new. You better stay close to me, unless you want to be eaten alive. That's what teenagers do you know, they eat other teenagers alive."

Leilah bent as far over as her tummy would allow, overcome by a painful sense of longing for Oak Tree, the Rudolf Steiner school she'd gone to back home. Leilah was sure Rudolf would never treat new students as Miss Caxton had just treated Frankie and her, making them into a spectacle for the rest of the class to ridicule.

"Come on," Frankie said, trying to pry Leilah loose from the tight ball she'd rolled herself into. "It's not that bad. These losers will forget about you soon enough. Look, they've already half forgotten."

Leilah peeked over the edge of their desk. Miss Caxton had her back to them again, writing out a timetable on the board, working around her giant name rather than rubbing it out. A few kids were still looking back at them and giggling, but most had started unpacking their bags and were comparing stationery.

"Why've you never worn a uniform before?" Frankie asked, trying her best to look serious. "You a home-school kid or something?"

"No, I went to a Rudolf Steiner school before this, and there was no uniform there. No exams or textbooks either and once a week we spent a whole period learning how to draw with our toes."

"Your toes?" Frankie said. "That's stupid."

Leilah nodded. It was stupid.

"This dress is so itchy."

Frankie looked at Leilah's pinafore and scrunched her nose disapprovingly. "Where'd you get that thing? It looks old."

Leilah's mom insisted they buy her uniforms from Kingston's second-hand shop, a damp little room at the back of the school, looked after by a grey-skinned lady who smoked while managing the cash register. Leilah's uniforms all smelt sour.

"It is old," she said, playing with the edge of her sleeve. "My mom's crazy."

Frankie laughed, and the sound of it lifted Leilah's chin, enough to see her new friend's hands resting on the table. She remembered the coolness of her fingers, and the straightness of her neck, and she raised her head a little more, to see Frankie's whole face, filling the room with its plainness.

At Oak Tree no one was treated as better than anyone else, and the kids were mostly kind. Anyone caught bullying was sent to the school therapist who sat patiently with them, encouraging them to draw or paint their anger until it turned into something beautiful. At Oak Tree, Leilah learnt to apologise and hug before she learnt to add or subtract. And even when the idea of math was introduced to her, she spent more time making things than doing sums. She made a cast of clay figurines to depict a world war. She painted the Greek gods and goddesses to memorise their stories. She learnt geometry by sketching complicated patterns with her compass and protractor. Subjects blended into each other like water colours, and the line between a good and a bad student was equally blurred.

Kingston Senior Primary was different. Leilah felt her insufficiency almost immediately, in the sideways looks the other students gave her, in their whispering and giggling, in Miss Caxton's loud voice and the ruler she held in her right hand, ready to come down on the head of any student who stepped out of line. There were no Coloured kids here, and having come from a brown neighbourhood and a half-brown family, Leilah wondered how that was possible. It was 1997 and though she'd heard news presenters speak of the new South Africa as a rainbow nation, Westville didn't look like a rainbow to her. There were only white kids in the class, and while Leilah could float along this pale sea and pass for one of its waves, she felt unsettled by the strange uniformity.

The school was a stacking of redbrick rectangles around two cement quads, flanked by two sports fields, one for the girls and one for the boys. At Oak Tree, Leilah had played basketball together with the boys, but here she could only play netball, a strange game, she thought, if you had to wear a skirt and couldn't run with the ball. Basketball players look strong dribbling across the court, but netball players – though tall and lean – looked powerless when they caught the ball, one foot pinned to the ground, flailing around in a cage of their own making.

Though co-ed, girls and boys seldom mixed. Classroom desks, which each seated two pupils, were grouped by sex; not an official school rule, but one that everyone stuck to. Anyone belonging to a group of three or five or seven was condemned to sit alone at a desk rather than share with the opposite sex, and so most groups were even numbered. Very rarely the odd boy and odd girl sat together in class, but they separated and disappeared at lunch, squeezed into toilet cubicles with their sandwiches, not belonging to anyone.

Kids were also separated by how smart they were.

"What level is she, Mr and Mrs Jacobs?" Principal Reid had asked Leilah's parents at their introductory meeting to Kingston Senior Primary. The man had looked puzzled, Leilah thought, his eyes darting between her parents and Leilah like they were from another country. As usual, her mother's round face had no make-up, her home-cut blonde hair was poorly brushed. She burped when she sat down, and made no apology. Her dad looked more formal at least, his salt-and-pepper beard neatly trimmed, his thick black curls combed to one side. He looked almost handsome,

Leilah had thought, his brown eyes matching his brown shirt and brown skin. Even his soccer-ball tummy appeared smaller, sucked in to accommodate his good leather belt, which he only wore on special occasions. Sitting between them, Leilah couldn't work out who Principal Reid found so strange, or if it was the three of them together that made him stare like that.

"He's Dwight."

"Ah—"

"And I'm Elke."

"Yes—"

"How should we know what level she's at?" Elke asked back, changing the cross of her bare legs and flashing the pale tops of her thighs, skin the sun didn't touch. She was wearing her faded green gardening shorts, and a pink vest that didn't cover her bra straps properly.

"Didn't her old school have levels?" Principal Reid asked, his already plump face ballooning in astonishment.

"No," Elke said. "The Rudolf Steiner system doesn't divide people into clever and smart. It doesn't divide people, period. Didn't you test her; wasn't that supposed to tell you what *level* she's at?"

Before being accepted into Kingston Senior Primary, Leilah had done three different tests at three different schools, and she found all of them confusing. Some questions were easy, basic adding and subtraction, while others laid out strange, nonsensical scenarios that she had to re-order and make sensical. How could a problem with so many possible solutions ever be answered wrong or right? She finished the tests feeling uneasy and unfinished and was surprised when Kingston accepted her.

"Those tests tell us something about a student's IQ," Principal Reid had said, straightening his tie. "But they're not conclusive. I thought you, as her parents, might offer some additional insight."

Leilah's dad looked up then, first at Elke then at Leilah, who was staring at a photo of Principal Reid's family hung high on the wall above him. "Excuse me Sir," he said softly, making first time eye contact with the man behind the desk. "Leilah's previous school was non-traditional, but it taught her everything you teach here, just a little differently. My daughter is a clever girl and a fast learner. Why not place her where you see fit for now and change her next year if necessary?" Principal Reid puckered his lips and eyes thoughtfully and with a nod of approval, stuck out his hand in the direction of Dwight, who returned the shake, but not the principal's gaze. He never looked strangers in the eye when saying hello or goodbye.

"Thanks Mathew," her mom said reading Principal Reid's first name from the plaque on his desk. "I'm sure Leilah will be just fine."

Leilah was placed in the "mixed ability" class, which came after the A, B, C and D classes. This stung a bit – was she stupid? – but when she met Frankie, she stopped caring. If having mixed abilities meant she could sit next to someone who wanted to sit next to her, she didn't mind.

"Why don't the Indian girls sit with the white girls?" Leilah asked between bites of an egg-mayo sandwich. It was first break, a week into the new year, and they were sitting on the highest step of the girls' pavilion, observing the patterns of friends. There were ten or so Indian girls and a handful of black girls in a field of two hundred, and they looked to Leilah like fresh cherries on an unbaked pie.

"Isn't that normal?" Frankie asked. "Don't people always sit separately?"

Leilah thought back to her old school and neighbourhood, trying to figure out if normal was the same everywhere. "I don't know," she said. "My dad's brown and my mom's German. Would they have to sit separately if they came here?"

Frankie sucked the last bit of juice from her apple and threw the core into a nearby bin, whistling triumphantly when it bounced off the edge and landed in the bag. "So, your dad's Indian?"

"No, he's Coloured."

"Oh," said Frankie, "we had Coloureds in Bloemfontein too."

"So, if there were Coloureds here," Leilah said, "would they have to sit separate from the Indian and the white girls, or just the white girls?"

Frankie threw her head back and laughed, showing off the delicate cleft in her chin that until now Leilah hadn't noticed. "They didn't teach you much at that funny school, did they? Too busy drawing with your toes." Leilah blushed and Frankie scooted closer towards her. "Look," she said, almost in Leilah's ear. "I think this place is different to what you're used to. I've never been to Cape Town, but where I'm from white people marry white people. There's one suburb in Bloemfontein, Heidedal, and all the Coloured people live and go to school in Heidedal. I think black kids might go there too, but the whites stick mostly to themselves. People like people who look the same as them, don't they?"

"I don't know," Leilah said, laying her arm next to Frankie's. "We don't really look the same."

"Ja, but we're new and we've got to stick together," Frankie said, pulling her jersey over her arm, though it was a hot day. "Have you seen that boy Dylan, from Joburg?

He's been here a whole year and he still sits alone, drawing stick men on his arms. They're not even good stick men. I don't want to be like him, do you?"

Leilah shook her head.

"So maybe don't say anything about your mom and dad being different. I don't mind it, but some kids might."

"But, won't people see that I'm a mix?" Leilah asked, confused.

"Not really," Frankie said. "You just look like a white girl with a tan."

"I guess," Leilah said. The conversation had begun to claw at her throat and she was running out of things to say. "Do you want to come to my house this weekend?" she asked, changing track. "We live right across the road from the beach."

"Sure," said Frankie. "I like the beach."

13

Chapter 2

While they looked for a suitable house to rent in Westville, and waited for their belongings to arrive from Cape Town, Leilah and her parents lived on the eighth floor of a furnished apartment block along North Beach. Leilah liked that the strip of beachfront was taken up mostly by hotels, ice cream parlours, and surf shops with only a handful of residential dwellings – some newly renovated, others cracking and sun bleached. For a short while at least, Durban felt like a holiday.

Leilah's block, Winston Heights, was one of the nicer ones she thought – burgundy façade, revolving entrance door and a mirror in the lift – but the plastic couch squeaked when she sat on it, and cockroaches scattered across the kitchen floor whenever the morning light flicked on. In Cape Town, she'd only lived in one place, an old farmhouse at the end of a cul de sac in Ottery, a dusty, outlying suburb, almost an hour's drive from any of Cape Town's turquoise beaches. When her family had gone to the coast, it was a special occasion – a whole day of simmering in the sun, eating warm tuna sandwiches, and making wigs out of seaweed. Living on North Beach was something different. There were no kids to play with, but there was also no day without the sea.

Now, for the first time, Leilah thought she understood what it meant to feel glamorous, sitting at the window of her new flat, watching and listening to the world below: couples kissing and arguing, ice-cream trucks singing, the ocean flapping in the distance. There was an amusement park directly across the road, with a Ferris wheel that sparkled at night. Next to it was a waterpark with slippery slides and a pathway of stepping stones curving elegantly from one side of the pool to the other. In Ottery, Leilah wasn't allowed to leave the cul-de-sac alone but here she navigated the elevator, crossed the street, and hopped across the pool without supervision, enjoying the moment of suspension between each stone.

On Fridays she got five rand from her dad, which she usually spent on candyfloss. She ate the pink fluff sitting on a bench below the Ferris wheel, looking at the lights change colour and scraping lumps of sugar from the back of her teeth. Once she bought a pineapple skewer from a wrinkled Indian man with a push-along cart covered in bells and pocket-size photos of his family. She chose a skewer with a dusting of red spice.

"Masala pineapples," the seller said with a cigarette-stained smile. "Only on North Beach!" The spice burned her lips and she had to throw most of the skewer in the bin, but she liked the way "masala" rolled off her tongue and she repeated it to herself many times as she walked back to the flat.

Leilah imagined North Beach to be much better than Frankie's hometown Bloemfontein, which she remembered as small and hot, with no mountains or coastline, and a dry wind that distorted people's faces. Leilah had only been there once, on the drive from Cape Town to Durban, and they'd stayed at a hotel with a pink foyer and a receptionist who never smiled. The petrol attendant who filled their tank also didn't smile, nor did the Wimpy waitress who poured their Coca-Colas. Leilah figured the whole of Bloemfontein must be grumpy and she wondered how Frankie, who smiled at most things and most people, survived there all those years. She couldn't wait to show her

North Beach. Candyfloss and spinning teacups would suit her better than a dry nose and joyless Cokes.

"Leilah, Frankie, over here!" Leilah's mom, waving furiously, had half her body hanging out of their Toyota Corolla.

"Hurry up," Leilah said, "before she gets out and really embarrasses me."

The inside of the car was cool, the aircon dial turned all the way up, a luxury Elke never afforded Leilah. She always drove with the windows wide open, even when it was raining, but now they were wound all the way up and the car's interior smelt like pine needles. A new air freshener hung from the front mirror, shaped like a Christmas tree.

"What a relief to be out of the heat," Frankie said primly as she climbed in. "Thank you so much, Mrs Jacobs."

"Please, call me Elke. Never liked being a Mrs, not even when I was teaching. You must be Frankie. Can't say I know much more than that but look forward to getting under your skin this weekend Frankie. I'm sure we'll get on great." Elke grinned and Leilah squirmed. Why couldn't her mom just say *how are you* and offer them a sweet?

"Mom," she mumbled, casting Elke a sideways look. "Please, just be normal."

"That's rich," Frankie said, squeezing Leilah's shoulder through the arms of the headrest. Elke smiled, wide as a wedge of watermelon, and when Frankie copied her, Leilah felt obliged to do the same. Her mom turned on the radio and tuned into the Indian music station, bopping her head to the tinny instruments and foreign lyrics like she'd known Indians all her life. She had pink lipstick smeared onto her cheeks, black lines under her wide green eyes, and a clip with a heart on it holding back her fringe. It must have been for Frankie's benefit, thought Leilah, and although the makeup looked like a child's painting, it felt nice that her mom had tried.

The first thing Frankie commented on when they arrived at the flat was the bed in Leilah's room. "That's going to be a snug fit," she said, plonking her weekend bag and taking in the rest of her surroundings. There was a dressing table at one end of the room, dark wood with a shiny finish, and a velvet upholstered stool that Leilah thought to be very grown-up. The only other piece of furniture was a two-door cupboard with floral knobs, white except for the fingerprint smudges around each handle. There was a small window above the bed, too high to see out of and not quite big enough to light up the whole room. A picture of an Arum lily hung skew on the wall.

"Where's your stuff?" Frankie asked.

"What stuff?" Leilah said, taking off her shoes.

"Your posters and things."

"I don't know, my parents are keeping it somewhere while we find a place to stay in Westville."

"Your dad didn't find a place before you moved?" Frankie asked.

"He did," Leilah said. "This is it." Leilah didn't like the way Frankie was looking at her room, which until now she'd thought of as cool, like a Holiday Inn. "Let's go down to the beach," she said, eager to leave before Frankie saw something else she didn't like.

Frankie sat on the edge of the bed and threw her blazer over her legs while she took off her underwear and slipped on her swimsuit. Once it was above her hips, she pulled her pinafore over her head, and unbuttoned her shirt. She was wearing a training bra underneath, two beige triangles covering a perfectly flat chest. Frankie stood up and pulled her swimsuit over her bra, looping the straps over her shoulders before unclipping the triangles and taking them off. She stood up, her body even straighter and thinner than Leilah had imagined, long pale lines leading into the floor.

"Don't you wear bras?" Frankie asked when Leilah pulled off her own uniform and stood in the middle of the room wearing nothing but a pair of panties.

"I don't need one yet," Leilah said, looking at her breasts, which were little more than a pair of chubby nipples. None of her friends back home wore bras. It was only one summer ago that she got her first bathing suit, before then she'd just swum in her bottoms. Feeling self-conscious, she grabbed her suit and pulled it on over her panties, the same way Frankie had pulled hers over her bra.

"All girls need bras," Frankie said, chuckling as Leilah tried to yank her panties down from under her bathing suit. "You've got to do one leg at a time silly. That way no one can see your fanny."

"Fanny?" Leilah repeated in a posh accent, sipping from an imaginary tea cup. "Oh fanny, oh fanny, oh fanny!" She fell to the floor giggling and lifted her legs straight into the air. "You do it if you're such an expert," she said and Frankie did, bending Leilah's knees one at a time as she pulled off her undies, which were covered in daisies, orange and yellow.

There was a Friday night special at the beachfront amusement park, thirty rand for all the rides you could ride, and Leilah had convinced her dad to pay for them by sitting on his lap and lighting his cigarette, like she'd done as a little girl. "Of course, sweetie," he'd said, pulling notes from his wallet, "as long as you girls stay safe."

Leilah pushed the money under the metal grate of the ticket counter. "Two please," she said, staring into the hollow eyes of the saleswoman and trying to hold her nerve. She wanted Frankie to see how grown-up she was – standing in the queue, handling money – but Frankie had wandered off to look at the Ferris wheel, leaving Leilah alone with the sour-faced woman and a fidgety string of people behind her, waiting to be served.

"You need a grown-up with you," the woman said. "Where are your parents?"

"I'm thirteen," she lied. "Your sign says I'm allowed if I'm thirteen."

"C'mon lady, just give her the tickets," a man behind Leilah said, leaning into the small of her back. "She's old enough, aren't you girlie?" She looked up and saw the bottom of the man's chin, connected to his neck in sunburnt folds.

"Park closes at nine," the ticket lady said pushing two perforated stubs towards Leilah while keeping her eyes fixed on the man behind. "Don't let me catch you hanging around any later than that. Next!"

They rode the spinning teacups and flying swings three times each before Frankie vomited a mix of candyfloss, cream soda and potato chips into a dustbin. She seemed okay once it was all out so they did the Sky Way before going home, a two-seater bench that floated high above the other rides in slow circles.

"Will be nice and cool up there," Leilah said looking at the dangling swing chairs. "Are you afraid of heights?"

Frankie rolled her eyes like she wasn't afraid of anything, but when the bench lifted them off the ground and the operator pulled down the bar to hold them in place, she squeezed Leilah's hand and didn't let go.

"How come you've changed schools so many times?" Leilah asked once they were off the ground and the sounds of the amusement park had receded. Frankie loosened her fingers but kept hold of Leilah's hand, looking at an unseeable point somewhere in the distance. They stayed like that for ages, Leilah adjusting to the silence between them, which Frankie usually filled with jokes and songs and clicks of her tongue.

"I had a friend in Bloem – Magda – and we did everything together," Frankie said eventually. "Her dad and my dad were big church buddies, always getting together and talking about the Bible. We just nodded our heads when they asked us something about God, and usually that was the right answer. That's what they wanted from us, to sit on our knees at their feet and nod our heads. We got away from them whenever we could, pretended to do homework so that we could sit in my room or hers and talk about normal stuff, like cartoons and all the things we'd do if we weren't kids. We did everything together at school – shared a desk, shared lunch, shared notes on the ugliest boys in class. On my twelfth birthday, my dad said we could go to the arcade. He gave me ten rand for tokens and from the tickets we won, I got Magda a teddy bear. She looked at me like I was the nicest person on earth when I gave her that teddy, like no one in the world could be her friend like I was her friend. It got cold while we were sitting on the pavement waiting for my dad to fetch us and Magda didn't have a jersey, so I put my arm around her and when she put her head on my shoulder, I put my head on top of hers and my hand in her lap to keep warm. It felt nice, I remember, our two heads like that, with the teddy between us. I must have closed my eyes because the next thing I knew my dad's car was in front of us, right there, by our feet, his lights were flashing on and off, and his hand was down on the hooter. I could feel the heat from the engine through my sandals and the horn sounded like someone screaming. We jumped up and got into the car, me in the front and Magda in the back, and my dad didn't say anything the whole way home. I thought something was wrong with my mom, or Magda's mom, but didn't want to ask because dad's face was so tight, and I couldn't tell if he was worried or angry. The next day I didn't go to school, and a week after that I was transferred. Magda couldn't visit me any more, and I couldn't phone her either. At church my dad held my hand until we reached our pew, always a few rows ahead of Magda, and he held it again when service was over, until we were back in the car. My parents never said anything about anything, except my mom once – *little girls aren't meant to love little girls* – and a few months after that we moved to Durban."

From above, the beachfront looked like the inside of a snow globe, colourful and distant. Leilah couldn't imagine the hollow-eyed ticket lady, or the sweaty man pushing against her, or a father hooting at his daughter. There was only the smell of fresh popcorn, Frankie's long fingers interlaced with hers, and the faraway cry of kids on the rollercoaster.

That night Leilah slept askew on the tiny bed, forcing Frankie onto the floor where she wrapped herself in two damp towels that had been hanging on the door. They spent the whole of the next day lying on the beach, limbs sprawled out as if they were making snow angels, and when they walked home, they passed a freshly dead man lying much the same way. Frankie stood transfixed by the blueing body – its faded red Speedo, its thin legs and big belly, its sunglasses tan – as if it were something in a museum. Though Frankie sleeping on the floor and the dead man sleeping on the sand made Leilah feel lonely, they were not what stuck out when she remembered that weekend. What she remembered more clearly than anything was the cool clutch of Frankie's hand while they floated above the city in their swing chair, how quietly they sat together after Frankie shared her story of Magda, and how easy the quietude had felt.

Chapter 3

"How's school, baby?" Dwight asked Leilah on the way to school the following week. Usually, her mom dropped her off and picked her up, but her dad needed the car for an out-of-town meeting that day, a fact he'd casually sprung on Leilah over breakfast. "Do you feel different than you did back home?"

Leilah did feel different, mostly towards him. She'd stopped talking to her dad about school and her classmates, and when he walked in on conversations between her and Elke, she stopped what she was saying and busied herself with homework. She never wanted to leave her home and had pleaded with him every night for months to find work in Cape Town instead. She'd left letters in his briefcase, listing people Dwight could ask for help, colleagues he'd mentioned, family members living abroad. She didn't know how much debt they were in or how many times he'd already borrowed money from the people on her list.

Distancing herself from her dad, Leilah felt like an ice cream melting. Dwight had always been the one she felt most like. They both looked at the floor when meeting someone new. They both liked three sugars in their tea. They both rolled their r's between their tongue and palate. They both had purple gums, not pink like her mom's. In Cape Town she liked it when Elke said she took after her dad but now, in Westville, she wasn't so sure.

"I feel the same," Leilah lied. "Just getting used to the changes. Do you feel different?"

"I feel the same, sweetie," her dad replied without thought. "I miss Motheo, but I'm happy to have you with me, and the dog, but don't tell Mum that, she'll think I'm a softie." He smiled as two long jets of smoke exited his nostrils and got sucked through the open crack in his window.

Leilah missed her brother too. He was from Elke's first marriage so he had a different dad, but he'd been there when Leilah was born so she never thought of him as anything but her whole brother, even though they looked quite different and they were ten years apart in age. Everyone liked Motheo. He could walk into a room of strangers and speak to any one of them without looking at his feet or saying sorry for no reason. When she was with her brother, Leilah felt a bit bigger than she was, even though he farted in her face and called her a pipsqueak. Leaving Motheo behind was one of the hardest parts of leaving Cape Town, especially now that he'd moved across the ocean to work in a place called Berlin, where his real dad, his white dad, lived.

"I also miss him," Leilah said as they passed a huge church with an electrified billboard inviting them to join Jesus. "Dad, do you miss church?"

"Church?" Dwight said with a chuckle. "Haven't been since Mum and I got married. Why do you ask?"

"At school we have to sing the Lord's Prayer at the start of assembly. Everyone knows the words, but I have to look at my hymn book. Why didn't Oak Tree teach me such an important song?"

"They didn't want you to sing something you didn't believe in." Dwight threw his cigarette butt out and wound up the window with smoke still inside.

"But what if I do want to believe in God? Aunty Millie said I'll go to hell if I don't and from the way the prefects look at me when I read from my hymn book, I think she must be right."

"Don't listen to Auntie Millie, she's got no business talking to you about hell. Do you want to go to church?"

Leilah rolled down the window and sucked in the humid air, though it wasn't much fresher than the thick smoke in the car. "I want to sing the prayer like everybody else," she replied. As they approached the school gates, Leilah bent down and pretended to arrange the books in her backpack. "Keep going," she said, head still down, "I'm not ready. There's a place for you to pull over a little further along."

"I hoped to come in and take a look at your classroom," Dwight said as the gates got further and further away. "Maybe meet your friends."

"My classroom's boring," Leilah said, her voice muffled. "And Frankie is my only friend."

"Okay baby," Dwight said. "No sweat." He drove a little further, then pulled over on the side of the road, into a yellow line. "There's nowhere to park so I'll just let you out here, okay?"

Leilah lifted her head slightly and climbed out of the car without speaking, still half bent over. Her bag scraped the tarmac as she swung it onto her shoulders.

"See you later, baby, I'll be back to pick you up at three."

"Bye, Dad," Leilah said. "You can pick me up here. I don't like waiting with the whole school." She slammed the door and walked away on the passenger's side. She could feel him watching her as she disappeared into a crowd of blue pinafores and crisp white shirts.

The day was long and worrisome. Leilah couldn't focus on her math test, or listen to Frankie's longwinded stories about nothing in particular. She couldn't even enjoy her chicken-mayo sandwich from the tuckshop, which was worlds better than the thick-bread-and-tomato lunches her mom made. The last and only time Leilah's dad had picked her up from school, she'd seen how the other kids had looked at him. Was their scorn for Leilah or Dwight, or were they both equally out of place in this new world of separated colours? Leilah bit her lips raw through the school day, and ran out of her final class without saying goodbye to Frankie. Her dad was half an hour late to pick her up, time she spent hidden behind a tree at the spot where he'd dropped her that morning. He offered some excuse about meetings running late, but she was too busy checking the mirrors for onlookers to care. She ducked into the passenger seat, and sank down until only her forehead was visible.

Sunrise Holdings took up the tenth floor of a glass façade building along Maydon Wharf, overlooking Durban Harbour. Though he seldom took the car, Dwight had his own parking bay, with a laminated name plaque stuck to the wall, and he pulled into it now, careful not to scrape his neighbours.

"Thanks for coming with me sweetheart. I just have one more meeting and then we can go home." He always said things like this – one more meeting, one more month of working late, one more pay check until you get your new bike – and Leilah knew not to believe it. "You can sit in the spare conference room, it's very nice, and I'll ask Naseema to make you a hot chocolate."

Leilah had accompanied Dwight to lots of different jobs. Construction sites, office parks, malls, even a church. She knew he worked on getting peoples' money in order but didn't understand why a job involving numbers could be so wishy-washy. Her dad was always vague when he spoke about work and money; how much he had and how much he owed remained a mystery. He only gave her mom what she needed for groceries and electricity, and if he didn't have it, there'd be a fight, followed by a dinner of buttered toast and tea. While Leilah never got used to the sound of raised voices, she'd grown accustomed to unsteady money. Her dad never stopped chasing the next big thing.

"Good morning, Mr Jacobs," Naseema said as the glass doors to Sunrise Holdings' reception area slid open. Leilah gasped as she stepped onto the plush carpet; she could feel it yielding beneath her feet. Big windows let in more natural light than she'd ever seen in one space, and unlike the stained chairs and cheap air freshener of Dwight's previous employers, this place looked and felt like she imagined successful places to look and feel.

"You must be Leilah," Naseema cooed, her voice soft and kind. "Your dad speaks about you all the time, how well you're doing in school. It's a pleasure to meet you."

The reception desk was unnecessarily high and Leilah had to stand on her toes to catch a glimpse of the sugar-voiced woman. She was pretty, a diamond-shaped face wrapped in a floral-print headscarf, her skin the colour of tea. "Nice to meet you too," Leilah mumbled, looking down at her scuffed shoes and noticing that her dad's were just as worn.

"Can I get you two a cup of coffee?" Naseema asked, her attention shifting from Leilah to Dwight.

"That'd be delicious, thanks Naz. And a hot chocolate for Leilah, if we have." Dwight looked at Naseema and Leilah noticed how his eyes circled the circumference of her face, as though he were looking at a painting he liked. "Nice hijab today," he continued, sounding different than he did speaking to Elke. "I like the flowers."

"Well, you know, us girls have got to keep things fresh,

don't we, Leilah?" Naseema grabbed an Endearment from the bowl on the counter and held it down to Leilah as she waited for an answer.

"I wear the same uniform every day. Why are you asking me?" Leilah ignored the chewy mint, and readjusted her backpack as if she had some important work to do. She didn't like the way *Naz* sounded coming out of her dad's mouth. It was too short and sweet. Too familiar.

Dwight took the mint, apologising for his daughter with a slow nod, and headed towards his office. "I'll bring your drinks now-now," Naseema said as they walked off, and Dwight hurried on, smoothing the back of his shirt as he walked.

"Take a seat, baby. Naseema will take you to the conference room when she brings your hot chocolate."

Leilah looked around her dad's cramped office for a place to sit. It was a small square, with a window that overlooked a narrow side street. "Smells like an ashtray in here, Dad," Leilah said, moving some boxes off an old grey chair so she could sit down.

"You're absolutely right, young lady, it does smell like an ashtray, a dirty one!" A short, well-dressed man was suddenly in the doorway, leaning against the frame with his hands slipped casually into his pockets. Dwight had just settled into his swing chair, and struggled out of it again, his tummy knocking the edge of the desk as he stood up. He looked at his boss, then at Leilah, and blushed.

"Ag sorry man, Mr Kassem," he said. "Smoking helps with the job."

"Please! Call me Khalid. So, tell me, how's it going? The whole office is raving about you, they say you're better at numbers than I am at closing deals. Ha! If you weren't on my payroll, I'd be offended." Mr Kassem chuckled and sat on the edge of Dwight's desk, moving papers and an ashtray to make room.

"Going well, Mr Kassem, I mean Khalid, Sir. I'm starting to make sense of the books, and I'm enjoying it." Leilah could tell her dad was fibbing.

"Good man," Mr Kassem said, nodding his head approvingly while looking out the window at the grey building opposite. "I knew you were right for this job, someone who can make the numbers work." He looked over to Leilah. "You're a quiet little thing, aren't you? Must get that from your dad." He was pointing his finger at Leilah as if she were a bird in a cage and she noticed how clean and trim his nails were, how smooth his hands. Leilah looked at her dad to say something for her but Dwight remained quiet. "Nothing wrong with keeping to yourself," Mr Kassem continued. "Just means you have to find a job, and a lifestyle, that suits you. Nothing like my job. I have to be out there shaking people's hands all the time, talking about some thing or another. It's my job to talk." Leilah had never thought of herself as having a *lifestyle*. It sounded like the island and palm trees on a bottle of sunscreen.

Naseema knocked on the door and poked her head in.

"Come in, Naz," Mr Kassem said, reaching his arms out towards her. "Is that for me?"

"It's for Mr Jacobs and Leilah but I can make you a cup." Naseema's feet remained outside the door, her blossom-wrapped face poking inside.

"Well then, bring it in. No one likes a cold coffee." Naseema came in and, taking small steps around the boss, walked to Dwight's side of the desk and placed the cups down amongst his piles of paper. "Don't be in such a hurry," Mr Kassem said as Naseema made her way back to the door. "Come here and give me a hug." He slid off

Dwight's table and wrapped an arm around Naseema's shoulders. "I'm so lucky to have both of you working for me." It was quiet until a pigeon pecked at the glass and broke the silence. Leilah's shoulders dropped as she remembered to breathe. "Would you look at the time," Mr Kassem said, peering past Naseema's nose towards his watch. "Bring that coffee to the conference room will you, Naz, I've got calls to make. Nice to meet you, young lady." Once he'd left the office and she watched her dad smoke a cigarette – one drag after another, before the old smoke had left his mouth – she knew for sure she hated him, this small suited man with the busy mouth and silky hands.

"Dad," Leilah said on the car ride home, "why are you are working for that man? He gives me the creeps."

"The *creeps*," Dwight said, smiling like she'd said something funny. "Why do you say that, baby?"

"He just doesn't seem like a nice man," Leilah said.

"He's an important man," Dwight said. "One of the best businessmen in South Africa, good enough to work for Jacob Zuma."

"So," Leilah said, unimpressed. "Who's Jacob Zuma?"

"He's a high-flying politician," Dwight said, a pride to his tone that Leilah didn't recognise. "He might even become president one day."

"Why does that matter?"

"It matters because I want to buy you and Mum a house. And if I work for a man that works for the president, I'll be able to do that."

"But lots of people who don't work for the president buy houses."

"Maybe," Dwight said, lighting another cigarette. "But I haven't managed to."

"But you work late every night," Leilah said. "Isn't that

enough to buy a house?"

"That's not how the world works, baby," Dwight said, flicking ash into an old jam can that Elke had stuck to the dashboard with Prestik.

"How does the world work?"

"It works if you know important men; big men like Mr Kassem and Mr Zuma."

"And you're sure Mr Kassem is a big man?" Leilah asked, thinking back to how short he was.

"He's the biggest man I'll ever work for," Dwight said, flicking his cigarette out the window instead of putting it into the tin.

Chapter 4

"You're a real coward, Leilah Jacobs!" Frankie yelled across the girls' sports field. Leilah was standing a few metres away and other girls were filtering onto the grass behind her, paying no attention to Frankie, though Leilah was sure they were listening. She always thought people were listening, so she spoke most of the time in whispers, driving Frankie mad. "You're a coward and liar!"

Leilah stared pathetically at her feet. It had started that morning, in the same corner of the quad where Frankie had first spotted Leilah. It was where they met every morning before school. "I learnt the water cycle by heart yesterday," Leilah had said, grinning proudly. "Now we can spend this whole weekend hanging out."

"Big deal." Frankie had replied.

Every time someone got an A on a test, Miss Caxton stuck a gold star on the achievements board and by the sixth week of term, Leilah had the most out of everyone while Frankie didn't have any. Jack Bertram, a chubby boy with cresting hair and flushed cheeks, started calling Leilah "teacher's pet" when she stuck her hand up to answer a question, so now she leaned over and whispered the answers to Frankie instead. No one called Frankie names – not after she told Jack Bertram to suck her middle finger – so she put up her hand for Leilah because Leilah liked hearing her answers out loud and she thought Frankie liked saying them. That morning in Geography class Miss Caxton had asked who could recite the water cycle. As usual Leilah had leaned over and with a whisper, explained evaporation and precipitation to Frankie, though she didn't seem to get it. Believing Frankie could look at the picture and turn it into words, Leilah had pushed a drawing of the water cycle in front of her and nudged Frankie to stick up her hand. She did, and when Miss Caxton said "Yes?" Frankie had said "Nothing" because nothing was apparently all she knew about the water cycle.

"I've had it with you disrupting my class, Francesca," Miss Caxton had yelled, moving quicker than Leilah had seen any lady her size move. Before she could say anything in Frankie's defence, Miss Caxton had Frankie by the ear, dragging her out the classroom like a bag of wet rubbish. Leilah hadn't followed. She'd just sat and stared at her drawing, repeating the water cycle to herself until it no longer made sense.

Now she stood in the open field, asking for forgiveness but saying nothing. Frankie looked too angry to forgive. Frankie never let herself feel embarrassed, not since Hennie Kotze called her a boy and kicked her in the crotch, but when Miss Caxton had dragged her out of class like that, Frankie's cheeks had turned the colour of shame. "I'm sorry Frankie," Leilah said, moving in big-small-small steps towards her. "It all happened so fast, I didn't know what to do."

"That's your problem, Leilah, you never do anything. You leave the hard work to me and act like you're the smart one. I buy us lunch at the tuckshop. I speak for you in class. I tell the bullies to leave you alone. What would you do without me, hey? I'm the only person here that you're not scared of *and* the only one that's actually willing to sit with you. Don't you think it's unfair, that you get to be weird while I get dragged out of class? Look! That lunatic nearly ripped my earring out. It won't stop throbbing." Gingerly, Leilah got closer and when Frankie didn't pull away, she held her friend's ear in her fingers like a butterfly.

"Do you want me to get you an ice lolly?" Leilah asked, knowing how much Frankie loved sugar. "The cold will help with the swelling."

"How are you going to get me an ice lolly?" Frankie shot back, though not entirely spiteful. "Half the school will be queueing at the tuckshop by now."

"Less chance of seeing Jack Bertram's nasty face if half the school is there," Leilah said, trying to smile. "Meet you behind the recycling bins?"

Frankie gave Leilah a once-over before answering, tracing her wide shoulders, her thick legs, her square feet. "Get me a blue lolly," she said after the excruciating examination, "and don't let it melt."

After they sucked all the sugar out of their popsicles, and compared the colour and length of their tongues, Frankie pulled a box of Lion matches out of her pocket. "Ever smoked before?" she asked, shaking the box and wobbling her head from side to side.

"Not really," Leilah said. "Once I put my dad's half-smoked cigarette between my lips and, another time, I rolled up a piece of paper, lit one end and sucked the other. Both tasted gross."

"Smoking matches is different," Frankie said. "It makes your head feel empty for a second; it's nice. Here, I'll show you." Frankie lit a match, inhaling the faint plume of smoke it made when hitting the strike pad. She lit another two and did the same thing, before leaning back against the orange recycling depot and closing her eyes. "Tastes like sulphur," she said passing Leilah the box. "Now you try."

Leilah thought of chemistry class, how bad sulphur smelt and how bad it would probably taste, then took the box and struck a match, sucking as hard as she could, eyes squeezed shut to stop them from burning. The smoke went in but didn't come out and it left a sour taste on her tongue, lemon mixed with chlorine. "I like it," she said, leaning back like Frankie.

"Of course, you do," Frankie said, opening her eyes for a second and sparing Leilah a glance. "Your eyes change colour you know?" she said after a while. "Sometimes they're blue, sometimes they're green and sometimes they even look grey. It depends on the weather. I figured it out the other day, when the clouds came in and your irises turned to concrete."

"Oh," said Leilah. "No one's told me that before."

The two girls stayed quiet against the recycling bins for the rest of lunch, Leilah occasionally opening and closing her eyes, letting the clouds imprint on the back of her lids and wondering which of her colours Frankie liked best.

Chapter 5

Over the course of their first summer together, Leilah learnt about Frankie and Frankie seemed to learn about Leilah too. They started to like and dislike each other in the way that friends do, spitting at each other one moment, giggling the next. Leilah let Frankie brush her hair, which was otherwise bound into a tight bun, Leilah's middle parting so straight that it cut her head in half. They sat together in Leilah's lounge after school, Frankie on the couch, Leilah on the floor between her legs, watching *Days of Our Lives*. Frankie had to pull hard to get the brush through Leilah's thick curls and frizzy underbits, but when Leilah got sucked into TV, she switched off, and Frankie could tug and yank to her heart's content.

They were always at Leilah's, first the North Beach apartment, then a rented house in Westville with faded peach walls and an oblong pool. They spent Saturday and Sunday afternoons lying around the pool like lizards, Leilah brown and stocky, Frankie pale and slender. Sometimes they reached across the warm terracotta tiles to hold hands, other times they lay at opposite ends of the pool, mad about one thing or another. It was mostly Frankie who got mad with Leilah – for being selfish, for slurping her cornflakes milk, for speaking like a mouse – but sometimes Leilah got angry too, and when she did, she threw stuff, once a honey pot that hit the ground and made a sticky mess, another time the half-orange that she'd been practicing her kissing on. *You're doing it wrong* was all Frankie had to say for the orange to come flying towards her, hitting her on the forehead and leaving a wet splodge.

Frankie's place was mostly off limits except for the

occasional Sunday when her parents, Sunette and Christo, went to see friends and left their daughter alone. "Come over *now,*" Frankie screeched happily into the phone the first time it happened, taking Leilah by surprise.

"I thought your parents hated me," Leilah said, afraid of what she might walk into.

"They don't hate you exactly," Frankie said. "They'd just prefer me to have normal friends, friends that go to church and don't speak to the ground."

"If your mom thinks I'm so awful, why does she let you hang out at my house every weekend? Maybe's she's the horrible one, have you ever thought of that?" Leilah hated it when Frankie called her abnormal.

"I think about that all the time," Frankie said. "My mom is horrible. Now hurry up and get over here, before the witch gets back and ruins everything."

Comforted by the idea that Frankie's mom was a worse person than her, Leilah put down the phone and ran out the door, her head swimming with made-up images of Frankie's forbidden home. When she got there, it was nothing like she imagined but also not unfamiliar. Frankie's house looked to Leilah like the background to a photo she'd seen many times. All the furniture had turned legs, the couch had no lumps and the walls were pure white. There was a polished cross on the kitchen wall, and above Frankie's bed a framed picture of Jesus, his hands and forehead bloodied, eyes rolled back in boredom or pain. The other three walls of her bedroom were covered from floor to ceiling in surfing pictures. The turquoise waves and Frankie's pink bedding made Leilah think of soft serve so that when she stepped into the cosy space for the first time, she licked her lips without meaning to.

"Do you like my room?" Frankie asked, her brow unusually furrowed.

"It feels like you."

After that Frankie invited Leilah over as often as she could, sometimes just for an hour when her mom went to the shops.

As summer was drawing to an end and Durban's wet air started drying out for winter, Basia and Norman flew to Durban to visit Leilah's parents. It was unusual for Dwight and Elke to host or socialise, but these two were more family than friends. Basia was Elke's only remaining schoolmate from Germany, and Norman had gone to a university for Coloureds with Dwight. Both friends were shaped the same, with legs that looked like toothpicks and gigantic upper halves, and both liked to drink and smoke hundreds of cigarettes. Leilah's mom joked that Basia and Norman were two halves to the same nut but could never fall in love for they would surely kill each other with their drinking and their smoking and their sameness.

"It will be fun to go away together this weekend," Elke said at the breakfast table on the morning of Basia's arrival. "Is Frankie excited that she's coming along?"

"Ja," Leilah said. "She's excited about driving in a Kombi."

"I don't know why Basia insisted on hiring such a big car," Dwight said into his bowl of cornflakes. "We could have squeezed into our Toyota quite easily."

"Don't be ridiculous," Elke shot back. "Basia and Norman would take up our car just by themselves. Anyway, she loves showing off her divorce money and I don't see you complaining when she brings you expensive whiskey." Elke caught Dwight's eyes just before they dipped into his cornflakes again.

"I can't say no to good whiskey. But I don't like the way

that woman looks at me when she gives me something, like a bug she can squash. She thinks I'm spineless."

"Then show her you aren't," Elke said, getting out of her chair to wash the breakfast dishes.

"Looks like you've put on some weight!" Basia roared from her seat at the kitchen table when Leilah got home from school that afternoon. She didn't get up but thrust her arms into the air so that Leilah would hug her, which she did with some reluctance, her satchel losing its balance on her hips and falling awkwardly over her head.

"She's a growing girl," Elke said, scooping her daughter into a proper hug, and giving her a small wink that said it was okay. "Basia's in your room, so you'll have to sleep on a mattress in ours. Is that okay?" The question was only for show. Leilah had been sleeping at the foot of her parents' bed for weeks now. The first time it happened, she'd curled into a ball on the bare floor but now a sheeted mattress leaned permanently against her parents' only bedroom window, blocking out the warm afternoon light. "What happened?" Elke had asked that first morning she found Leilah on the floor. "I can't sleep with all the new noises," Leilah replied, and her mom had left it at that. Though Leilah blamed Elke for almost everything that was wrong with her, she appreciated her mom's acceptance of her peculiarities. Frankie would never be allowed to be a such a scaredy-cat. From what she knew of Christo and Sunette, they would – or had – beaten the wobblies right out of her.

"We'll leave straight after school tomorrow," Elke said to Leilah. "Why don't you get all your packing done now so that you're not rushing in the morning? Go on, I'll come check on you in a bit."

"Stay!" Basia shrieked, hopping up from her chair and

spilling beer onto her purple kaftan. "I want to hear all about Durban!"

"Liar," Elke said, grinning. "You don't want to listen; you just want to talk. Let the poor girl go, I'm here to entertain you, Frau." Together the women started laughing, heads thrown back, bosoms shaking like big bowls of jelly. Leilah took one step backwards, then another, slowly, slowly, until she was out of sight. She felt small in Basia's presence and was happy that her mom had kept the mattress arrangement quiet. Usually, Elke treated family secrets like any other conversation point, throwing them out with no care of where or how they would land. But with Basia, her mom was different, more restrained. It was like she was trying to be one of those moms in the TV shows – joyful, accommodating, funny, sweet. Leilah was surprised to realise that she preferred her mom the normal way – tactless, terrible at landing jokes, and incapable of smiling without some sadness in there too.

In her room, Leilah took off her uniform and looked in the mirror. She had a bit of a waist, but below it her tummy pouted over her panty line and the tops of her thighs touched. Her bum stuck out more than the other girls at school, and her jaw was wide and square, like that of a grown man. She tugged at her soft flesh, pinching and pulling and trying to peel it off. When her fat didn't budge, she muttered rude things about Basia, whose kaftans lay all over Leilah's bed, each big enough to make a tent.

"No dogs," instructed the man at the guesthouse reception. Fritz, their old pavement special with a bum leg, was sitting at Elke's feet, half whimpering, half growling.

"What do you mean no dogs?" she said. "We drove three hours to get here. My dog is with us. What are we supposed to do with him?"

"Not my problem, lady," the man said, his neck thickening. "No dogs, no Indians, no Coloureds, no blacks. Those are my rules. Take it or leave it."

"Say that again," Elke said, her hand moving around to shield Leilah, who was standing a bit behind, stiff as a lamp pole.

"No dogs, no Indians, no Coloureds, no blacks. Take your dog home and you're welcome to come back."

Leilah felt the guesthouse welcome area shrinking. A wall clock ticked too loudly to her right, cicadas were screaming in the grass outside, Fritz's whimpering became unbearable. Her lush surroundings – the palm trees, the blue skies, the Indian Ocean in the distance – felt suddenly threatening. She didn't trust the colours, the breeze, the humidity. It all seemed a cover-up now, for this man who didn't want them. Without knowing what she was doing, Leilah kicked Fritz, and with a yelp their old dog ran outside. Elke's grip on Leilah's shoulder tightened and twisted, and together they turned and walked out without saying another word.

"No dogs allowed," Elke said when they reached the Kombi. "We'll have to keep driving until we find something else." They were parked in a small bay at the back of the guesthouse, out of the owner's sight. Dwight was smoking a cigarette in the driver's seat, Norman was in the passenger's, bent round and listening animatedly to one of Basia rambling stories. Frankie was standing outside, throwing pebbles against the ground to see if they would bounce.

"No dogs?" Basia repeated, leaning out the window. "That's absurd! Let me go in and talk to the owner. Look at Fritz, he can barely walk. What harm could this poor mutt possibly do?"

"No frau," Elke said firmly. "I tried. Let's go." Elke

picked up Fritz and placed him gently on the seat next to Basia, then held Leilah's hand as she hopped into the back. Frankie was close behind, still clutching a pebble. "We'll find something," Elke said, looking at the two girls but focusing on Leilah. "Don't worry."

"Let's go to Ifafa," said Norman. "I stayed at a place there once, real nice with a pool and big braai area. Very close to the beach."

"Ifafa?" Dwight asked. "Doesn't sound like a very serious place."

"Well," said Norman smiling, "who wants to spend the weekend at a serious place? And it's close, maybe an hour's drive from here."

"Sounds good," Elke said, jumping into the Kombi alongside Basia and patting her on the knee. "Just like the old days, hey frau, going where the road takes us."

"Bah!" Basia's cheeks wobbled as she protested. "Nothing compares to hitchhiking through Europe in the sixties. And nothing, absolutely nothing, compares to being in your twenties. You'll see, my girl, you'll see." She craned her neck to grin at Leilah, and Leilah felt the curious urge to smack her.

Norman's suggestion was a collection of stone cottages arranged on lawny hills around a big pool, close enough to the ocean to smell the fish. There was no official reception area, but upon arriving a short Indian man in khakis and a Billabong t-shirt approached their car out of nowhere and, with a big smile, asked how he could help.

"Got something big enough for four adults and two kids?" Elke asked.

Leilah watched the man look across the hodgepodge of faces in the car, worried that he might kick them out too, even though he was darker than Norman and her dad combined. She still couldn't understand how things along this coast of South Africa worked, who was allowed to do things and who wasn't, who was acceptable and who wasn't.

"Sure, sure," the man said lightly. "My name's Rafik. Come, come, let's get you sorted."

"Yes!" Leilah exclaimed, climbing over the seats and pulling Frankie with her.

"What about our stuff?" Frankie asked, looking confused. Leilah knew Frankie didn't like it when her mood changed so suddenly. She'd tried to ask Leilah about it once, and Leilah's hurt had been immediate. She'd curled her arms and shoulders around herself like bat wings, and refused to say anything. So now Frankie didn't ask anymore, and Leilah – whose mind confused her as much it seemed to confuse Frankie – loved her more for it.

"We can get our stuff later," Leilah said once they were out of the Kombi's sliding door. "Or Rafik can take it for us. He's nice, isn't he?"

"How should I know?" Frankie said. "We just met the man."

The two girls ran from the Kombi down the hill to the pool, which was pale green and had a mermaid mosaic at its centre. There was a boma at the far end, with a bar and braai area, and Leilah started poking her head around in there, opening the freezer to see what she'd find. A frozen steak was glued into one corner with old, greying ice and right at the bottom lay an almost-empty bottle of peach Schnapps. Leilah blocked her nose to avoid the smell of years-old meat and leaned in, her feet leaving the ground for a moment as she reached the bottle and pulled it out. "Think it's okay to drink?" she asked Frankie, who was looking at her quizzically now, as if seeing Leilah for the first time.

"Don't see why not," Frankie said, grabbing the bottle, which – covered in a fine layer of frost – looked like hidden treasure. "Yikes it's freezing!" Frankie squealed, almost dropping the bottle. "What if it freezes our insides?"

"Don't be silly," Leilah said, giggling. "My dad drinks vodka out the freezer all the time. Spirits don't freeze, too much alcohol in it. Drinking it cold is the classy way to do it."

"What do you know about classy?" Frankie asked, poking Leilah playfully in the ribs.

"My aunty taught me. She wears petticoats and stockings, and smokes cigarettes from one of those long holders with gold in them."

"I bet it's not real gold," Frankie said.

"Is too," Leilah said, twisting the lid off the Schnapps bottle and taking a swig. It was cold and stung going down her throat but when it reached her tummy, everything turned warm. Her insides seemed to stretch a little wider, in a nice way, and her eyes filled with tears that blurred her vision and made the pool appear greener and brighter. She took another swig.

"Hey, give me some," Frankie said, grabbing the bottle and taking her own sip. They sat down behind the bar, with knees to their chests, passing the bottle between them until it was all gone. "What happened at that first guesthouse that made you so quiet?" Frankie asked, turning to Leilah and smoothing away some of her frizzy hair that had gotten loose. "You don't have to tell me, but if you want to, you can. I won't tell anyone."

Leilah kept her body the same but turned her head to face Frankie, and for a long time they just looked at each other, unflinching, as if watching their favourite cartoon.

"The owner didn't want any Coloureds staying at his place," Leilah said, head swimming. "He didn't want me there."

"He really said that? That he didn't want *you*?" Frankie's cheeks had turned red.

"Not exactly. But only because he couldn't see the Coloured in me. I don't think anyone can. What do you think he would have done if Norman or my dad had been there? Do you think he would have hurt them?"

"Are you kidding? Norman would have squashed him like a bug. That man's a giant. And, anyway, the laws have all changed. No one's allowed to hurt you for not being white, not anymore."

"Do people stop hurting people just because the government says they must?" Leilah asked, bringing the bottle to her lips though there was nothing left in it.

"Ja," Frankie said. "I think so."

"Then why did you tell me to keep my dad a secret?" Leilah asked.

"Because I didn't want us to sit separately," Frankie said after a pause.

"But if the laws have changed, why would we need to sit separately?"

"Why are you asking me so many questions?" Frankie asked, twirling a piece of hair between her fingers like she did when she didn't know the answer to a math problem.

"Because I'm confused," Leilah said. "At my old school there was a black girl in my class that I ate lunch with. But at Kingston, the blacks don't sit with the whites. And I haven't seen a single other Coloured person living in Westville, never mind a mixed person. I feel like a freak there."

Frankie shuffled closer to Leilah, and stretching her thin

arms as far as she could, wrapped Leilah inside them so that their foreheads touched. "You're not a freak to me," she whispered. "Now, let's go for a swim, while I still feel so warm."

"In our panties?" Leilah asked, lifting her head and breaking into a smile she hadn't felt coming. "I thought girls were only supposed to swim in bathing suits?"

"Ja, but this is a special occasion, and we're the only ones here."

Together they pulled off their t-shirts and shorts and, holding hands, ran and jumped into the pool in tight balls, laughing as they hit the water. They dove down to the mermaid and ran their fingers along her mosaic scales, again and again, until their fingers wrinkled and their teeth began to chatter. Around them the sky was turning a deep shade of pink, and thick clouds had gathered low in the sky, their bottoms also pink. It started to rain, thick pellets of water striking the pool's surface and falling into the girls' upturned mouths. They only got out when they heard Elke calling for dinner.

Under the boma, and before they got dressed, Leilah gave Frankie a hug. She felt even thinner without clothes on, her ribs pressing into Leilah's arms, covered in a wet layer of goosebumps. Through the thrum of rain on the boma's tin roof, Leilah could hear the feint ba-bump of Frankie's heart and Elke's dinner call rumbling down the hill. The two girls separated and pulled their clothes on in silence and just as they were about to leave, Leilah leaned over to kiss Frankie on the lips. They were slightly parted, and tasted like peaches.

Chapter 6

"What did that guesthouse owner really say to you, Frau?" Basia asked, a slim cigarette hanging from her lips, flecks of mascara dotting her fold-over eyelids. The adults were sitting around a table at their holiday cottage in Ifafa. Frankie was sleeping down the hall, and Leilah – who couldn't sleep in the strange bed – was sitting at the entrance to the corridor. From the shadows she could see and hear everything, and with schnapps still outlining her view of things, she thought the four looked like characters from a movie. A dim light hung above the table, casting a soft orange hue across their aging faces and accentuating the dark blue rings under Basia's glare. A bottle of whiskey, half empty, rested between them. Norman grabbed it and started pouring liberally for everyone except Elke, who Leilah had never seen drink.

"He was a racist," Elke said.

Leilah put her hand over her mouth to stop it from gasping and giving her away. She'd never heard her mom call someone a racist.

Norman, who had his hand under the table and was stroking the tops of Basia's thighs, looked up and smiled. "So what?" he said. "Everyone's a racist, why did we have to leave?" He took a sip of his drink, then grabbed a handful of dripping cubes from the ice bucket at his feet and split it up across the whiskeys.

"We had to leave," Elke said. "He didn't accommodate..." she paused. "People of colour."

"You mean Coloureds?" Dwight said. He had both hands around his glass and wasn't smiling or frowning. He looked, to Leilah, unfeeling, less like her dad, and more like a man.

"Ja, Coloureds. Or blacks or Indians or dogs. I wasn't lying about the dogs." Elke slid her hand across the table and tapped the wood with her short nails, like she was trying to get Dwight's attention, or maybe stop him from getting angry. Her dad wasn't an angry man, Leilah knew, except for that one time he got really mad about work and threw his beer against the kitchen wall. It only happened once, and no one spoke about it, not when it happened, and not after. It was like an alien had taken over his brain for a minute, and then left as quickly as it had come.

"No one would ever accuse you of being dishonest," Dwight said, his long, rounded forehead catching the overhead light. His voice sounded like it was cracking, and Leilah could hear drops of rage leaking through. He didn't look up from his glass, and ignored her mom's fingers coming towards him. Leilah wished he'd reach out and touch her.

"Are guesthouses allowed to keep out people because of race?" Basia asked, sucking whiskey through her ice cubes, seemingly unaware of how gross it sounded

"It's his place, sweets," Norman said. "Right of admission and all that. Not sure I'd let us in either." He laughed, and Basia joined in, though her heart didn't seem to be in it.

"But what about the famous Rainbow Nation?" she asked, looking at Elke and avoiding Dwight. "What about the end of apartheid and white men running the place?"

"Give me a break," Dwight said, louder than usual, the cracks in his voice widening. Leilah fought to sit still. "You think anything changes in three years? You think anything changes in a hundred years? South Africa hasn't changed. Black men might be in government but white men still own this place. Meanwhile Norm and I are stuck in the middle like idiots, not light enough to appease the whities, not dark enough for affirmative action. Nothing's fucken changed." He downed his whiskey and rattled his glass in Norman's direction for a top-up.

"When did you become such a cynic?" Norman asked, leaning over and pouring. "I thought you didn't see colour, or didn't see yourself as Coloured. You know it's all rubbish, right? Under our skin we're the same, same bones, same brains, same need to fuck. Isn't that right, Basia?" He put down the bottle and returned his hand to her thigh, which looked as soft as down, and just as white. Leilah squirmed.

"You are right," Elke said. "But you can't say race doesn't matter. Look at Hitler, he killed six million Jews and used race to justify it."

"The Jews?" her dad asked, looking up without meeting anyone's eyes. "Why's it always about the Holocaust?" No one answered. The schnapps warmth was all gone and now Leilah felt embarrassed for her dad, and the silence that surrounded him. "Because Jews are white," he said. He was making circles with his glass on the table and watching the whiskey swirl. "That's the only reason everyone still talks about it."

Leilah had heard her mom shouting about Hitler and the Holocaust before – she was mad that it wasn't being taught at Leilah's school – but she'd never heard her dad get upset about people called "The Jews". The anger looked strange on him, like a foot struggling into a glove.

"Jews aren't white," Elke said, her eyes narrowing.

"Aren't they?" Dwight said. "They look white to me."

"So?" Elke said. "Leilah looks white. Doesn't mean that she is." Her father started saying something in response but stopped. Leilah held her breath, wondering if her mom would say something more about her. "Hitler's men stacked the dead bodies three by three," Elke carried on. "One layer over another over another. He wasn't just evil, he was efficient. You don't think people should remember and talk about that, so that it doesn't happen again?"

"I think there are lots of things people should remember that they don't," her dad said. "I think Jews, at least, have a history. They know who they are and the world knows who they are. What do people know about Coloureds? What do Coloureds know about being Coloured? Maybe if six million of us were killed and stacked like firewood, people would see us as our own thing, not just some group stuck between whites and blacks."

Leilah didn't even know what a Jewish person looked like, not until now: white-looking but not really white, just like her. If anyone ever asked her directly, maybe Leilah could say she was Jewish? They weren't on the list of people the guesthouse owner didn't want, which meant her dad was right. They were white, or at least whiter than half-Coloured.

"You know my one grandmother was Griqua, my other one a mix of Swiss and Malay?" her dad said, breaking Leilah's train of thought. He was speaking more slowly now; the angry alien was disappearing, and its place, some sadness. "My mother had blue eyes and skin lighter than yours, Elke, but her sister was the colour of teak and her eyes just as dark. All those different histories forced to stand together under the 'Coloured' umbrella." Her dad's air quotes lingered in the air a while, before he returned to his glass. "Even the term - what does *Coloured* mean?"

Elke didn't say anything. Dwight never spoke this much, even when he drank, and Leilah suspected her mom wanted him to keep going, even though the things he'd been saying were like bullets leaving a gun. Elke looked at Norman, like she wanted him to respond, but her dad's giant friend was fiddling with his shirt pocket, as if there was something important inside. "Isn't the black umbrella just as bad?" Elke asked eventually.

"No," her dad said. "Because under the black umbrella there are Xhosas and Zulus and Sothos. There's pride there, even under oppression. When do you ever hear a Coloured person talking about his heritage, unless it's about some Swiss or equally white grandpa who was gracious enough to knock up their black granny?"

"What do you mean?" Basia asked, looking directly at Dwight for the first time, a faint look of interest cutting through the milkiness in her eyes.

"I mean Jews and blacks and Indians know who they are while Coloureds still define themselves by proximity to white people. Deep down, we all wish we were white." Dwight was speaking firmly and slowly, and Leilah marvelled at how certain her dad looked, the purse of his lips, the firm set of his jaw. She committed the rare image to memory.

"Is that true, Norman?" Basia asked again, her dismissal of Dwight's opinion as ugly as her swollen ankles.

"Ag, I don't know," Norman said. "You lost me at Holocaust. These kinds of conversations don't do anyone any good." He tried to smile.

"The white umbrella isn't too great either," Elke said, the whites of her sober eyes still white. "I hate being German. I hate my accent, my green eyes, my blonde hair. I wish I had curls like you, and a history the world didn't know about. Every time people look at me, or hear me speak, they see that moustache and his four-legged insignia." Elke only used German when she swore and in her mouth the words sounded round and familiar, not foreign at all. Leilah wondered if she had a Coloured accent she couldn't hear, one that might give her away.

"I like your green eyes," her dad said, reaching his bare feet under the table to meet her mom's and smiling at her through the dim orange light. "Don't pay any attention to my ranting. I'm just a grumpy old man who's had too many whiskeys."

"You're not old, or grumpy," Elke said, stroking his toes under the table with hers. "How about a dance?"

"Great idea!" Basia said, springing up from her chair. "We're here to have fun! Norman, top up Dwight's drink and let's all lighten up, shall we?"

"What do you say, chommie?" Norman said, getting up and walking over to her dad's side of the table. "I saw a record player in the TV room, let's see what they've got. Maybe some Louis Prima or Hendricks, if we're lucky." Norman squeezed Dwight's arm and, in the squeeze, Leilah saw an acknowledgement between the two men, and something like loss.

Later that night, while Basia spooned the empty whiskey bottle on the couch and Norman spooned her, Leilah sat outside her parents' bedroom and tried to make sense of the moans she could hear through the door. She'd never heard them make love, not ever, and though it made her tummy churn, she didn't want to pull away, fearful they might hear her and stop.

"You were unusually open tonight," Elke said when they were done. "Anything else you want to share with me?"

"I think Leilah's ashamed of me," he said and Leilah felt something in her drop, a stone plunging to the bottom of a dark pool.

"Why do you say that?" her mom asked, too casual, like she was asking how he wanted his steak done, or his hair cut.

"She hides when I drop her at school. She walks ahead of me at the supermarket. She doesn't talk to me anymore. God, she barely even looks at me." Her dad was speaking so softly now that Leilah had to put her ear on the door to hear him.

"She's the same way with me," her mom said. "It's her age. Teenagers are shitty."

"No," her dad said. "It's more than that. She still sees you enough to get mad at you. With me, it feels like she's turning off a switch. I don't think she wants to think of herself as my daughter."

"But Dwight, that's normal. It's healthy for kids to cut the cord."

"Ja, maybe," Dwight said, but Leilah could tell he wasn't buying it. She heard the springs of the bed creak, and knew it was him turning onto his side, away from her mom so that his thoughts would belong only to him again.

When she heard her parents' faint snore, Leilah tiptoed to the kitchen and opened the fridge. There was a beer inside and she took it out, twisting the cap off the way she'd seen her dad do. She put the bottle to her lips and drank until she felt she would choke. She glugged another two times until the beer was empty, then walked over to the couch to make sure Basia and Norman were still sleeping. They looked like seals, their blubber slopping together, and she had to refrain from poking curiously at the flesh on Norman's hips, which hung out from under his hiked-up shirt. She stumbled a little as she walked to bed, fearlessly navigating the dark corridor that until now she'd found terrifying, its end too black to see.

Chapter 7

Leilah didn't mention the kiss in the weeks following Ifafa. She wasn't sure if it had really happened, a doubt made worse by Frankie's own silence on the matter. When Frankie talked about the weekend, it was always about the two boys they'd met on the beach, who were tall and blond and offered to share their cigarettes with them. Leilah, who was not as good at smoking as Frankie, didn't really like spending their whole Saturday with the strange boys, but Frankie seemed so at ease in their presence – chatting about school and Durban like she was a big fan of both, taking long drags that she inhaled without coughing – that Leilah went along with it. She held the smoke in her mouth for as long as she could and blew it out as casually as she could, but still the boys told her she was faking it and when they laughed, Frankie laughed too, though it was half-hearted and weak and didn't sound like her at all.

Sometimes in class Leilah found herself looking at Frankie's lips. She marvelled at how thin they were, and how soft and full they had felt. It frightened her, this mix of soft and hard in her friend; it made her think that Frankie might be keeping secrets from her, which wouldn't be fair since they were supposed to tell each other everything. Not that Leilah told Frankie about the mattress at the foot of her parents' bed, which she moved to her own room whenever Frankie spent the night. "Smells like you," Frankie had said once, smelling the sheet. After that Leilah made sure to wash the bedding before every sleepover, cramming her Friday or Saturday mornings with detergent and pegs, both of which she hated. The detergent stung her nose and the wood pegs felt wet and mouldy from the dank Durban summer.

Tired of doing the laundry, and keen to assure Frankie that she didn't need to hide stuff from her, Leilah decided to have a secret-sharing sleepover the same weekend school broke for winter holidays. It was June. The air was starting to dry out, and though they'd just moved for the third time that year, Leilah was feeling better than she had in a while. When she didn't think about her dad, or the sadness she'd heard in him while eavesdropping in Ifafa, she could get through a day without wanting to run and hide. School wasn't so scary any more, and with Frankie at her side she'd grown relatively comfortable around her other classmates, though she still remained wary of Jack Bertram, the handsome but meanspirited jock who teased her for being a nerd. Leilah even had an admirer, Aarush, a very tall, very dark Indian boy with black, almond-shaped eyes, and the best bowling arm in their grade. He left love letters in her desk, which she read in the toilet before showing them to Frankie. They both laughed at him, and called him ugly, but somewhere in herself, Leilah liked the love notes, and hoped they wouldn't stop.

Leilah's new house had a pool which had been drained before they moved in and was still waiting to be filled. She liked to imagine her and Frankie playing in the big empty bowl, running along its edges to see how far they could go up the wall, sitting at its centre and pretending to be invisible. She was sure this would be a good place to tell each other everything. On the last Friday of term, she bought them two Cokes and, with uniforms still on, led Frankie down into the centre of the pool. "It's champagne," she said shaking her bottle vigorously, coaxing Frankie to do the same. When they popped the lids, sugary foam sprayed everywhere, all over the pool floor, their faces and each other's uniforms. Laughing and sticky, they ran around in circles, collapsing eventually from exhaustion and joy.

Once they'd caught their breath, Frankie pulled two Craven As from her breast pocket. They were soggy and covered in dirty fingerprints but remained unbroken. Frankie held them up to the sun like a trophy, as if waiting for Leilah to congratulate her. But she didn't. She didn't like cigarettes, didn't like it when her dad smoked in the house and made everything stink, didn't like it when he left a pile of butts in his ashtray next to the TV, and she especially didn't like it when her mom screamed at him for being so inconsiderate. When Elke got mad, she got loud. She'd scream while arranging Dwight's shoes in a neat pair at the foot of the couch; she'd scream while pulling back the curtains and opening the windows; she'd scream as she picked up the dirty ashtray and walked it to the kitchen bin at arm's length, as if throwing away a cockroach.

"They're menthol," Frankie said when Leilah didn't react. "It's like chewing Stimorol and having a cigarette at the same time. Isn't that cool?"

Leilah kept her eyes on the two misshapen smokes and after a while started to see individual shreds of tobacco shining gold through the thin wrapping paper. Maybe they aren't so bad, she thought, but that did nothing to solve her biggest problem with smoking, far bigger than not liking cigarettes. She didn't know how to smoke.

"Frankie," she said after a long silence. "I don't know how to inhale. At Ifafa I just held the smoke in my mouth for as long as I could, and then blew it out again. Didn't you hear those two guys teasing me? I'm no good at this kind of stuff, I'm no good at being cool."

"They weren't teasing you for not being cool. They were teasing you because they liked you." Frankie lowered the cigarettes along with her eyes.

"Really?" Leilah was confused.

"Ja. Guys like you. I bet you anything that asshole Jack Bertram likes you too. He's just too dumb to admit it. You know he failed two years of school? That's why he's so much bigger than the other boys. He walks around like he owns the place but actually he's too dumb to be with kids his own age. And you know—"

"Frankie," normally Leilah let her friend ramble, but at that moment she didn't care about Jack Bertram and his two extra years, she could ask about it later. Right now, there was something more important she needed to know. "How can you say boys like me? I'm ugly."

"Who told you that?"

"I don't need anyone to tell me. I can see it in the mirror. I look nothing like any of the pretty girls in school. Did you see our class photo? My calves look like thick logs. My face is square, my eyes are squinty and my skin is yellowy-brown, like a banana about to go off. What boy would ever like that?"

"You think too much about yourself, Leilah. No one cares about your banana skin, and if they do, maybe it's because they like it. Maybe some people like different, did you ever think of that?"

"Do you?"

"Sure," Frankie said, a shy shadow creeping into her face. "Most of the time." She grinned. "Wanna stop talking rubbish and learn how to smoke like a real girl?"

"Ja," Leilah said, grabbing both cigarettes off the floor and passing one to Frankie. "Teach me."

Frankie took her time talking Leilah through the steps,

telling her exactly how long to suck for, encouraging her to breathe in deeply, to open her throat and ignore the initial discomfort. Leilah – nervous of what might happen to the smoke if she got it down but couldn't bring it up again – wasted the first few drags, but under Frankie's guidance, got halfway down the cigarette and went for it. She needn't have worried about the smoke getting stuck because the moment it went down, she started coughing uncontrollably. Coca-Cola spewed out her nose, and spit flung from her mouth along with the fumes, which tasted even more foul coming out than they had going in. She waited to stop coughing and took another drag, then another and another, and by the time she reached the filter, she concluded that smoking was disgusting but not so disgusting that she couldn't keep doing it. Leilah stood up to throw the butts into the garden and had to steady herself on the ledge of the pool. Hundreds of spots blurred her vision, her legs were wobbly and for a strange-but-not-unpleasant moment, she couldn't make any sense of her surroundings. She would have fallen flat on her face had she not been holding onto the pool wall.

"What's wrong with you?" Frankie asked, half giggling, half concerned.

"I'm dizzy," Leilah replied. "What do they put in those things?"

"Ag, don't worry so much," Frankie retorted. "Half the world smokes and they're all okay, aren't they? Just look at your dad." Leilah thought of Dwight, the gaping pores on his nose, the deepening lines around his lips, the yellowing of his fingers and eyes. If smoking made her look more like him, she ought to stop immediately. Instead, she threw the butts as far as she could, sat down and asked Frankie for another one. "Sure. But we'll have to buy a new pack."

Together they rollerbladed to the closest shop and with sugary voices convinced the shop owner that they were buying for their parents. They skated hurriedly away, Frankie's skinny legs splayed like a giraffe drinking, Leilah's bum sticking out even further than usual, trying to balance the forward lean of her torso. They found a quiet cul-de-sac and spent the afternoon sucking through half a pack, one smoke after another until they were both ready to vomit.

"Wanna go home?" Leilah asked, unable to take another drag.

"Please," Frankie said. "I'm starving."

It was the first time Leilah had heard Frankie talk about her appetite, or express any desire to eat. She spent the skate home thinking of all the things she'd like to make her friend: toast with fishpaste and gherkins, tomatoes cut in half and covered in grated cheese, Ricoffy with lots of sugar and milk. The sharing of secrets would have to wait until the next day. All she wanted to do now was make Frankie food and watch her eat it.

The next morning Leilah woke first and rolled to the edge of the bed to look at Frankie lying on her back, straight as the day Leilah had met her, the duvet pulled right up to her chin. Her eyes were closed and she looked peaceful, her skin smooth across her cheekbones, the muscles of her jaw relaxed. Leilah liked this version of her, quiet and unflinching, and hoped she would stay that way, later when the truth came out. Leilah shivered, rolled back to the centre of her bed, and lifted her pillow over her face so that she couldn't see the day.

"What are you so miserable about?" Frankie asked at breakfast.

Leilah was sitting silent and rigid in her chair. "I don't

feel so good," she replied, pushing her undercooked eggs around on the plate. "My stomach feels strange."

"Want something different to eat?" Elke asked. She was standing at the Tupperware cupboard, swearing as she tried to find a lid and base that lined up.

"Maybe some Weet-Bix," Leilah replied, irritated that her mom wasn't looking at her. "Your eggs are too runny." "What do you mean too runny?" Elke turned to face the breakfast table. "I thought you loved soft eggs. Don't you like slurping up the yolk in one go?"

"No, *you* love doing that." Leilah face crinkled in disgust as she visualised her mom sucking her eggs at restaurants. The other tables always looked at them like they were animals when she did that. She wished her mom had better manners, that she didn't eat so loudly and quickly, that she didn't cut her hair so short or use lipstick to colour her cheeks like a clown. Elke didn't know anything about being a lady.

"Gosh," Elke said, her face screwing up. "You are grouchy this morning. Go watch telly and I'll bring your Weet-Bix in there." She crouched down next to Leilah and put a hand on her forehead to check for a fever. "I remember when your whole face fitted into one of my hands," she said. "Now look at you, you're almost a woman."

"Are you saying I have a big head?" Leilah asked, pushing Elke's hand away. "Never mind, I don't care what you think. I said my stomach was sore, not my head. You never listen to me, Mom." She shot up and dragged her feet to the lounge, looking back a couple of times along the way to make sure Frankie was following.

"You're not being nice," Frankie said when they were sitting alongside each other on the couch eating sweet, sloppy cereal. "I don't know what crawled up your butt last night, but you're not being nice."

Leilah didn't know how to say that she was nervous about spilling her guts. What if Frankie laughed at her for being so scared of the dark that she had to sleep at her mom's feet like a dog? What if Frankie told the whole school that she was a baby? Surely, then, Jack Bertram would find her and beat her up, make her pay for being such a freak. Surely, then, she would never make new friends and school would become her prison, day after day eating lunch in a toilet cubicle, crouched on her haunches so that no one would see her feet, pins and needles creeping up her legs. No, she decided, she wouldn't tell Frankie her secret unless Frankie told her something first. Something big, something she could hold against her if necessary.

"Let's go down to the pool again, when my parents leave to buy groceries," Leilah said, trying to sound as nice as possible.

"Okay," Frankie said. "But only if we can smoke."

"Of course we'll smoke. We've got ten left over from yesterday, what else would we do with them?" She wanted to sound like she didn't care about anything, but her pitch was too high. She sounded brittle. Frankie lifted the edge of her bowl to her lips and in one long go, slurped up the rest of her milk.

Down by the pool they sat opposite each other, Leilah with her back to the wall, Frankie with hers to the house. They were each smoking, and Leilah felt almost comfortable, holding the smoke down for an acceptable amount of time, blowing it out in a long, thin line. She'd learnt the previous day to tighten her lips when she exhaled because it gave her more control. She could move her head up and down, or side to side, as she blew out, making lines in the air that started tight and white and dissipated into nothing. The longer she took to exhale, she realised, the lighter her head felt when the cigarette reached its end, and she was beginning to like that feeling of her head being a balloon, detached from her neck and body. The sun was just warm enough that she could smell the papayas ripening in a nearby tree. She closed her eyes and willed herself to float above Frankie and the pool, above her many fears.

"You know that story you told me about Magda?" she asked, keeping her eyes closed.

"I remember," Frankie said.

"You know I'd never tell anyone that story, right?"

"I've never really thought about it. Who would you tell anyway? I'm your only friend."

"Am I *your* only friend?" asked Leilah, her balloon head starting to lose air.

"In Westville, yes, I suppose you are."

"So, you can tell me anything then, since I'm your only friend. Your secrets I mean, stuff you wouldn't tell anyone else."

"Like what?"

"Like whatever, something no one else knows."

"Will you tell me something too?"

"I will," said Leilah, opening her eyes and finding her focus. "But you have to go first." Frankie shuffled around so that she was sitting next to Leilah instead of in front of her. Folded, Frankie's legs reminded Leilah of a pretzel, twisting easily into each other, creating a maze of skin and bone that Leilah got lost in now, following each bendy line to its end. She closed her eyes again, waiting for Frankie to speak. She'd expected Frankie to laugh at the idea of sharing secrets, but the way she sat so still next to her – the same way she had before speaking about Magda – Leilah knew something was coming.

"I wet the bed," Frankie said. Short and ugly. Leilah felt like she'd been kicked. Frankie's secret was too big. She pictured her mattress at the foot of the bed, saw herself hanging the sheets on the line, her mom standing quietly next to her, passing her the mouldy pegs. It all looked so ordinary now. "I try to hide it from my mom and dad because they don't like it; they think I'm doing it for attention. I make my bed in the morning while everything is still wet and when I get home, I scrub. With bleach and hot water, the stain goes away, but the stink never does. Sometimes I wake up at night and I can smell it, even when my sheets are dry. My bed is like a boy's toilet, soaked with old wee."

Leilah couldn't speak. She could only stare at Frankie's fingers, which were trembling around the filter of her Craven A. Slowly, she brought the cigarette up to her lips and pulled on it, and blindly Leilah followed the motion, letting her eyes rest now on Frankie's lips, which were thin as ever, and paler than she remembered. She kept staring at those pale lips, at the white smoke ejecting, at the fingers returning for another drag, and after Frankie had taken three long pulls, Leilah started talking.

"I had a friend when I was small, in Cape Town. He was bigger than me." She stopped. Her cigarette had burned all the way down to its filter, and was singeing the tops of her fingers. Frankie pried it loose and squashed it out alongside her own.

"Go on," she said. "Tell me about your friend."

"He was actually my brother's friend."

"Your brother?" Frankie asked. "You never told me you had brother. What's his name?"

Leilah was surprised. She thought she spoke of Motheo often, of how cool he was and how much he knew about the world. But maybe she'd just been thinking it. "My brother's name is Motheo. He's much older than me, ten years, so when we moved to Durban, he moved to Germany, to get a good job. His dad is different to mine, so I guess he's only my half-brother, my mom's half."

"Is his dad white?" Frankie asked.

"Ja, his dad's German, like my mom. But he left my mom when Motheo was still a baby so my dad is actually his dad. He adopted Motheo when he was six or something."

"Ja, but he's still white?" Frankie said, making a real point of it.

"I dunno. If colour is how you look and who your parents are, then ja, I suppose he's white. But Motheo calls my dad *dad*, so he can't be totally white."

"White's white," Frankie said in her bossy voice.

"I don't know," Leilah said. She was irritated by Frankie's belief that she knew everything about everything. "And it doesn't matter anyway, that's not what I'm talking about right now. Do you want to hear my secret or not?"

"Yes, I want to hear it. I told you mine, didn't I?" Frankie reached over and lifted Leilah's chin so that it was parallel to the ground. "Now I can hear you properly," she said. "Go on, tell me."

"This friend, who was Motheo's friend but also my friend, didn't like doing things with all three of us together. I wanted to. I wanted to play the same games they played, to sit in my brother's room and listen to them talk about school and girls, to go with them to the shop and play the arcade game in the corner. But they never wanted me to play with them, they said I was too small, that I didn't understand the same things they understood. I used to sneak to the shop and hide between the chips and sweets watching them play Pacman. They weren't that good; I could've beaten them if they'd given me a chance."

"Is that your secret, that you used to stalk your brother and his friend?"

Leilah blushed. "No, but maybe it's part of it. Secrets come in parts, don't they? And you don't know what all the parts are until you start telling it. This is the first time I'm telling it."

"Okay," Frankie said, "carry on."

"My brother's friend's name was Otto. Once, we went on holiday to Swaziland, our family, the dog, and Otto. We stayed in these huts that looked like big beehives, and there was a pool with stalks that picked at worms in the grass around the pool. I didn't know how to swim yet, so everyone took turns holding me in the water. Otto too, except he held me differently, with his one hand between my legs. My parents and Motheo put their arm under my legs like a chair. But Otto, he put his hand between my legs, and sometimes he moved his fingers. After that holiday, he started spending more time with me, at night when my family was asleep, and sometimes during the day when both our families were together at the house, when it was busy. He kissed me and stuff."

"Was he your boyfriend?" Frankie asked.

"I think so."

"But you told me you never had a boyfriend."

"I wasn't sure if he counted."

"How old were you?"

"Four or maybe five. I started school the year after the pool thing."

"And how old was he?"

"Fifteen, like my brother, except he had a moustache, and that made him look older. Once, he let me touch his lip after he'd shaved and it felt like a cactus, a soft one."

Frankie took a breath as if she wanted to ask another question, but kept quiet. Her fingers spider-crawled across the small space between them and touched Leilah's hand, which had gone cold, same as the pool floor. "I don't know if he was supposed to do that stuff with you, Leilah."

"Well, you're not supposed to wet the bed. That's why they're called secrets." Leilah pulled her fingers away from Frankie's and folded her arms tightly across her chest. Her breasts – which seemed to grow bigger every week – felt tender under the pressure, and she squeezed even tighter, down to her ribcage.

"Are you sure you don't want to tell someone else, your mom maybe?"

"Why would I do that? Why don't you tell your mom your secret? Moms don't understand anything."

"You're right about that," Frankie said, pulling two more cigarettes from the box and handing one to Leilah.

"Think you can light your own one this time?"

"I can do it," Leilah said, unfolding her arms and taking the smoke. "You're not allowed to tell anyone Frankie, promise me. Our secrets stay here, at the bottom of this pool."

"Okay," Frankie said after what felt like ages. "I promise."

Leilah lit her cigarette and leaned back against the pool wall, holding in the smoke until her head took flight.

Chapter 8

The weight of her secret sat silently between Leilah and Frankie once the winter holiday was over and the two girls returned to school. They still shared the same small wooden desk, still split their lunches, still teased the boys behind their backs, but Frankie no longer answered questions on Leilah's behalf and they stopped sitting behind the recycling bins, smoking matches and holding hands. Frankie didn't ask to brush Leilah's hair any more.

When Rose arrived, two weeks into the new term, the gap between Frankie and Leilah grew even wider and quieter. Rose was dark skinned and light spirited, with an easy smile and always a pack of Jellybeans in her blazer pocket. She was more beautiful than any black girl Leilah had seen, almost as tall as Frankie, with precise collarbones and a fine jawline. Her hair was unbraided and stood in a neat pile above her head, like a puff of candyfloss. Her ankles reminded Leilah of seashells. It was unusual for a student to arrive midyear, even more unusual for a Zulu girl with no apparent ties to Westville. No one approached or talked to her and, after a week, Frankie asked Leilah if they should invite her to be their friend.

"Won't people think we're strange, making friends with a black girl? I don't want to give Jack Bertram another reason to hate me. He follows me sometimes, you know, when we're not together. Follows me for a few metres and then pretends to be doing something else. He creeps me out."

"You're paranoid," Frankie said, poking Leilah in the ribs.

"Am I? You said he was two years older than us. I think he could be dangerous."

"Dumb and dangerous aren't the same thing." Frankie wasn't even looking at her.

"But he gets so mean when I do well in tests. My mom was a teacher and she said the kids who stayed back in her classes were always messed up, like they didn't really belong there. She said she felt sorry for them."

"I'll never feel sorry for Jack Bertram; he's a total dickwad. She looks nice, doesn't she?"

"Who?"

"The new girl, Rose. I think she looks nice."

"Hadn't really thought about it," Leilah lied. She'd done her best to ignore Rose, whose breathing she could hear from the table behind them, calm and steady. Her presence made Leilah uncomfortable. "I heard Jack say *kaffir* the other day. All the boys standing around him laughed, like it was a joke. I thought that word was bad. Why did they think it was so funny?"

"It's just a word. My parents said it all the time back in Bloemfontein, and me. I don't any more because your dad's cool and I don't want to disrespect him or anything, but it's just a word, only means what you make it mean."

"My dad's not a kaffir," Leilah snapped, her fingers scattering a pile of eraser flakes she'd brushed into a small pile on the desk.

"No, but someone in your family must have been. Brown people don't just pop out of nowhere. So, are we going to ask Rose to sit with us or what?"

"Whatever," Leilah said, "I don't care."

When Rose joined, the three took turns sitting in pairs. Leilah had to get used to being alone at a desk, which she seemed to do more and more as Frankie and Rose grew closer. On one of those days that she was alone, a small paper plane floated over her shoulder and landed on her workbook. She looked around to see Anastasia and Natalie smiling and winking at her, silently nudging her to open the flying package. She unfolded it carefully, thrilled and scared that Anastasia – who could kiss any boy in school – was looking at her so expectantly.

Rose is a dirty black, the note read. *Don't sit with her. Sit with us.*

Leilah crumpled it immediately, looking forward to see whether Frankie had noticed. She could hear Anastasia giggling, Miss Caxton drawing on the board with a screeching piece of chalk, a cricket ball cracking on the playground. She got up and left the classroom, pointing in the direction of the toilet on her way out. Surprisingly Miss Caxton let her go without comment. Outside, Leilah slid down the wall of the stairwell and sat on the floor, scared of the air she was breathing, scared of things she couldn't name.

She never mentioned the note to Frankie, and every time Anastasia or Natalie approached her, she lowered her eyes and shrank. If she could make herself even more pathetic, she reasoned, they wouldn't take offence that she hadn't written back, wouldn't mind that she wasn't sitting with them, would be relieved that she wasn't theirs to deal with. She stuck to Frankie and Rose during breaks, tuning out and saying little, and after school ran straight home. She convinced her mom to buy her hair gel, and started gluing her wet hair to her head each morning. With her bun so tight, the hair never really dried and on Fridays when she finally let it loose, it stank like a gutter. Her mom started commenting on the smell when she kissed Leilah good night, so Leilah started mushing herself into the far corner of her bed, against the wall, where her mom's nose couldn't reach. She stole a bottle of pale foundation from the pharmacy that made her look like a ghost and when Frankie invited Rose to the mall without her, she started to feel like one too.

Two months after Rose arrived, Elke told Leilah she was leaving. "It'll just be six months," she said on a Sunday evening, relaxed on the couch, like it was no big deal.

"Why?" The scratch in Leilah's nose was so instantaneous that she had to pinch it to stop herself from crying.

"Because there's a massage course I want to do and it's in a place called Sedgefield, which is a day's drive from here. Leilah," She sounded more serious now. "I want to start working again."

"But who will pick me up from school?" Leilah asked, her mom's desire to work again barely registering. She hated the idea of her dad taking over. It would make him more visible in her life.

"Dad will be at work, so you'll have to start catching the bus."

"The bus? Only black kids catch the bus."

"What's that got to do with anything?" Her mom's voice was getting angry now but Leilah didn't care. She was angry too. Mothers weren't supposed to leave.

"I'm not black. I'm going to stick out like a sore thumb. What if the white kids see me? They'll think I'm poor, or that you don't care about me. Aren't you worried about that?"

"No, Leilah, I'm not. And it upsets me that you are. Since when do money and skin colour matter?"

Leilah could almost taste how much her mom disliked her. Her mouth started to salivate and she felt like she wanted to vomit. She swallowed hard and continued, determined not to give Elke the upper hand. "I'm the only girl in school whose parents look nothing alike. I'm the only girl in my class wearing second-hand uniforms. And now I'll be the only white girl catching a bus. It's not fair."

"You're not white, and life's not fair. Consider this your first lesson in being a grown-up and stop complaining about meaningless shit."

"But I'm not a grown-up, and you're leaving me here like I am. We've only been in Durban six months and you're leaving me here like I've got it all figured out. But I don't, I don't have anything figured out."

"I'm not leaving you forever. It's only six months and Dad will still be here. The time will fly, I promise."

"These last six months have felt like forever, so don't tell me the time will fly. Six months is ages for me. I won't have anyone to talk to in the afternoons or to check my grammar, or make me sandwiches. Dad doesn't do any of that stuff, he's always at work and anyway he doesn't know how to do lunch and homework stuff."

Elke's face softened. "My sweetheart, you're almost thirteen years old. You make better sandwiches than dad or I could ever dream of making, and your grammar will survive six months without me. I'm not that good at it anyway. I just pretend to be so that you keep asking me for help." Leilah was taken aback by the way Elke was talking to her. She'd let the divider between mother and daughter fall, and Leilah waited anxiously for her to pick it up again. Instead, she kept going. "I know it's hard for you to see now, but me doing this course will be good for you, because it will be good for me. You're getting older Leilah, and I need something else to do with my life, something that isn't you, or Dad."

"Can't you just start teaching again?" Leilah asked, getting desperate.

"I never really liked teaching. And it's been so long since I've stood in front of a class, I don't think I have the confidence to do it again."

"You're being selfish," said Leilah, her voice unsure of its cruelty. "You're leaving me alone as if I don't exist, as if you're not a mom."

"You won't be alone." Elke sounded like her mother again. "Greta will be here to help with lunches and looking after the house. I expect you to clean up after yourself while I'm gone. Please don't treat Greta like a maid."

"But she is a maid," Leilah said, her cruelty gaining confidence. "And I don't like Greta. You can't just leave a stranger in your place and expect everything to be fine." She turned on her heel and left Elke alone in the kitchen, smoothing an imaginary tablecloth on the countertop.

Greta was the live-in maid that came with their most recent rental home and, knowing that she was going away, Elke had asked her to stay. Leilah felt a bitterness towards Greta from the start. They'd never had a full-time domestic before, let alone one who stayed with them, and the idea of seeing this woman every day, a woman she didn't choose, made Leilah so angry that she didn't care to question why.

She hated the way Greta hobbled around the house, wrapping and rewrapping an old blanket around her waist like a bandage. She hated having her at the dinner table and the smell of her hair product. She hated that Greta was black. Some mornings when she went into the toilet and smelt Greta's shit, the word *kaffir* played over in her mind and though she never said it out loud, she felt it – the belief that she, Leilah, was better than Greta, the maid. Her defence was to pretend that Greta didn't exist. She avoided eye contact when they ate together and made no effort to greet her when she got home from school. When Leilah's first period arrived and tore her stomach in half, she stuffed toilet paper into her undies and rolled around on the floor for hours, determined not to ask Greta – the only woman – for help. Through that first afternoon of pain, she practised the speech she would give her mom, whom she resented and needed more than ever. She practised the soft voice with which she would speak, the voice of a small child left unattended. She was sure that if she said the right things, if she expressed her pain in just the right manner, her mom would not hesitate to come home and look after her.

Elke had no reception in the house where she stayed so, every evening, she walked to the only working payphone in the small village she now called home. Every evening Leilah sat by the phone at the allocated time and on those rare occasions that Elke didn't make it to the tikkie box for some or other reason, Leilah spent a sleepless night imagining all the terrible things that were being done to her mom in the dark.

She sat at the phone now, clutching her stomach and waiting for it to ring. Part of her wanted it to stay silent, wanted her mother to fail, but then another thought swept in, the thought of being forever alone and forever sore, the way she was now. Her dad pulled into the driveway a little before 7pm, his headlights filling the lounge with an unfriendly yellow. The smell of frying mince thickened the air and made Leilah gag. The phone rang.

"Hi, sweetheart." Her mom sounded breathless and happy and Leilah was overcome by the feeling that she'd swallowed a ball, big enough to fill her up, but totally empty, a hard circle of nothing.

"Hi," she said.

"You sound funny," her mom said, sounding less happy.

"What's going on?"

"Mom…" Leilah paused, forgetting what she'd practised.

"What? What's going on?"

"I got my period." Leilah was surprised by how deep her voice sounded, nothing like she'd planned, nothing like a child's. Her mom kept quiet so she continued. "It's sore, and I don't have pads, but I'm not dying." Leilah could hear Elke clearing her nose of fresh snot. "Don't get upset," she continued, struck by her mother's rare show of fragility. "I'm okay."

"You actually do sound okay," Elke remarked with phlegmy surprise. "But I think I should still come home. Do you want me to come home?"

"No, stay there if you want to stay. Just tell Dad to get me pads. And something for the pain. I won't go to school tomorrow so he'll have to write me a note and tell a good lie."

"What should we say you have?" Elke asked and Leilah could tell she was smiling.

"We could say Greta poisoned me with one of her oily bolognaises."

"Leilah!" Elke was half-laughing now. "Don't be so mean. Dad loves her mince."

"Well, it's making him even fatter," Leilah said, watching as Dwight struggled out of his car, waving awkwardly at her through the window as he did. "We can say I fell off a ladder or something. Then I won't have to do PE this week, maybe this month, if I'm lucky."

"What's wrong with sport?" her mom asked. "You love playing outside."

"School sport isn't playing Mom. It's a popularity contest and I'm not popular, or hadn't you noticed?" Her mom went on a tangent about the Latin beginnings of "popular" – something about people – and Leilah was happy to hand the receiver over to her dad when he walked into the lounge and put down his briefcase. She dodged his hug and hurried to her room where she lay flat on the floor with her hands on her stomach, trying to feel where the period pain ended and the hard, empty ball began. She wondered why her mother's happiness made her so sad and, failing to find a satisfactory answer, decided she must be a terrible person.

Down the hall Dwight lit a cigarette and, hearing the click of the lighter, Leilah knew they were talking about her. Her dad smoked everywhere and anywhere except when he was on the phone, an odd place to draw the line she thought since the person on the other end couldn't smell his smoke. Still clutching her tummy, she walked to her parents' room and picked up the receiver next to their bed, making sure to hold the mouthpiece away from her face so they wouldn't hear her breathe. Leilah had become an expert at eavesdropping. It evoked the same thrill in her as watching an R-rated film.

"You're meant to be looking after her!" Elke was shouting. "It's 7pm. She's been home alone for hours, Dwight. Why didn't you rush home with pads and painkillers?"

"I didn't know this had happened. If I had, of course I would have come home. But she didn't call me. No one called me."

"Do you come home this late every night?"

"Most nights, same as before," Dwight shot back, choking on his smoke. "I have to work. Don't get mad at me because you're not here."

"Please Dwight, don't lecture me." Her mom sounded

dejected. "Leilah's been hiding under my skirt since she could walk. I have no life outside her, no friends, no job. When was the last time we went out dancing? I gave everything up because she needed me, she needed me all the time. All I ask is that you pick up the reins for six months. Do you think you can do that or do I have to throw in the towel?"

"What do you mean throw in the towel?"

"I mean quit the course and come home."

"Do you want to quit?" Leilah imagined her dad's eyebrows raising, making two neat v's that pulled his soft eyelids towards his hairline.

"No, I don't want to come home." Elke sounded so confident in her answer that Leilah wanted to reach into the phone and grab her neck. "This is the first time in my life that I have a room to myself," she continued. "I wake up and only have to make one breakfast – mine – and in the evenings, I sit on the stoep and listen to the insects. I like being by myself."

"More than you like being with us?" Dwight sounded like a pleading child now, the same way Leilah had wanted to sound.

"No, not more than you, different to you," her mom said. Leilah struggled to hang on to the receiver, aware of the line she was crossing by eavesdropping on this most intimate of conversations but, as with her parents' love-making in Ifafa, she couldn't stop listening. Her ears burned, but she was also excited that in her absence their relationship sounded like a relationship, making her believe that perhaps they still loved each other, not a soap-opera kind of love with lingering kisses and eyes that locked across a room, but a love worth arguing over.

"Then you should stay," Dwight said, "but what should

I do about Leilah? She's a teenage girl with her first period. I have no idea how to approach her."

"Start by asking what she needs." Elke's voice was crisp and clear, and Leilah realised how comforting her sureness sounded, and how much she missed it.

"When has that ever worked?" Dwight asked. "She's as bad at knowing what she needs as I am." The line went dead; her mom's money had run out.

That night, Leilah made her regular journey to the foot of her parents' bed but moved back to her own before Dwight got up. Over the next five days she lay silently on the couch and watched TV, getting up to make sandwiches and change pads, which were too big for her underwear and made her feel like she was wearing a nappy. Each evening her dad worked later and she spoke less until – on the final day of her period – Leilah tried to count the words she'd said since waking and realised she hadn't said any. She wanted to call Frankie and ask her to come over but it had been too long since they'd last sat alone together at her house. Not since that afternoon in the pool. She got up and went to look for Greta, who was sitting in the kitchen folding laundry and listening to the radio.

"You still sore?" Greta asked, the gap between her front teeth seeming to grow wider.

"No, I think it's over now. I'm making tea. Do you want?"

"I'll have coffee, the way you like it. Hot milk, no water."

"Milk coffee's not for you," Leilah said, and immediately she felt guilty.

"Who's it for then?" Greta looked at her, unblinking.

"Me, my mom, and my dad."

"Well, your mom's not here so I'll have hers." Greta

returned her attention to the laundry, and made a clicking sound deep in her jowls.

Leilah turned on her heel and filled the smallest cup she could find with milk. She faced the burring microwave while Greta hummed along to church melodies, her voice too pretty for her face, Leilah thought, as if it belonged to someone else.

Sipping her coffee, Leilah thought about Motheo. She wished he'd come to Durban to visit her, especially now that their mother was gone. Her brother had always teased her but he also hugged her and made her laugh when their parents fought, inviting Leilah into his room and closing the door so she wouldn't have to hear Elke screaming. She picked up the receiver and dialled Motheo's strange cell phone number, which she'd learnt by heart.

"*Hallo*," Motheo answered, his accent different to what Leilah remembered.

"Hi Mo," Leilah said in a small voice. "It's me."

"Sis!" he said, like Leilah was someone special. "It's so good to hear your voice. You okay?"

"Ja, I'm okay, why wouldn't I be?"

"I don't know," Motheo said. "Mom not being there must be hard. She mentioned that you were upset about her course."

"I'm surprised she cares," Leilah huffed. "She was a real bitch about the whole thing, like leaving was no big deal. And now I have to take the stupid bus home from school."

"I grew up taking the bus, and you grew up taking the train," Motheo said, sounding more grown up than Leilah wanted. "What's so bad about that?"

"I stick out on the bus Mo; all the black girls stare at me."

"Sticking out isn't so bad, is it?" Just like Elke, like nothing in the world was worth crying about.

"Maybe for you," Leilah said. "You like being the centre of attention, and you're good at it. But I hate it. And Mom knows I hate it."

"Sis," Motheo said, his voice gentler. "You know I told you that story about Mom wanting to raise us with a tear in one eye and a smile in the other?"

"I remember," Leilah said. "But I still don't get it. How can one eye do something different to the other?"

"I don't think you're meant to take it so literal," Motheo said. "Once, when I'd just turned eighteen, I swore at her because she kept waking me up at 6am on Saturday mornings to transplant a tree, or carry bricks, or clean the pool, all things I could have done at 10am, like a normal person. She didn't seem to mind that I told her to *fuck off,* but she did tell me the story about the tear and the smile. She said she didn't want kids who didn't know how to suffer. I know she does strange things sometimes, but that's just her way of toughening us up, for the real world, you know?"

"But I'm in the real world already, and it sucks."

"Why does it suck? Are those Westville kids giving you trouble? You know I'll come down there and break their necks if they are. I've got no problem breaking necks."

He didn't, Leilah knew. She'd seen Motheo beat up a kid who'd tried to kiss one of his friends without her permission. She'd even seen him raise a fist to Dwight, when he got too drunk one night and started swearing at Elke. He didn't actually hit their dad, but his fist was ready to, and his eyes had looked like little fires. "No one's being mean exactly," Leilah said. "I just don't feel like I fit in here. Did you feel different in Ottery, being, um, German?"

"I'm not really German," Motheo said, his accent back to normal. "But I know what you mean. Some of the Ottery kids called me *whitey* but I don't think they meant it in a bad way."

"That's because there's nothing bad about being white," Leilah muttered.

"Sis, listen to me," Motheo said, his voice sounding old. "There's nothing bad about being who you are. One day, you'll see that. One day, you'll be grateful for that tan you've got, even in winter. I wish I had that."

There it was again. Her *tan*.

"Okay," Leilah said, trying to sound better than she felt. "I'll just wait for one day then. Apparently, that's when all the good stuff happens."

"It'll come sooner than you think. Just hang in there. And do me a favour, wait until you're eighteen to call Mom a bitch to her face, will you? She makes like she doesn't care about that stuff, but she's got her own shit going on. We all have."

"We can say goodbye if you want," Leilah said, her heart sinking. "I didn't mean to bother you."

"You're never bothering me, sis. I'm always here if you need to chat."

Leilah put down the phone and went back to her room. Her milk coffee was cold and a skin had formed across the top. She poured it down the bathroom sink and looked at herself alone in the mirror before scratching red lines down her cheeks and neck and watching them puff up.

Chapter 9

"Want to do something together this weekend, baby?" Dwight asked one morning at the breakfast table.

"Like what?" Leilah asked, taken aback by how good the invitation sounded.

"We could go to the beach and have breakfast at Wimpy, like you used to do with Mum. Would you enjoy something like that?"

"Ja, okay," Leilah said, allowing a small smile of thanks to creep into her face.

The North Beach Wimpy was one of the few places Leilah felt safe going with her dad. It was far enough away, and she liked the smell of sea air mixed with bacon. They found a small table at the back of the smoking section and sat down, Dwight lighting a cigarette while Leilah hid behind a menu and scanned the other tables. There was no one from school that she could see, and the crowd wasn't entirely white, though she and her dad were the only mixed table. Everyone else sat in groups of matching skin tones.

"What are you *lus* for?" Dwight asked once his cigarette was out and Leilah had come out from behind her menu.

"You mean what would I *like*?"

"Ja, what would you like?"

Leilah saw fine, almost undetectable sorrow lines gather between his eyes, and took a breath, shocked by how unkind she'd become. "Bacon and eggs I guess," she continued, looking straight at Dwight. The whites of his eyes looked even yellower than she remembered, and a small brown spot had formed next to one of his irises. "Do you want to share a plate of chips?"

Dwight returned her gaze and they both smiled shyly,

their lips identical in their fullness. "You don't have to ask me twice, you know how much I love chips, and when Mum's here I'm not allowed to eat them. She thinks Durban is making me fat."

She's right, Leilah thought. Her dad's tummy had grown rounder and firmer, though his hips remained slender and his bum barely there. She never understood how she got a round bottom while his was so flat. Wasn't a big bum a marker of their brownness? She wanted to ask but wasn't sure her dad would get it. Did he notice he was brown when he looked in the mirror? Did he notice anything beyond spreadsheets and cigarettes?

"We only have macon," the waitress said when they ordered. "It tastes almost like bacon, but it's Halaal, for the Muslims." The waitress was black, and moved between the tables as if nothing fazed her, collecting a glass here, wiping a table down there, committing orders to memory instead of writing them down. Leilah was jealous of her ease, the certainty with which her shoulders carried her head.

"What's it made from?" Dwight asked, disappointed.

"It's mutton, Dad, you'll like it." Leilah didn't want to keep the waitress longer than necessary. Her eyes were already wandering to other tables, checking glasses and ashtrays, nodding to a man who had his hand up, a gesture to wait, she was coming. There was glamour in the control she had over the space, Leilah thought, her small frame holding all these people and their Saturday mornings together.

"Okay, let's have macon and eggs then. Doesn't feel right, mutton pretending to be pork, but I guess if the Muslims are happy, I have to be too."

"Dad!" Leilah shrieked. "That's rude."

"I'm just playing, baby, don't take everything so serious."

"Two macon and eggs and one plate of chips," the waitress confirmed before turning on her heel and seeing to her other tables. Leilah kept looking as she walked away, the sway of her hips, the up-down of each bum cheek.

"So baby, tell me how you are? How's school, are you settling in there? You don't talk about it much, not to me anyway."

"School's school, Dad, not much to tell. There's this new girl, Rose. She's sitting with us now, with me and Frankie—"

"Frankie and me."

"Yes, Frankie and me."

"Is she nice?"

"She's nice enough, sucks up to Frankie mostly. They have their own thing going on."

"Oh. Well, I hope you don't feel like an outsider. You know what they say about threes."

"No, what do they say?"

"Two's company, three's a crowd. Haven't you heard that expression before?"

"No. It takes more than three people to make a crowd. That's lame."

They fell quiet. Leilah shuffled her feet below the table and Dwight lit another smoke. A group of surfers had gathered on the section of promenade in front of the restaurant, and Leilah looked at them, their zipped-down wetsuits, their tanned torsos, their white-blond hair. They laughed as if they wanted everyone to hear them, to hear how carefree and happy and handsome they were. Leilah ducked her head, not wanting them to catch her staring.

"Dad," she said, "are we kaffirs?"

"What? You're not supposed to use that word."

"But the boys at school use it, and some of the girls.

Frankie even used it, before she moved here. It's normal in Westville."

"I'm not sure about normal," Dwight said, rubbing his hands together and looking towards the ocean. "Do you know what it means?"

"It means black."

"Maybe people here see it that way, but I don't. It's actually an Arabic word, *kāfir*, and it means non-believer, someone who doesn't believe in God."

"*Kāfir*," Leilah repeated, noting how much softer the pronunciation sounded. "So, if I believe in God, then I'm not a kaffir, not a kāfir?"

"It's not that simple, baby. That word has come to mean something different here. Racist people use it to describe Africans."

"But Aunty Millie used it once, back in Ottery. That was the first time I heard it."

"Aunty Millie is a racist."

"But she's Coloured."

"Brown people can be racist too, baby. Aunt Millie doesn't like being in the middle so she criticises black people because it makes her feel stronger, makes her feel..." he paused. "More like a white woman."

"Are we like that, in the middle?"

"I like to think of myself as Dwight. And you as Leilah. What do you think?"

"I don't know. I never thought about it until we moved here. Why did we move here, to Westville I mean? It's so different from Ottery."

"I wanted you to go to a good school and Kingston is one of the best public schools in the country. I never had that, the best."

"Why?"

"Because I'm Coloured and under Apartheid laws, Coloured people weren't full people."

"Are you full now?"

"Not yet, baby, but I'm getting there."

Leilah looked over to the surfers again. They were all holding soft serves, ice cream melting down their chins and hands. They looked suddenly out of place, not as beautiful as they had before, their happiness on display like that.

"Want to go for a walk after breakfast?" Leilah asked, picking up her dad's lighter and lighting his cigarette for him.

"Oh, I'd like that very much," Dwight replied, dropping the lit cigarette from his lips so that he could smile.

They walked side-by-side along the promenade, Leilah only slipping behind him when they passed the skate ramp, where Leilah knew boys from school liked to hang out over the weekend. She pretended to go into the toilet so as not to upset Dwight, who waited for her at the water's edge, just far enough to get his toes wet.

The next week Leilah felt something different. She no longer sprang up each morning to escape her dad's room before he woke. Instead, she lay still when she opened her eyes, staring at the ceiling and trying to remember her dreams. When her dad's alarm went off, she peeked at him over his duvet, and smiled when he opened his eyes. By the groans he made in the morning, Leilah realised Dwight must be in some pain, so she got up and made coffee, which they drank together, he still in bed, she perched on the window sill, the sky lightening behind her. She pushed aside the fear that someone from school was always watching her, and focused instead on the small seed of certainty that had planted itself somewhere between her ears or maybe between her hips. She couldn't put her finger on it but it was there, the belief that she was a girl with clean edges, someone that others might one day like.

To her surprise, the feeling lasted through school on Monday, through first, second and third bell. By lunch time on Tuesday, she stopped waiting for it to disappear, and didn't even mind sitting alone at a desk. She watched Frankie and Rose from behind, their necks both long and slender, Rose's hair giving her additional height while Frankie's short, neat bob made her look like a cartoon character, fun-coloured and harmless. Leilah tore a piece of paper from her notepad and after decorating the edges with hearts and flowers, wrote them an invite to her house that weekend. A picture of their friendship started forming in her mind – Leilah, Frankie, and Rose, the crowd – and it looked to Leilah like a believable picture. She could see them walking up the street alongside her house, sharing a cigarette and laughing at Jack Bertram's stupidity. She could see them together, not two-plus-one but three.

She folded the note into a small square, slipped it into an envelope that she'd pasted together with Pritt and slid it along the ground to Rose's feet. Rose picked it up and smiled over her shoulder at Leilah, a smile so small and honest, that Leilah felt guilty for not welcoming her the way Frankie had. She thought of Greta too, and how similar her skin tone was to the neighbours and friends she'd had back in Cape Town. She gave each of her wrists a pinch and vowed to never think the word *kaffir* again, but once she'd made the promise, the word kept running across her mind, faster and faster until it lost all its meaning.

At break the girls sat on the stairs above the field, which was being set up with tents for the Grade 7 sleepover that weekend.

"I forgot that was this Saturday," Leilah said, her heart

dropping. She couldn't spend a full night in her own bed, let alone in a field of strangers. "Are you guys going?"

"We have to go," said Rose, her confidence so beautiful that Leilah wanted to push her over, or love her, she couldn't decide which. "It will be our first disco."

"Disco?" Frankie looked at Rose and grinned. "No one says disco."

"What is it then, a *social*? That's so white."

Leilah was shocked that Rose knew the race of different words, as if she knew something about all the races, and all the words too. Observing her – the casual sparkle in her eye, the steadiness with which she ate her sandwich – Leilah thought she must know a lot.

"What about 'party'?" Leilah chimed in, a thin wave of excitement running down her spine as she considered the implications of a party – a dress, two proper friends, a boy asking her to dance. A disco ball.

"Do you want to go?" Frankie asked, touching Leilah gently on the elbow.

"Yes. Why not? We could get ready at my house. I mean, if you guys want to? It's just my dad there, and he's so quiet, we'll hardly notice him. I think we could probably steal a swig of his brandy; I know where he keeps it. And his cigarettes. I know where he keeps those too." Leilah was talking too quickly for her mind, the words pouring out without consideration for her nerves and fears. She was overtaken by the feeling that she could do anything Frankie and Rose could do. She could sleep in a field. She could invite her friends to her home. She could talk like a member of the group, not an outsider whispering at its edges.

"Sounds like a plan," Rose said, hopping up from her seat, shaking her bum, and clicking her fingers happily around her ears. "Except the cigarettes. I don't smoke."

"We'll teach you," said Frankie, the first time in a while that she'd put her and Leilah together in a sentence. "It's easy once you get the hang of it."

"No," said Rose. "I don't want to smoke. It makes your hair stink."

Again, Leilah was taken aback by Rose's certainty around those things she liked and those she didn't. It didn't clash with the smile that was almost always on Rose's face, the lightness of her movements, the Jellybeans in her pocket. Her sweetness and sureness seeped into each other and led Leilah to wonder if, perhaps, smiling was not a sign of resignation but resolution.

"Oh, it makes your hair stink, oh no, oh no, oh no." Frankie was teasing Rose now, nipping at her waist with the tips of her fingers, ducking and weaving when Rose tried to nip back. They started laughing together and Leilah leaned back against the cement step to close her eyes and listen to them. The sun felt good on her face, and the sound of tent pegs being hammered into the ground across the field took on a soothing thrum. She imagined the three of them squeezed into a tent, eating marshmallows before bed and falling asleep with sugar-crusted teeth. "What about brandy?" Frankie asked. "Will you have some of that Miss Goody-Two-Shoes?"

"Brandy I'll try, but just a taste. My moms would kill me if they ever found out."

"Your moms?" Frankie asked.

"Ja, my moms. Didn't I tell you I have two?"

"I think I'd remember that," said Frankie, snorting a little and looking at Leilah to back her up.

"I don't remember you telling us," Leilah confirmed. "Maybe you dreamt about telling us. I do that sometimes. And then I can't tell which conversations are real and which are imagined." She thought of kissing Frankie in Ifafa; of holding her hand; of sitting in the pool and making promises not to tell. She wondered if these pictures of them together were real, or if she had dreamt them into being.

"Maybe," said Rose, "but I doubt it. I don't remember my dreams. You guys should come to my house after school and meet my family. Want to?"

"I can't," said Frankie. "My mom's taking me to some lame church thing this afternoon. I'd rather die, but if I don't go, she won't let me come to the party this weekend."

"I can come," said Leilah, leaning forward to catch Rose's reaction.

"Good," Rose said, only hesitating for a second.

"Or we could do it when Frankie can come too?" Leilah felt stupid for inviting herself by herself, as if she was someone Rose wanted to spend time with.

"No man," Rose pushed back. "You don't need your bodyguard there. My moms don't bite. Not hard, anyway."

Rose's house was nicer than Leilah's, a double storey with pastel-blue walls and a red brick driveway. The front façade reminded Leilah of a butterfly, each side identical to the other with white shutters trimming the upstairs windows and an arched doorway with mint-green aloes on either side. The aloes were in bloom and Leilah had to stand still for a moment as she and Rose walked down the driveway, captivated by the red-hot pokers against the pale-blue paint. The lines and colours were as perfect as a magazine cover.

"Come on slowcoach," Rose said, turning back and waving Leilah towards the front door. "I'm hungry."

"Is this really your house?" Leilah asked, her feet still glued to the ground.

"It's not my house silly, it's my mom's."

Leilah had never considered that her mom's house was not also hers. She'd never really considered her home as something that anyone owned, but rather as a collection of rooms and things she was familiar with, even in the dark.

"It's really pretty," Leilah said, forcing her feet in small steps towards Rose and the fancy front door. "I've never been to a house this pretty." Rose looked at her quizzically before turning her attention to the front pouch of her backpack and pulling out a set of keys. They were strung together by a beach-ball keyring, its gaudy colours at odds with the butterfly house to which the keys belonged. Leilah wondered if she was the beach ball and Rose the house, or if perhaps Rose also knew what it felt like to clash with one's surroundings.

"My darling!" The door swung open before Rose could unlock it, and out stepped a petite woman with short white hair and engine-red pumps. She hopped over to Rose and engulfed her in a long hug and, before Leilah had a chance to react, the tiny woman was in front of her, taking Leilah's hands in her own. She was so short that when Leilah's eyes looked instinctually downwards, they met the woman's gaze instead of the ground. "I'm Trudy, Trudy Taylor. You must be Leilah. It's so nice to meet you." Trudy stood on her tiptoes to wind her thin arms around Leilah's neck and, as if by magic, Leilah hugged back, not pausing to consider whether she should or not, whether she wanted to or not.

"Jeez Mom," Rose said, "give Leilah a chance to get inside before you scare her off with your bear hugs."

"I-I don't mind," Leilah responded with a small stutter that Trudy seemed to enjoy. "It's nice to meet you, Mrs Taylor. I really like your house."

"Oh stop!" Trudy said as if embarrassed, although Leilah noticed that her cheeks didn't flush. "You haven't even seen inside. Come on, there's plenty of food in the kitchen. And please, Leilah, call me *Miss* Taylor. I've never been married and never plan to be." Her tone was neither soft nor scoffing and Leilah wondered if she'd ever sound so confident. It wasn't until Trudy rushed ahead of Rose into the spacious front den that Leilah noticed how different they looked. Trudy was white, not as white as her hair but white nonetheless. How could this woman have given birth to Rose, whose plume of black kinks looked as alien next to Trudy's shiny bob as the orchids lining the entrance table? Leilah felt an overwhelming sense of joy as she teased out an image of Rose's charcoal black dad and compact white mom, more beautiful than her own family, but mixed, just like her.

"Where's your dad?" Leilah whispered as they made their way along a wide corridor with pressed ceilings and light wooden floors.

"I don't have one," Rose replied, her answer bouncing off the empty walls. A curiosity burned in Leilah's throat, forming questions she dared not ask for fear of upsetting Rose, who she was liking more and more. Leilah tried to think of something simple to say, a stone too small to make any ripples. But she couldn't. Small talk didn't come easily to her. She always blurted out stuff she shouldn't, odd things that made people squirm or sneer. Like telling a class of strangers that she'd never worn a uniform. Or kissing Frankie the first time she'd felt drunk. Or vomiting into her mouth when Anastasia called Rose a dirty black. Newness made Leilah feel like her mind and tongue were not her own, but belonging to a monster, one that could enter a room at any moment and destroy the secrets she relied on to protect herself. Her defence was to avoid anything unfamiliar and yet here, in this new and sparkling house, with this new and baffling family, she didn't want to run.

The tall corridor opened into a bright kitchen with cloudy countertops and a long central island covered in fruit bowls. Photographs were stuck to the fridge with alphabet magnets, one of Rose under a Christmas tree holding a present, and another of Trudy at a desk covered in paperwork, her hair still blonde, her eyes not quite as sharp.

"Where's this?" Leilah asked, pointing to the image of Trudy with the papers.

"That was my very first office," Trudy said coming over to Leilah and placing a hand on her shoulder, her nails all equally cut and painted in sheer pink. "The first of many."

"What did you do in the office?" Leilah asked.

"I started a gym, and then another one, and another one. Now I have over a hundred all over the country. It's my own little fitness empire." A squeal of laughter escaped Leilah and her hand flew to her mouth, trying to smother the sound. Star Wars had an empire. Mr Kassem had an empire, or at least a reception area big enough to suggest he did. But Trudy, with her pink orchids and fingernails? It seemed unlikely.

"What's so funny about that?" Trudy asked as she pried Leilah's fingers away from her mouth one by one. Irritation crinkled across the older woman's brow. Her lips lay in a straight, angry line. Leilah stopped smiling and looked down, her face warming as she tried to form a polite response.

"Oh nothing, nothing's funny, Miss Taylor," she said, stumbling away from the fridge. "Sorry, I just, I've never met a gym owner before, it's cool, really cool, *so* cool. I mean, I walk past the gym at the shopping centre some afternoons and look inside, and everyone's skin shines and everyone looks so strong. I just, I never imagined I'd meet someone who owned a place like that, a place full of shiny giants."

"Shiny giants?" Trudy started laughing and her face re-opened. "Oh, that's good Leilah, that's very good. I might just use that in my next ad campaign. Who wouldn't want to join a club full of shiny giants? That's my gym, you know, the one in the Westville Mall that you walk past. You're welcome to pop in any time you like. Maybe one day you'll be a shiny giant too. Anyway, must run, lots of work to do. Bye darling." Trudy walked over to Rose to kiss her cheek, and Leilah thought her stride looked longer than before.

"You're weird," Rose said once her mom had left. "Not that it's a bad thing, but I think you should know, just in case someone brings it up one day and you're not ready to be told – you're weird."

"What makes you think I'm ready now?" Leilah asked.

"Maybe you're not, but it's better I tell you than someone who thinks they're normal, like that girl Anastasia. I know she's popular and everything but I think she's boring, the same as every other girl who's got a life as good as hers."

Leilah grinned, delighted by the roll of Rose's eyes when she said *normal* and the sound of Anastasia's name on Rose's lips. It sounded so common, not wielding any power.

"*So* boring," Leilah chirped, dropping her bag to the floor and leaning on the counter in the direction of Rose's coolness. She grabbed an apple from a fruit bowl and took a big bite, closing her eyes as she listened to the sweet white flesh crunching between her teeth.

"I'm sorry about my mom touching your face," Rose said, more solemnly than Leilah had heard her before.

"She's sensitive about her business. I know you weren't laughing at her, or were you?" The slight tilt of Rose's head suggested she might actually like Leilah and wasn't trying to catch her out.

"NO. I mean, no, not at all. I laugh when I get surprised and can't think of what to say. I've never known a woman that's owned a business. My mom was a teacher, and I think her mom was a maid. She always likes to rub that in my face when I don't make my bed. Like I'm too good for something my dead gran did a million years ago."

"You're not supposed to say *maid*." Rose looked solemn. "It's domestic, or housekeeper. Some people even say Minister of Home Affairs."

"Oh," said Leilah. "I thought maid was right. My mom says maid, but only when she talks about her mom. Greta she just calls Greta. That's our, um, domestic."

"So, your mom *used* to be a teacher?"

"Ja, when I was very small, I think. I can't remember exactly when she stopped."

"What does she do now?"

"She just stays at home."

"So, she's a housewife?" Rose had been fishing around in the fruit bowl but now she looked up and studied Leilah.

"Not any more actually." Leilah felt mysteriously irritated. "She's in Sedgefield right now, learning how to massage people, how to be a masseuse." It was the first time she'd used the word *masseuse* and though she wanted it to roll smoothly off her tongue, it came out sounding sticky and unpleasant. "A mas-seuse," she repeated, but it didn't sound much better.

"I don't think my mom would do a job like that," Rose said. "But it's cool that your mom does. Cool that you can get a free backrub whenever you like." A memory came to

Leilah of her mom painting her face with an imaginary paintbrush before bed. She remembered how nice her fingers felt, rough from gardening but not in any hurry, the lines slow and steady, up her nose, across her eyebrows, along her hairline and around her jaw, stroke after stroke until Leilah fell asleep.

"Ja, I guess." She wanted to change the subject. "Hey, so, this weekend should be fun. What do you think of getting ready at my house? I don't have great cloths or makeup but it's easy to get away with stuff when it's just my dad. Frankie and me smoke cigarettes all the time when he's home."

"I told you I don't like cigarettes, but I do want to see your house. And don't worry about clothes and makeup, I've got lots of that. Trudy likes to shop." Rose winked and signalled Leilah to follow her. "Let's go upstairs and look at stuff you could wear to the disco. Our first disco!" Hearing Rose squeal with delight, Leilah realised she liked this stuff too, clothes and things, stuff Frankie would roll her eyes at. Leilah liked feeling like a girl.

Rose led the pair back along the corridor, into the den and up a curling flight of stairs with a newly polished railing. Layla stopped when they reached the landing, noticing more photos, framed and arranged in neat rows. Rose as a baby sleeping in her cot; Rose's first day of school, Trudy standing proudly alongside her, making a thumbs up; Rose in front of Table Mountain; Trudy riding a bicycle with Rose in a little seat behind her. Somewhere in the collection there was a faded photo of Rose standing next to a black woman, holding her hand and looking up towards her, as if waiting for a green light. The woman was almost the same black as Rose, with dark flecks across her cheeks. She was looking straight into camera, squinting from the sun, her feet planted parallel on the ground. She looked unbudgeable.

Rose whistled from somewhere deep in the house, and Leilah turned to look for her, continuing down a wide, pink corridor. Leilah thought of her much shorter passage at home, how she ran from one end to the other to get to her parents' bedroom at night, terrified of what the dark tunnel contained. She wondered if she'd have a house like Trudy's one day, one she could walk through unafraid, wearing a silk nightie. Leilah could hear Rose singing from a room at the far end of the corridor, and she walked towards the sound, looking back at the photo wall a last time, at the woman's feet, and the little girl's upward gaze.

A radio was playing in Rose's room and she was hopping around to the beat, pulling stuff from her cupboard and laying it on the bed. There were already a bunch of dresses out, their patterns bleeding into each other so that Leilah couldn't tell them apart. Dazzled by the mush of colours, she walked over and fell face-first into the sumptuous pile, which smelt like coconut, and felt just as sweet. "Is that lady in the photo also your mom?" Leilah asked, her voice muffled by the fabric.

"I can't hear you," Rose replied as she walked over to the bed and perched on its corner.

"I asked if that lady in the photo, the black lady, is also your mom? At school you said something about having two moms." Leilah had turned her face to the side and each time she inhaled, a piece of tulle followed her breath and tickled her nose. Her arms lay along her sides, her feet dangled off the edge of the bed.

"Yes," Rose said. "That's my first mom. Trudy is my second mom. My first mom works for my second mom, as a domestic." Leilah was impressed by how few words Rose used to explain all this. The simplicity made it easier, and harder, to understand. "Do you want to meet her?" Rose asked.

"Yes," Leilah replied quickly, lifting herself off the dresses. "Do you see her often?"

"I see her every day," Rose said. "She lives downstairs, in her own little place, but not separate from us or anything. I'll call her." Rose walked over to a grey box on the wall, and pressed a button that made it crackle.

"*Yebo*," said a firm voice through the intercom.

"*Sawubona, Mama*," Rose said, followed by other stuff in Zulu that Leilah didn't understand. She pressed the button again and the crackling stopped. "She's coming now."

"Just now, or *now* now?" Leilah asked.

"Now now," Rose said.

"Is it weird having moms of—"

"Of what?"

"Of different races?" Leilah looked at her feet.

"I don't have anything to compare it to," said Rose. Her confidence was still there but her mind seemed to have wondered somewhere less cheerful than jellybeans. "Is it weird for you, being a mix?"

"Did Frankie tell you that?"

"Ja, but only because I asked. You're the only white girl in class that doesn't get sunburnt after PE." Rose used her slender black fingers to put air quotes around white.

"In Westville it's weird. Most of the time I feel weird."

Rose stayed quiet for a while. "My surname changed to Taylor when Trudy adopted me, but at school I still use Mthethwa. Harder to pronounce but it's what kids expect – for a black girl to have a black surname. Makes my life easier."

"Doesn't Trudy mind that you're pretending?"

"Pretending to be black?" Rose started laughing and Leilah joined in, swept up in the silliness of it all. Had she been making a big deal out of nothing? Was the question of who she was only scary because she kept asking?

There was a knock on the door and Rose's first mom entered. She was taller than Trudy and her movements were slower, more considerate. She studied Leilah before sticking her hand out and saying, "You're pretty."

"Am I?" Leilah asked, her cheeks as hot as the sun.

"Don't be so shy girl. The world doesn't like shy people. I'm Zenzile, and you are?"

"I'm Leilah."

"Nice to meet you, Leilah. I've heard some small things about you, but Rose didn't mention you were pretty." Leilah couldn't tell if being pretty was, in Zenzile's eyes, a good thing. She was the spitting image of Rose, her hair as light on her head, her neck as slender, her ankles as fine. She wore a plain blue t-shirt tucked into a black three-quarter skirt, with a frilly apron cinched around her waist .

"I'm sure you've heard more about Frankie than about me," Leilah said, looking between mother and daughter self-consciously.

"No, I don't think so," Zenzile responded. "When Rose talks about Frankie, she talks about you too. She talks about you together. As together." A smile sprang on to Leilah's face, so fast she thought she'd been slapped. "You're blushing again. Stop that and show me what you plan on wearing. I want to make sure you girls look decent."

"Hayibo ma! We're not those kinds of girls. Leilah, try this on." Rose was holding out a pale-yellow dress, velvet, with spaghetti straps and a round neckline. Leilah held it against her uniform and looked in the mirror.

"Do you think it will fit me?" she asked.

"You won't know until you try it on," Zenzile said, so matter-of-fact that Leilah started undressing right there in front of her. She got down to her undies and socks and thanked her lucky stars that she'd listened to Frankie and bought a training bra. The dress struggled over her shoulders, but with Rose's help, Leilah managed to slip into it. "That's the one," Zenzile said when the dress was on and by the way she said it, Leilah knew she must be right.

Chapter 10

The girls' sports field was filled with row upon row of canvas two-man tents with festoon lights strung up around the perimeter. Flood lights on either end of the field cast long shadows across the grass and any faces that crossed it. To Leilah, the scene looked like something out of a science-fiction film, a place where light and dark were at war, and only those who adapted to both could survive.

Frankie and Rose walked ahead, looking this way and that, surveying every detail, while Leilah could only look at one thing at a time, a dread growing in her that worsened the bigger the picture got. In the days leading up to the disco, a tiny sprout of hope had grown in her, a belief that she might make it through the night without her mom or dad nearby, that she might dance and drink sweet punch and sneak off for cigarettes, like the teenager she dreamed of being. But arriving at the school and seeing how different it looked at night, how many dark corners there were for people to hide in, the sprout of hope wilted and her hands started to shake. She forced her attention to the fine rim of light that framed Frankie and Rose's silhouettes, and kept walking, fiddling with the hem of her velvet dress so that her hands wouldn't give her away.

An escape plan started running through her head – a reason to go home, when to start faking it, where her dad would fetch her so that no one would see them together. Like her dad, she was good at telling small lies, but as she practised the lie in her head and visualised how much pity to invoke, the dread only got worse and she was torn between the demons that lurked in the school field and the demons her friends might become if they knew she was such a coward. Leilah decided to hold on a while and see how it went. She was sharing a tent with Frankie, so wouldn't have to sleep alone, and Rose had done her makeup so perfectly she looked the closest to pretty she ever thought she would. Secretly, she wanted Aarush, her admirer, to see her like this, and to write her a little note the following week to say he thought she was beautiful and that he would have liked to dance, had he had the courage to ask. She could see his handwriting, the exaggerated arc of his c, the sweeping tail of his g, and had already decided to keep such a note to herself rather than share it with Frankie as she usually did. She no longer wanted to mock Aarush's legs, even though they did look like a stick insect's.

The girls found their tents along the outskirts of the temporarily erected settlement. They were flanked by the school's perimeter fence and Leilah fixated on the street lights along Westville Main Road while Frankie and Rose offloaded their bags. A light fog hung in the evening air, catching the glow from the street lights and reducing visibility to a couple of metres. Leilah held her hand out in front of her and saw the edges her fingers blur in the murk.

"Come on, Leilah!" Frankie said, tugging at her elbow from inside the tent. "Put your stuff down so we can go see the hall. I think I just heard the Spice Girls!" Leilah had never heard or seen Frankie this girly, her hair held back with two dainty clips, her lips smeared in watermelon lip gloss. The sound and image of her friend cut through the fog, and Leilah decided that she could shelve her fears long enough to see the hall, and maybe even dance. She threw her overnight bag into the tent and smoothed the front of her dress.

"Okay," Leilah said taking Frankie's hand in one of hers, and Rose's in the other. "Let's go." The three held onto each other as they climbed the tall stairs of the pavilion, flashing their panties to the night with each exaggerated step. A disco ball hung from the centre of the school hall, shooting small squares of white light across the walls and ceiling, and eliciting an unexpected thrill in Leilah's stomach. An additional strobe light flashed red and green beams across the floor and a smoke machine spat out puffs of white smoke whenever the beat dropped. The DJ was a skinny young man with peroxided tips and hollow eyes, his fingers moving knowingly between the dials of his mixer while his torso bopped mechanically back and forth, as if disconnected from his legs and feet.

Though the hall was just as murky as outside, Leilah relaxed once she stepped into its warm, flashing belly. Something in the smoke and lights and music detached her from her feelings, and she allowed herself to step ever so slightly away from Frankie and Rose into her own space. She saw Anastasia's silhouette at the far end of the hall with Jack Bertram hanging off her, the crest of his hair gelled obnoxiously high. He caught her looking at him, and passed his eyes from the top to the bottom of her before looking away. Some of the sickness Leilah had been feeling crept back in through her ears, and she moved quickly back to Frankie's side, trying to ignore the way Jack had looked at her.

"Wanna go to the bathroom and have a swig of the brandy I stole from my dad?" Leilah asked, looking between Rose and Frankie with as much bravado as she could muster.

"Ja, what a question," Frankie said.

They walked arm in arm to the bathroom and finding it empty, took one, two, three swigs each from a flask in Leilah's rucksack. While Rose and Frankie were checking their makeup, Leilah swigged two more. As warmth spread down her throat and into her groin, she moved easily back towards the hall, the velvet dress shifting like warm water across her nipples. "I feel fantastic!" she screeched to no one in particular, and she sounded nothing like the Leilah she knew and disliked. This brandied version of herself was loud and surefooted, her chin pointed forward, her hands at her sides instead of fiddling stupidly around her mouth. Like this, nothing could touch her, not Anastasia, not Jack, not Kingston Senior Primary, not even the night.

She stepped back into the hall and felt that she was it, the beginning and the end of everything, the only pair of eyes that mattered. She spotted Aarush sitting on a chair in the corner sipping slowly from a glass of Coke, his stick insect legs folded. Without thought, she walked up to him and reached out her hand. "Wanna dance?" she asked, impressed by how disinterested she sounded. Aarush choked on his Coke and turned away from her to clear his nose of bubbles. Leilah bopped while she waited, her feet glued to the ground like she'd seen the DJ doing. Aarush jumped up, still wiping the cola off his face, and stuttered something that Leilah couldn't hear over the music. She took his hand and pulled him to the heart of the dancefloor, and with arms as endless as a rainbow, she wrapped herself around Aarush's neck, and let her nose slip under his chin. He smelt like cologne, not as spicy as her father's but still musky, like the small pink sweets at the bottom of a Lucky Packet. Leilah felt Aarush's hands weave gingerly around her waist, trembling ever so slightly. She moved closer in towards him, propelled by his shyness and the feeling that in his arms she was the bigger person. They swayed from side to side barely moving their feet, Leilah sucking in the brandy and cologne, Aarush's chest so still she wondered if he'd stopped breathing.

"I really like you," he said, leaning down and whispering into Leilah's ear.

"I know," she said. "You told me in your letters." She felt invincible.

"D-do you like me?"

"I don't know. Maybe." She stood on her toes and with steady movements leaned in to kiss him. The strobe slowed everything down so that the one second it took to reach his lips felt like two, and the two she spent kissing him felt like four. When her feet landed back on the ground, she turned on her heel and trotted back to Frankie and Rose, who were looking at her through the lights and smoke, Rose smiling, Frankie fiddling with her hairclips before yanking them out and throwing them to the floor.

"What was that all about?" Frankie asked, almost shouting.

"What?" said Leilah, also half-shouting. "I felt like it."

"Whatever, he's gross. You shouldn't have done that." Frankie's head had fallen to one side, as if her usually straight neck could no longer hold it up.

"You're not the boss of me, Frankie." Leilah didn't mean to sound so vicious, but the warmth in her belly had grown into a snake that wanted to bite something. She sashayed out of the hall and when the cold dark wall of outside swept over her, she knew at once that she'd made a mistake. All the warmth drained from her face, and with fear seeping back in, she pulled out her flask. It was empty, just a few warm drops left that stung her lips. She started running, with an urgent need to replenish the burn that had made her kiss Aarush, but once she reached the field, she couldn't remember where their tent was. She kept running into the maze, down one row, then another. She was looking for something familiar but all she could remember was the image of Frankie and Rose silhouetted under the glow of a street light. Street light! They were on the end of the field closest to the main road. Leilah ran to the far end of the tent maze to get some perspective.

She reached the edge, her heart racing. The big tree that she, Frankie, and Rose sat under when it got hot was a little way off. She walked over and sat on a bench under the tree's wide arms, aware that she was in shadow but comforted by the big pools of floodlight just a few metres away. She put her hand to her chest and took a few deep breaths, closing her eyes and trying to picture her tent again. She saw it now, in the lane where the school field and the main road met, four tents from the corner. She'd refill the flask, go back to Frankie, say sorry for kissing Aarush and ask her if she wanted to dance. Not a slow dance or anything, unless Frankie wanted that. She wouldn't mind slow dancing with Frankie.

As she sat contemplating Frankie's long neck – would she fit under her chin like she had with Aarush? – Leilah heard a leaf crack. Or was it a twig? She couldn't say before the steps grew quicker and more determined, and then the cracking was right behind her and in the dark, she felt a blow to the space between her shoulder blades. Before she felt any pain, she was on the ground, her arms twisted behind her like she'd seen on *Law and Order*. Her body stiffened and the twist tightened. Her lips smeared into the dirt.

"I know you're a mongrel," Jack Bertram's voice growled into the back of her head. "I saw you and your darkie dad at the beachfront. I watched you the whole time."

A string of images ran rapidly through Leilah's mind –

pictures of her and Dwight eating breakfast at Wimpy, walking side-by-side along the beach, laughing at something she couldn't remember now. Had she hugged him, or kissed him, or done anything to suggest she was his daughter? How did Jack know? Who would he tell? The hand on her back grew heavier and when Leilah tried to push herself up, she found that she couldn't. Jack pushed harder and more dirt filled her mouth. Leilah wondered how long she could go without breath and, as she wondered that, Jack pulled her dress up and stuck his hand between her legs, up and into her until it hurt.

"Do you like this?" he asked, spitting into her ear. Leilah tried to speak but there was too much sand gritting between her teeth and soiling her tongue. "I bet you like it more than you liked that curry muncher Aarush. Don't let me see you kissing that mutt again." Jack made a scoop with his fingers before pulling his hand out of her, and using Leilah's back as a launch pad, lifted himself to standing. She turned her face to breathe and watched as he sauntered off down the tent lane, silhouetted by the street light just as Frankie and Rose had been.

Elke

Chapter 11

The view from Elke's stoep was a neat vista across the forest of stinkwoods separating her from the village. For three months she'd spent Monday to Friday there, eight hours a day, learning the theory and practice of bodies – fat ones, skinny ones, skew ones, straight ones. Every day she had a body beneath her fingers, a set of bones and flesh that she learnt to silently converse with.

Evenings and weekends were her own, and she tended to spend them alone, turning down invitations from the others on her course to go for dinner or walks or beers at the village pub. Being away from Dwight and Leilah made Elke realise how much she liked her own company, which was surprising since she'd never thought of herself as particularly likeable. She knew she was poor mannered and blunt because people let her know – not so much with their words as with their uncomfortable stares and silences, signs that she was too loud, or too honest, or simply too much. The people on her course seemed to like her more than most, which she attributed to their own strange natures. It took a certain kind of person to rub bodies for a living and, amongst such people, Elke felt comfortable saying *I want to be alone.*

She had never considered herself a healer. When she thought of healers, she thought of shamans and sangomas, and perhaps the odd shrink, those special few who could see more of a person than they wanted you to see. But when she touched a back for the first time, when she ran her fingers along a spine, and traced the angles of a shoulder blade, a current passed between the stranger's body and hers and that made her feel special, made her believe she could heal.

She was in a group of eight students, of which there were two others who she considered suitable to this kind of work. One was Sam – a voluptuous woman so jolly that at first Elke couldn't take her seriously. She made stupid jokes to fill the silences that settle between strangers, a trait that had always irritated Elke. Why did people find quiet so disagreeable? So, it was with some scepticism that Elke lay on the bed to be worked on by Sam for the first time, her mouth and nose wedged into the awkward hole that always smelt of old breath. When Sam's hands touched Elke's back, that same current that made Elke feel so powerful passed from Sam into her, and she took a deep breath to stop herself from writhing. Sam – jolly, appeasing Sam – had it too. A body's mood travelled through her, just as it travelled through Elke. Elke decided they could be friends.

Michael was the other student suited to body work and he didn't mind letting you know. He wore loose cotton pants that clung to his hips with an overused drawstring, and if he wasn't barefoot he was wearing Jesus sandals. He burned incense and clutched crystals and spoke like a river with no pauses between his words. But none of it was insincere and when Michael worked on Elke for the first time, she fell asleep within seconds and woke feeling as though her skin and the air were the same entity. For a moment she floated off the massage table and looked at this lanky man standing over her still body – his hands hovering up and down her spine, his bare feet rocking ever so slightly from heel to toe – and she knew Michael was a body whisperer too.

The rest of the class also worked on her, and she on all of them, but it was only Sam and Michael whom Elke respected and, as the course wore on, she started to wonder if they respected her too. Was this ego, she wondered, every time she imagined their muscles rippling beneath her fingers, and if it was ego, would it get in the way of her instinct? She always alternated between self-belief and self-disgust.

One morning Sam picked up on Elke's turmoil. Outside, the sky was grey and the clouds hung low. "What's up with you today?" Sam asked. "Your hands feel funny." She was lying face down on the massage bed and Elke heard her suck the insides of her mouth, clearing the spit that had gathered while she spoke. Folds of fat spread from either side of Sam's spine and a deep bra line ran across her puffy shoulder blades. She giggled uncomfortably with the question, and Elke relaxed somewhat, laying a hand on Sam's rippling mounds in a gesture meant to comfort her. Elke wondered if Sam gabbled and giggled because she thought that's what people needed and if Elke was honest, that was what she needed – someone who laughed instead of sighing, as if the world were not so heavy after all.

"Do you ever get the feeling that you're good at this?" Elke asked. "Good at bodies?"

"I wouldn't say I'm *good*," Sam said immediately, her humility prancing around the room like an ostrich. "But I feel calm, like being under water. I can't talk and I don't want to talk. It's the only time I feel okay being quiet, like I won't disappear if I don't say something."

"Oh," said Elke.

"Do you believe you're good at this?" Sam asked, turning onto her back now so that she could look Elke in the eye. Her breasts were out, soft as dough, and she made no attempt to cover them up, which again put Elke at ease.

"Yes," said Elke. "When I feel connected to the body beneath me, I do think I'm good. Not everyone can do that, feel connected to someone without knowing who they are or where they come from – or do you think I'm kidding myself, believing I'm special?" Elke didn't usually put herself on the line like this, waiting for someone else's appraisal of her. But Sam was someone who seemed to know a few truths, who could see things others couldn't, and for this, Elke trusted her.

"I don't think you're kidding yourself," Sam said, laying her hands across her breasts as if noticing for the first time that they were exposed. "I felt that connection when you worked on me for the first time. I also felt you judging me." Sam grinned, toothy and teasing. "Am I right?"

Elke dropped her head and chuckled, her eyes glued to Sam's bare skin which in this muted light reminded her of fresh snow. "Doesn't everyone judge everyone?" Elke asked, peering out from under her freshly cut fringe.

"That they do," Sam said, rolling back onto her stomach.

Elke rubbed her hands together for a minute and placed two warm palms below each of Sam's shoulder blades, splaying her fingers like bird wings. She pushed in and under the blades and stayed like that for a while, exerting as much pressure as she felt Sam needed. She hadn't learnt this from anyone but imagined it felt nice, a pair of strong wings holding you in place. Sam inhaled and exhaled deeply, one, two, three times. The third time Elke felt something leave her, some grey and heavy thing, and Sam's body grew even softer, her folds tumbling a little further over the edges of the bed.

While she sat on the stoep of her cottage and waited for 7pm, when she'd make her way to the village payphone and call home as she did every day, Elke ate boiled eggs on rye bread, with dollops of mayonnaise and thick slices of tomato coated in salt. She listened to the shuffle of bugs as she ate, the crickets singing, the drip-drip of the outdoor tap. In the stillness, the day's contents slipped slowly from her mind, and she realised again how easy solitude was for her, how normal it made her feel and how much she enjoyed it.

Despite this, a worry was brewing. The last few times she'd spoken to Leilah, her daughter had sounded distant. She'd been speaking in clipped sentences and hushed tones, and there was none of the usual banter between them, no hint of the irritability she'd come to expect from Leilah, whose journey into adolescence made her increasingly insufferable. Elke was starting to miss Leilah's stroppiness, the pause on the line when she rolled her eyes, the annoyed smack of her lips. She needed some sign that her daughter was in there, her fists raised to the world, even though it frightened her so. Over the last two weeks, she'd been too agreeable, and Elke needed to know why.

She washed her single plate and spent a few minutes stroking Ben, the cottage cat. Ben came and went as he pleased, adopting each new tenant as if they were his own, his commitment to one or the other as fluid as his tail. With her jacket and walking boots on, Elke made her way down into the stinkwood forest, shining her flashlight as she walked, aware of how safe she felt out of the city. There was nothing here to hurt her but spiders and snakes and she wondered if Leilah could like this kind of darkness, a dark without humans, with a view of the stars.

She reached the tikkie box, an old rusted rectangle on the edge of the village with *Lenadia4Freddie* scratched into the scratchpad. She ran her fingers across the lettering, irritated by its sentimentality but also wishing that Dwight would hold her hand more. The coin made a noise as it travelled into the guts of the phone, and each number she pushed made its own sound, culminating in a tune of ten notes that was unique to home.

"Hallo." Greta's deep voice travelled effortlessly through the phone, the gap in her teeth acting like a tuba.

"Hi Greta, it's Elke. How are you?"

"Hi madam. I'm good. Thank you." Elke usually insisted that Greta not call her madam, but she didn't want to waste her coin on that now.

"Greta," she said, choosing her words more carefully than she usually would. "Is Leilah okay? I know she can be difficult, but apart from that, does she seem okay to you?"

"She doesn't speak to me, madam. She doesn't speak to anyone."

"Not even Frankie?"

"Frankie hasn't been here madam. Not for two weeks."

"What happened two weeks ago?" Elke knew she should be speaking to Dwight about this, but she also knew how much he struggled to confront Leilah about her feelings. When Leilah said she was fine, he believed her, or he didn't, and nodded anyway.

"She and Rose and Frankie were here at the house, putting on dresses, doing makeup. She looked good. She was smiling." Elke wanted to stretch out Greta's sentences, to make them longer and more helpful. She took a breath, ran her fingers along the scratch pad again, and rearranged her feet.

"And then? What made her stop smiling? Anything you can tell me would be helpful, Greta. She doesn't sound right. I'm worried."

"Hard to worry from so far away, madam. She's not my Leilah, so I don't know what is right and what is wrong with her."

"No," said Elke, "I suppose you don't. Please call her for me. Thanks." She listened as Greta put down the receiver and shuffled off, slower than usual, Elke thought irritably. She heard the faint call of Leilah's name, and then the patter of her daughter's bare feet.

"Hi Mom." Her voice was so far away, it seemed to echo.

"Hi sweetheart. How are things?" Elke squeezed softness into her tone, afraid that her usual brashness might scare off the bird peeping into the receiver. At the same time, she wanted to reach into their Durban home and shake Leilah awake. Shake this small frightened thing until she grew big and brave.

"I got an A on my maths test. Miss Caxton thinks I'll move up a class next year." *Next year*, Elke thought, *high school*. She shivered and wound her scarf tighter around her neck.

"That's excellent, sweetie," she replied in a revolting squeal, nervous for reasons she couldn't articulate. A spider fell in front of Elke's face, its busy legs alight in the glow of her torch, its web too fine for Elke to see. She stared at it for a moment, suspended with the tiny creature in silence. "I miss you," she said, her attention still fixed on the spider, which was disappearing quickly into an empty sky, as if it needed no anchorage at all. Her eyes burned as she lost sight of it and her free hand shot up to scratch the itch along the bridge of her nose. She'd never told someone she missed them. She'd never been told she was missed.

"Oh," Leilah said. "You'll be fine. Want me to fetch dad?"

"You don't want to talk any more?" There was no response and for a moment she thought Leilah might share something with her, something to suggest they were two bodies spun of the same cloth, always tugging at each other, regardless of time and space.

"We speak every night Mom, what could I tell you that I didn't say yesterday? Thanks for calling. Hold on for Dad." The receiver dropped and Elke heard her walk off, down the corridor until there was no sound of her left. Elke listened to the quiet; a bird of prey called some way off, followed by Dwight's uneven shuffle. She knew before he spoke, by the way he mumbled as he sat down at the phone table, by the clink of his ice, by the clearing of his throat, that he was drunk.

"Hi, how you?" Dwight seldom called Elke by her name. When Leilah was around, he called her *Mum* and now that she wasn't, Elke had no name.

"Have you been drinking, Dwight?"

"Oh please, I've had one or two scotches."

"Something's wrong with our daughter." The ice in her husband's drink clinked. He sipped and swallowed. "Dwight? Put your fucking drink down and listen to me. Leilah isn't happy. Something happened. She..." Elke's voice cracked and she gave herself a little punch on the cheek. "She sounds like she's breaking in two, but slowly, so no one notices."

"Fuck it, Elke." There it was, her name. "You know what your problem is? There's always a war coming in your head. You won't let anyone be happy."

"You know what your problem is, Dwight?" Clink, slurp, slurp, clink. "You think you're the first piece in an arrangement of dominos, and you have to stay upright or the whole lot will fall down. So you don't do anything, you just stand still, hoping that no one else moves. But I'm not a fucking domino Dwight, and neither is Leilah. That's your other family, that Coloured one remember, the one you were so eager to get away from." Elke didn't like Dwight's sister Millie, her urgent pleas to be more like God, an imaginary white guy perched in the clouds.

"My Coloured family? And what is Leilah if not my *Coloured family*."

"That's not what I meant."

"Don't talk kak. You always say what you mean."

Elke felt the hot air rush out of her. Her toes began to fidget in her shoes, searching for comfort and warmth. "Please, just look out for our daughter. Look properly, Dwight. I'll call you tomorrow." She put down without waiting for his response and tried listening to the forest sounds, sounds she loved and which usually loved her back. But in her ears, another noise was growing, a faint and constant ringing that drowned out all the crickets.

Chapter 12

That night as Elke tried to fall asleep, Leilah's square face kept pushing into her mind. Her daughter's shy but stubborn gaze was fading away, and in its place, a plastic smile. Then Dwight appeared, his drunk yellow eyes, his whiskey-wet lips. Her jaw was clenching and her shoulders remained raised and taught, no matter how many breaths she took. This was Dwight's fault, this absence in Leilah. He'd let her float off, and now Elke lay alone, unable to enjoy this one short period of solitude, wondering instead how to re-anchor her daughter.

She walked to the kitchen and poured a glass of water. Was it unfair that she'd been enjoying herself here, speaking to her family once a day but otherwise unencumbered? Or did she have to obsess about them as she did now, worry, get hot with rage as she was now? Did this make her a good mother? Elke thought of her own mom, Maria, and the apron she wore every day except Sundays when she went to church. Maria was inseparable from the house, and from housework. As a child, Elke thought she must enjoy it, all that scrubbing, and carpet beating, and mending. She'd been a maid before she'd married Elke's father, Klaus, so Elke assumed cleaning was an accepted part of her mother's nature. It was only once she had her own spouse, children, and home that she learnt the mundanity of ironing the same shirts every week, knowing they'd just re-wrinkle.

Elke then thought of herself as a daughter – thirteen, Leilah's age, breasts sore from growing, skin as unpredictable as the future. At thirteen, she'd just moved to Cape Town from their small German village of Ahronsburg, and Maria had little time to soften Elke's fall in this strange new land. She'd been too busy cleaning house, trying to build a life that would make Klaus happy, or at least comfortable enough to leave Germany's sins behind him. Her mother hadn't seen the indignity Elke suffered as she started to bleed and become a woman, and how it knitted into the shame of where she'd come from. No, in those early days of leaving Germany behind, Maria only had eyes for Klaus, and much like Leilah seemed to be doing now, Elke had disappeared.

Elke built on the little English she'd learnt in Germany, and read books – children's books first, adult's later – learning the language of the free. Her parents enrolled her in the German school, but she was careful not to make friends, aware of the growing desire in her to be anything but German, even if that meant being South African. She kept quiet in class, read during break, and walked herself home every afternoon, each week learning a new route, a new mountain path where she could peddle time before having to go home. She grew infatuated with the great mounds of rock that were her new neighbours – Table Mountain, Lion's Head, The Twelve Apostles – rocks that had been there for millennia, growing too slowly for it to hurt. She found a field of chincherinchee at the base of Lion's Head, small white flowers with long green stems that rubbed together in song if you got close enough to listen. She lay between them, the damp ground seeping into her uniform, and let the strange sound engulf her. There, hidden, she felt the freest she could feel in this new land, free from the bounds of her foreigner's body.

By fifteen, Elke had become fluent in English and was intrigued by another Cape Town language, Afrikaans. It was a variation of Dutch, but she found it far more intoxicating than Dutch, not white Afrikaans but brown Afrikaans, the kind spoken by a people known as "Coloured". She'd never understood why brown people would be named *Coloured*, for surely everyone was a colour of some sort, and therefore all coloured? She didn't speak about this to anyone. Who could she speak to at her white German school, or in her white immigrant neighbourhood, or at home where her parents grew increasingly opaque, scared of the southern sun and everything it brought to light?

Elke started detouring through the Bo-Kaap on her way home from school, a place of multi-coloured houses that sat above the city centre on the steep slope of Signal Hill. She soon learnt it was a Muslim neighbourhood by the long gowns worn by both men and women, by the haunting calls to prayer, by the smell of food cooking through open doors, smells that reminded her of Scheherazade, far-off and exotic. Elke had heard her father talk about the forced removals that were happening all over the country at the time but she'd never heard him speak of the Bo-Kaap, this brown community surrounded by whites, seemingly unscathed by the nationalist government's separation tactics.

After a few weeks, Elke felt as though she was starting to learn the rhythm and pace of the Bo-Kaap and its language. In the mornings, at first light, old ladies sat on their balconies feeding the pigeons. The birds gathered in the cobweb of phone and electricity wires that spread across every street, flocking down in synchronised patterns each time a handful of breadcrumbs hit the pavement. They'd surround the feeders until the breadcrumbs were all gone, and then return to their wires, waiting for the next handout. Elke liked to sit still under the street lights and listen to them fly, the trill of their wings flapping in unison. Once the pigeons returned to their wires, the feeder would look at her and smile, some more sceptical than others, though never unkind or expectant that she should leave.

In the afternoons, the light was different. The soft hues of the morning sun were replaced by stark, almost blinding colour. Each house was painted a different shade of rainbow, and in the 3pm light, those colours began to scream, jolting Elke awake until the next day. The routine of pigeons, school, and colour broke her sense of detachment into manageable pieces.

As she grew more accustomed to the faces along her usual route home, Elke decided to push deeper into the Bo-Kaap, aware of how white she was but still relatively naïve to the invisible lines separating her from them. *They* were a place she could hide from her parents, and for that reason alone, she liked being amongst them. She made her way up the Bo-Kaap's steep central artery, hopping from one cobblestone to another to distract from the tedious incline. At the top she reached a small café selling cigarettes, Cokes and fresh samosas, and after waving to the small man inside, she turned left in the general direction of the neighbourhood where she lived. She came upon a park where a group of boys her age was lingering, eyes darting this way and that as if they were doing something that might get them into trouble. "Hi girlie," they called as she walked past. "You're as naais as a tamatie slice." Elke kept looking straight ahead, at the flat line of Table Mountain and the heat waves that shimmered around its edges on days as hot as this. Though she was eager to get away from the strange boys, she quite enjoyed being called a tomato slice, a veggie-fruit, plump and juicy. It was a far cry from the pale, plain, blonde girl she saw in the mirror every morning, and the unfeeling glaze over her once-sparkling eyes.

The road started to narrow to a width that wouldn't accommodate two parked cars, which was no problem since there were not many cars. Those that did sit outside their homes were battered but spotless. One had flat tyres and was held in place by bricks, but even without feet it looked proud, small gardens of moss and weeds growing around its base.

"Hey, what you doing looking at my car like that?" The woman's voice came from somewhere above Elke's head. She peered up, squinting into the hot sun, her cheeks wet with sweat. The owner of the voice was fine boned and short, wrapped in a black hijab with gold trim. Her eyes were dark brown and close together, her face the colour of cinnamon. The woman might have been intimidating were it not for her eyebrows, two thick black lines arching across her forehead, moving animatedly in different directions even as she scolded. "I said, what is a thing like you doing in my street?"

"Walking home," Elke said, as if she had as much right to be there as anyone else. "I live just over there, on the opposite side of the slope."

"We don't get many visitors from the *opposite side*," the woman said, eyebrows still dancing. "You look hot. Want to come in for tea?" Elke started walking towards the woman before she'd given her an answer, up a narrow set of stairs to the first-floor balcony from which the eyebrows were calling. By the time she reached the balcony, the woman had turned and was walking down a dark corridor towards a light at the far end. Draped all in black, feet hidden, she looked like she was floating.

Elke stepped into the corridor and let her eyes adjust to the dark. The coolness felt soothing on her sunburnt skin, and she pulled her school shirt away from her neck so that it might get inside her too. She walked to a small sunlit kitchen, where the woman was scuttling around boiling water and fetching tea cups from a cupboard above her head. She was too short to see inside the cupboard, but seemed to know the shape of every piece of crockery, feeling this one and that, before pulling out two cups and saucers, delicate sets with curly handles and lips, embossed with red roses.

"Here, sit," the woman said and Elke sat at one of the two benches saddling the chipboard table. "I'm Fatima, but you can call me Tittie." Elke supressed a chuckle. She couldn't imagine Tittie's titties, not under all that black cloth.

"I'm Elke. Thanks for inviting me in. It's hot out there today."

"Where you from?" Tittie asked.

"The other side of the slope, like I said."

"Naai man, where are you really from?" Tittie was holding a can of condensed milk that she'd pulled from her small bulbous fridge. She looked at Elke for a moment before returning to the tea cups and pouring a dash of the thick sweet liquid into each.

"I'm from Germany. My parents moved us here for a fresh start. Or at least that's what I've been told." Klaus and Maria didn't look any fresher. They looked to Elke like two cabbages wilting side by side, their bodies still firm but their faces starting to sag, giving away their decay.

"A fresh start from what?" Tittie asked, laying Elke's tea cup in front of her and sitting on the bench opposite. In the warm light of the kitchen, Elke noticed that Tittie's dark eyes shone hazel.

"The war," Elke said.

"Which war?" Tittie asked, blowing her tea.

"Um," Elke replied, trying to hide her surprise. "Hitler's war."

"Oh ja," Tittie said, flippant, like Hitler was just another guy. "We have our own war going on here. Can't keep track of everyone else's."

"May I ask why you invited me in? A stranger I mean."

"You looked like you needed a cup of tea," Tittie said. "Was I right?"

"Ja..." Elke paused. She'd only just started to say *ja* in place of *yes* and although it wasn't too far off from the German *Jawohl,* she felt self-conscious saying it to Tittie now.

"Ja, and...?" Tittie was smiling.

"Ja, I did need a cup of tea. It's hard work climbing these streets. They're as steep as the mountains."

Tittie chuckled. "Not quite as steep, but I guess you could say we're part of the mountain up here. I like being on the hill, keeps me fit."

"Isn't that car outside yours?"

"It belongs to my brother - he never wanted me to get my license. Why, when everything I need is in walking distance? My mosque, my spice shop, my friends. It's enough." Elke thought of the arduous journey from Germany to South Africa aboard a ship; the tight room she had to share with her parents, the weeks it took them to arrive, the terrible food, the loneliness. Her dad always told her that she had traveller blood, that she'd never be happy staying in one place, but looking at Tittie now, she believed she could be happy in a small world of steep streets and people who knew her name. "What were you doing walking up my street?" Tittie was looking at her the same way she had from the balcony, her eyebrows arched in teasing curiosity.

"I don't like going home after school. My mom makes me sad."

"All moms make their daughters sad. You'll do the same to yours one day."

"Do you have a daughter?"

"Jirre. You ask a lot of a questions for a laaitie."

"What's a *laaitie*?"

"A young person."

"You think I'm young?" Klaus always spoke to Elke the same way he spoke to her mother, with big words and forceful gestures. She'd never really felt like a child.

"You're younger than me, aren't you?"

Elke guessed Tittie to be in her thirties. "So do you have any children?"

"My brothers are my kids," Tittie replied with a surrendering grin. "It's hard work, looking after two grown men who can't make their own bed or breakfast. And I look after the neighbour's kids sometimes, you know, when their mommies have to work, or go shopping, or whatever. I'm always home. So, they know they can come here any time. You can too, if you like."

"I'd like that," Elke said. "I'd like that very much."

Following their first meeting, Elke spent long afternoons at Tittie's, watching soapies on her tiny television, helping her to cook, and listening to her speak Bo-Kaap Afrikaans when her friends came over and caught up on the gossip. At first Tittie's circle treated Elke with suspicion, but the more they saw of her, the less they seemed to scowl. After a few months, Elke was being invited to meals at other houses and felt comfortable heckling the young boys who kept calling her tomato slice. Elke's parents didn't care that she spent most school afternoons away from home. Her mother seemed grateful for the hours alone, and Klaus was fixated on his work, a small jewellery shop with stones in every cut and colour, shiny little things that never aged or ceased to sparkle.

Tittie's kitchen became her kitchen, and the Bo-Kaap – where Elke's skin colour felt less of an affront than it did anywhere else – became her preferred home. Amongst Tittie and her circle, Elke changed from a teenager into a young woman, her accent adopting a slight Malay-Afrikaans drawl, her skin darkening to an orangey brown, her hair smelling more and more like cardamon.

As Elke lay in her Sedgefield cottage remembering those years with Tittie, she reached instinctively for the soft fat that had blossomed around her waist, and rubbed the lines across her forehead that deepened each year. She pushed the image of Leilah from her mind, and replaced it with images of herself, then and now, decades apart yet two of the same. Though her wrinkles and fat told a story of time gone by, she was still Elke perched on a hill. She was still Elke who'd run away from home.

Chapter 13

"There's something up with my daughter," Elke said to Sam the next morning when they met on the village path towards class. "She won't talk to me, not properly anyway. She sounds more and more like a robot." Sam bent down to pull her crumpled socks up in her gumboots, losing balance as she tipped over her large midsection, and grabbing the hook of Elke's arm to steady herself. Elke stopped and waited for her to finish, having learnt some weeks ago that rushing Sam was fruitless, and could even drive her to tears. She was sensitive about the time it took her to do things, time thin people took for granted, and though Elke had little patience for such sensitivity outside of Leilah she did her best not to get irritated.

"Why don't you go fetch her?" Sam asked.

"Isn't that a bit extreme? What teenage girl wants to be plucked up by their mother and shipped to the forest?"

"Wish my mom had done it," Sam said, unwrapping an old Quality Street that she'd dug out of her pocket. She gestured to Elke in an offer to bite the toffee in half. Elke shook her head and waited the three minutes it took for Sam to chew the toffee and pluck the sticky bits from her teeth. "I wish my mom had pulled me from school and asked me what was wrong," Sam continued, a finger still digging into the back of her mouth. "I was left to fend for myself, hanging on to whatever thread of self-worth I could while my class laughed and called me fat. You'd be amazed at how many variations there are on *pig*." Sam stopped to take a breath. Her cheeks were flushed from the walking and clumps of damp hair stuck to her

127

forehead. "I think the reason teenagers are so awful is because they're not ready to leave their parents' side when the whole world is telling them they have to. I mean, what does anyone actually know at thirteen? Not enough to stand on your own two feet, surely? It's the loneliest, most confusing time in a girl's life, and at that very time that she needs her mother to take her hand and not ask anything of her, Mom looks at her like an alien, like something she didn't make herself."

Elke's eyes began to sting again, that same angry-sad sting that Dwight had stirred in her the previous night. Sam's words rang true, but that made them all the more maddening. Again, she felt pressured, bullied even, to leave this place that she loved to play saviour to her daughter because Dwight couldn't – wouldn't – step up to the plate. She clenched her fists and thrust them into the air, and without a word jogged the rest of the way to class, happy to leave Sam, and her sensitivities, behind. She kept her distance from Sam for the rest of the day, avoiding all eye contact, and taking lunch on her own. It was only once the sun started to dip behind the trees, and the sky's blue started to relax, that she walked over to her friend and gave her a hug, squeezing her rolls like they were delicious sponge cakes.

Elke dug in her pocket for a coin and, instead of calling home, dialled Frankie.

"Hallo." Sunette answered, Atlantic cold.

"Hi Sunette. This is Elke Jacobs, Leilah's mom."

The two women had met a handful of times at drop-offs and pick-ups. They knew immediately they'd never be friends, lines drawn in the sand before either woman had to invite the other for tea.

"Hi Elke." Still cold. "Leilah's not here."

"No, I know. I was actually calling to speak to Frankie. Do you mind putting her on?" A dishwasher was going in the background, emphasizing the long pause.

"I don't know if that's appropriate. It's almost 7pm, on a week night. What could be so important?" Elke considered that she might actually loathe this woman, her taut lips, her paisley shirts, her belief that children should be stowed away by eight. Everything about Sunette felt like a finger sticking itself down Elke's throat. She closed her eyes and turned to face the wind that blew into the village every evening.

"I'm worried about Leilah," Elke said more quietly, her hatred making way for fatigue. "Frankie sees her every day at school, so I thought she'd be a good person to ask. I just want to check if my daughter is okay, that's all Sunette, it won't take long. Please." The problem with asking cold people for favours was that you inevitably started feeling cold yourself. Elke balanced the phone between her cheek and shoulder and blew into her hands. Her nose felt like a popsicle.

"Why don't you just ask Leilah how she's doing?"

"You know I'm away Sunette. I'm trying to work out if I need to come home. Please." Elke didn't know if her pleading was for show or if she was indeed this desperate. The twenty-four hours since she'd spoken to Dwight stretched like a dimly lit tunnel behind her, and she felt tired all of a sudden, ready to cry if crying were something that comforted her. The receiver left Sunette's ear with a crackle, and suddenly Frankie was on the other end, Sunette saying something in the background about keeping it short.

"Hi Elke." Frankie stopped calling her Mrs Jacobs

from the first time Elke had asked her to. She didn't offer it up timidly now and wait politely to be corrected. Elke loved that about Frankie, her belief that she was as good as any adult. "This is a funny surprise. Leilah said you don't have a phone so I suppose you're using that red tikkie box?"

"How do you know it's red?" Elke smiled.

"Leilah told me." Frankie said this like it was nothing but hearing it felt to Elke like a hug being returned.

"Yes, that's exactly right, the red one. How are you, Frankie?"

"Ag, you know. School is crap, but that's life, isn't it?" Elke could only grin.

"I need your help, Frankie. Leilah has sounded off the last couple of weeks, too nice, you know what a mean?"

"But she is nice." Elke could sense that Frankie was treading water, that she knew what she meant. Most people saw Leilah as a pushover, but Elke knew Frankie saw that spring in her daughter's spine, the thing that kept her standing upright even when her eyes were glued to the floor.

"You're a smart girl, Frankie, I think you know what I mean. Can you tell me what happened two weeks ago?"

"We had the school disco."

"Did something happen there?"

"No, not really. Leilah went home early. She called Mr Jacobs from that portable phone you guys have, and he came to pick her up. I don't think she likes sleeping anywhere except in her own room." Elke thought of the mattress at the foot of her bed with Dwight, how neatly Leilah always folded the bedding each morning, as if she wouldn't need it again.

"And after the party, at school, how did she seem?"

130

"She hasn't really spoken to me since the party. I dunno where she eats lunch, but she doesn't sit with us on the field any more. And when the final bell rings, she runs out before me or Rose can speak to her. She's there, but not really. It makes me feel weird so I just leave her alone."

"Okay. Anything else?" Frankie's breath quickened on the other end; her fingers fiddled with the phone cord. "What else Frankie?" Elke repeated. "If you know something, you need to tell me."

"I promised her I wouldn't tell anyone." Frankie sounded sad, her boyish confidence all gone and its place, the sound of a young girl losing someone she loved. Elke cleared her throat, feeling embarrassed all of a sudden, as if she were entering a space where she didn't belong. "Frankie," she said once she'd regained herself. "Some promises are meant to be broken, especially if it's to help someone we care about." Elke spoke as gently as she could now, scared that her coin would run out before Frankie told her the full story, or that any change in her breathing or tone might do the unimaginable and stop Frankie from talking.

"Leilah told me something during the winter break." Her tone was resigned. "She said you guys had a friend in Cape Town. Owen, or maybe Otto? Sorry, I can't remember exactly." This was the first time Elke had heard Frankie apologise for anything. The hairs on her neck bristled.

"Yes," said Elke. "Otto is our son's best friend. What does he have to do with anything?"

"Leilah said he was more like her a boyfriend than a friend, and I thought that was strange because we're not supposed to have boyfriends so young and also because Leilah told me it was a big secret, something you and Mr

Jacobs weren't supposed to know."

Elke's grip around the body of the phone receiver was tightening. She hated it for being so hard, she wanted to squeeze it into nothing. "Frankie, I know it's difficult, but I need you to tell me, word-for-word, what Leilah said. This is important, sweetheart, maybe one of the most important things you'll ever do." She felt guilty for putting so much pressure on Frankie but if there was one thing she knew about this little sprite from Bloemfontein, it was that she could be a grown-up, if asked to be.

"She spoke about a holiday you guys took, to Swaziland. She said you all went, with the dog, and with Otto. She said there was a pool where you were staying, and that everyone took turns holding her in the pool, because she couldn't swim yet. She said you and Mr Jacobs and Leilah's brother, I'm sorry I can't remember his name…" Frankie sounded as if she might start crying, her adulthood waning with each new word that passed into the phone.

"It's okay, Frankie, take your time. My son's name is Motheo."

"She said you and Mr Jacobs and Motheo held her different to how Otto held her. She said he held her with his hand between her legs, not under her legs like a chair. She said after that holiday Otto wanted to spend more time with her, but only at night or when the house was too busy for you guys to see. She said he kissed her and stuff. She didn't say what *stuff* was."

The clumsy sentence poured into the phone and a weight landed on Elke's shoulders. Otto. Shy, fat Otto. When she thought of him, all she could picture was his big brown eyes and curly eyelashes, the way he blushed whenever anyone noticed him or asked how he was doing. He was Motheo's best friend, another son. Elke made him roast potatoes for lunch and let him drink Fanta during the week, something her own kids weren't allowed to do. She hoped the sugar would make him less timid. She picked him up from school and phoned his mom, Beryl, to ask if he could stay over, and he did every weekend, on a blow-up mattress next to Motheo's bed. Every Saturday or Sunday he and Leilah sat next to each other at the breakfast table, knocking elbows as they ate their oats. He was ten years older than her but still a child, barely fourteen when he came home with Motheo for the first time. He was fiddling with the straps of his satchel when he told Elke his name, his chin glued to his collarbone to avoid eye contact. She had trusted his shyness; she had trusted it completely. Now, images of Leilah and Otto sprang into her mind. The two of them spent hours together, alone. He took her cycling. He let her play in his room when Beryl invited them for dinner. He played with her in the garden while Motheo fiddled with his motorcycle. Did he bath her?

"Frankie," she said, pulling her voice up from some place she didn't know. "Are you sure?" She could see everything – the bed wetting, the night terrors, the fragile sexuality Leilah exhibited, even as a little girl. The clarity of the truth was oddly comforting, though not enough to stop her lungs from closing in.

"That's what she said." Now Frankie sounded like a child, younger than her years, and Elke pinched herself for asking so much of the girl.

"Thank you, Frankie," Elke said, as reassuringly as she could. "You did the right thing telling me, I'm very proud of you. There's just one more thing I need to ask. What happened two weeks ago, at the party?"

"I don't know anything about that. You'll have to ask

Leilah." There was something in the way Frankie answered that didn't ring true, a kink in her tone, but Elke couldn't ask more questions, or stomach another answer.

"Okay. Goodbye." She put down the phone before Frankie could answer, and stood alone in the blackened night.

Chapter 14

Elke took the long way home, avoiding the stinkwood forest and its many shadows. Ordinarily she loved the walk back from the tikkie box, the crunch of leaves, the smell of wet soil, the solitude. But the sense that she was a whole person had gone, and in its place was all the pain she imagined her daughter to feel. She followed a winding jeep track, passing the village corner store, a meadow of cows, and a cluster of small square homes, their chimneys smoking into an inky sky. The scene reminded her of Germany, and of Klaus.

Nowadays her dad would be considered a good guy. During the Second World War he smuggled Jews into Scandinavia and tried to slow down the production of Hitler's weapons at the engineering company where he worked. After the war, when the Americans came into their village to deliver food parcels, Klaus walked straight up to the big army vehicles and welcomed them to their small town of Ahronsburg, his face smooth and fearless. Elke was only six, and she marvelled at how virtuous her father looked outside, different to the man he was inside, the man who locked her in the basement for holding hands with a boy, who spanked her bare bottom with his bare hand, who got hard when she sat on his lap. It was during that time in the basement that she learnt to get along with the dark, to see the details in it, and to not be afraid.

Elke had always steered clear of men like her father, men with blue eyes who gesticulated as a way of gaining trust, men who liked to speak about doing the right thing, men who manipulated the truth. Her first husband turned out to be gay, the boyfriend after him was so straightforwardly violent that Elke had no problem leaving him the first day he hit her. And Dwight – he'd come to her like a baby bird kicked from his mother's nest, asking Elke to take care of him. His thick hair and humbly stooped shoulders had sealed the deal.

But as wary as she'd been of men like her dad, she'd let another kind of snake into her home and he'd been twisting himself around her daughter for how long? Six months, one year, three years. Otto first came home when Leilah was four. They left Durban when she was twelve.

Eight years?

She saw Leilah swimming naked in the pool as a small girl, her bum already round and beautiful, her small but sinewy body capable of anything. At home, she was fearless. All the shyness she exhibited in the presence of strangers evaporated and she ran their small garden like her kingdom. The neighbourhood kids followed her around, some a couple years older than her, listening carefully to the strict rules she liked to lay down for whatever game they were playing that day. She climbed trees and scaled the roof. She tied little boys to the swimming pool fence regardless of whether she was cop or robber. In those early years, Leilah was the child Elke wished her to be – free, sunburnt and strong.

Had she let these daylight scenes blind out the night? Did she overlook the time Leilah woke up in so much pain that Dwight had to drive her to hospital? The doctor found no medical reason for the tummy cramps so he sent them home with a quizzical look and painkillers. Should she have paid more attention to the begging and shaking that set in every night before bed, so vigorous they bordered on theatrical? *Please stay with me Mommy. Please this one more time. Tomorrow I'll be a big girl.* She did stay with her most nights, reading to her or stroking her face until she fell asleep, and at midnight Leilah's screaming would start, or she would make no sound at all, but be curled at the foot of Elke's bed in the morning, her face smothered in hair. She'd turn over and smile, and the sun would catch her, and Elke breathed relief, for there was her happy daughter again, the one who could rule a kingdom.

Chapter 15

The bus ride back to Durban was long and cramped. Elke sat next to a woman who believed everyone would lead a good life provided they take her advice; the aircon was turned too high so that she kept waking during the night with blue fingertips. Elke didn't have enough of her own money to buy a plane ticket and she didn't want to explain anything to Dwight until she got home. What could she tell him, if not the truth about Leilah? She didn't want him to find out over the phone as she had. Dwight's skin was thinner than hers and this would hurt him in ways Elke didn't want to imagine.

Durban's central bus station was buzzing. The Coloureds she'd grown accustomed to in Sedgefield were gone and, in their place were Zulus, walking – Elke always thought – with the tall pride of a people descended from King Shaka. Even the squattest and fattest of Zulu women walked with straight spines, a trait that stopped Elke from seeing black suffering as any different to her own. The ocean of movement at the station was claustrophobic, and she saw no joy in sitting on a bench and watching the world go by. All she'd taken with her was an overnight bag, which she tossed easily over her shoulder, and started walking. It was a couple of kilometres to the beach, and it was still early morning when she arrived, the sweepers just beginning to clear the promenade, the seagulls and pigeons waiting eagerly for breakfast scraps.

Elke took off her shoes and walked into the sea, letting

the ends of waves wash over her feet, which were swollen and red from hours of sitting. The Indian Ocean stretched out in front of her, its tepid waters shining grey in the early light. The empty body of a jellyfish landed somewhere next to her on the yellow sand and was taken away again as the sea receded, its tentacles having lost their sting. Elke watched it float away, and walked deeper into the sea, letting her calves, her knees, her bum get wet, floating her hands on the water like lilies. She closed her eyes and listened to the gulls, to the swoosh of street sweepers behind her, and to the pull of the ocean in front of her. She dug her feet deeper into the wet sand so that she'd be stuck more firmly in place, and started swaying the top half of her body in circles, clockwise then anti-clockwise, eyes closed, hands floating. In these circles, Elke forgot she was a mother - if only for a moment.

Elke scratched in her purse for the last remaining note that she had and paid the taxi driver, apologising for the wet mark she'd left on his backseat. She made her way up the drive and pulled her keys from her bag to unlock the front gate. The bunch felt odd in her hands, her beaded elephant keyring smaller than she remembered. She had to look at each piece of metal for a while, remembering which key unlocked what, and as the right one slipped into the lock and turned, Elke felt a clawing at her throat. She stood still for a moment and tried to cough the claw up but it didn't budge.

She could hear the faint sound of Greta's TV playing

in her room at the back of the house but other than that everything was silent. Not wanting to catch Greta or Fritz's attention, she tiptoed through the house, avoiding the dog's resting spot in the kitchen and making her way up the stairs towards the bedrooms. She paused at the room she shared with Dwight, put her bag down at the door and continued along the passage to Leilah's room, the corridor seeming to close in on her as she walked. Leilah's door was closed and Elke pushed it gently open, afraid she'd find her daughter there instead of at school, unsure of her words even though she'd been practising what she'd say on the bus. She'd tried to imagine the whole encounter from start to finish, visualising which of her two blue pinafores Leilah would be wearing that day, how tightly her hair would be glued to her head, how she'd be carrying her backpack, and where her eyes would look. With a picture in mind, she tried to imagine the words that would come out, who would speak first and how they would sound, who would cry first - and might one of them even smile. Elke asking the right questions, Leilah feeling safe enough to answer them honestly, Elke cradling her pain. She had no choice but to think of it neatly, for to think of the next few days, months, years of uncertainty was not possible now. It would have paralysed her.

She was relieved to find the room empty, the best-case scenario still intact in her imagination. Elke stepped inside, and closed the door behind her. The fresh smell of shampoo hung in the air, and the bed was made, the ends of the duvet pinched to suggest Leilah had done it herself. Elke felt a little pride, happy that Leilah didn't expect Greta to clean up after her. Not knowing what she hoped to find, Elke opened Leilah's desk drawers one by one, picking out each piece of stationery, and examining it for clues. She'd filled these drawers for Leilah, staples and a stapler, stamps of tortoises and stars, paper in different shades and thicknesses, pens with fine tips and pencils whose nibs didn't break. Leilah spent hours alone at the desk, writing letters to no one in particular, stamping papers for no other reason than to see blue tortoises imprinted onto pink paper. Looking at it now, Elke wondered if it was the only place where Leilah felt safe.

"Hi Fatima, can I speak to Dwight?"

"Of course, Mrs Jacobs, please hold on a moment."

Elke winced, annoyed by the use of her surname and tired of correcting the sweet receptionist, the lady with the mints whose hijab looked like royalty. An inane song started playing while she waited to be connected and Elke pulled the receiver away from her cheek. The ringing in her ears had been steadily loudening, and the polite music clashed with it, two mismatched instruments screeching at each other.

"Elke?" Elke felt a lightness flutter through her, hearing her name in Dwight's deep voice, and she pulled the receiver closer, as if the harder she listened, the longer she could hang on to this sound of him, before his world was irrevocably altered. "How come you're calling me now? Is everything okay, is Leilah okay?"

Again, Elke fluttered, an affection for Dwight swelling between her hips, this man who loved their daughter just as much as she did. The claw in her throat let go a little and the ringing in her ears took on a more muted quality. "Leilah's okay. Or, at least she will be."

"What does that mean? Where are you?"

"I came home."

"Why?"

Elke thought for a moment. To get him home before Leilah returned from school, she would need to tell him why she was there. She could not lie, for what good would that do any of them now? "Do you remember Otto?"

"Of course I remember Otto. Why ask me that? What's going on?"

"Otto molested Leilah." She hadn't meant to say it like that, not in so few words. It left no gaps to fill, no time to break up the pain. The truth always sounded so commonplace. "I'm sorry," she continued when he said nothing in response. "I didn't want to tell you over the phone, but I didn't know what else to do. I still don't know what to do. Dwight, what do we do?" Elke's speech quickened. Her thoughts became a room of dark figures, moving from one corner to another, through each other and past each other, impossible to separate or pin down.

"How do you know?" Dwight asked, his voice so deep it sounded like a grunt.

"I phoned Frankie and she told me," Elke said. "I had to know what was wrong with our daughter. I told you, Dwight, I told you something was wrong." She regretted it immediately, the sideways blame, but couldn't find the will to take it back. She left it hanging between them, for him to absorb. Maybe Dwight could be the sponge and absorb everything, slowly and quietly, like he always did. Maybe if he could absorb all this pain, Elke could be free.

For a long time, no one said anything, and then, it came. "I found them together once," Dwight said, his voice hoarse, the claw having reached into him now. "I found them in Leilah's room. They were lying on the bed side by side, both with their pants down. I picked her up straight away and walked into the garden. I remember pulling up her pants while I carried her and she giggled, as if there had been some silly mistake. She put her arms around my neck and said *daddy it was just a ga*me and I wanted so badly to believe her, that I did, I believed her." Dwight stopped now. He'd been speaking so quickly, the sombre plod of his usual tone all gone, and in its place quick desperation, as if what he was saying had been brewing in him for years. "When I put her down," he said after a long pause, "she ran straight to the neighbours, running like she always did, like she couldn't fall. She looked back and smiled just before she disappeared, and I told myself again, nothing bad could be happening under a smile as beautiful as that."

It was quiet again. Elke had the sense that the distance between her and her partner was stretching. "Don't come home," she said. "I want to talk to Leilah alone." Elke could hear how hateful she sounded, but she didn't care. If she had found them, she would have known, she would have sensed, surely? The ringing in her ears was shrieking at her now. She dropped the phone into her lap, and through the round mouth with the little holes in it, she heard the faint desperation of Dwight.

I'm sorry. Please don't leave.

She placed the receiver on its cradle, walked to their room and unpacked her bag. In the toiletry drawer that they shared, she rolled up Dwight's facecloth and lay it between her things and his, and as she closed the drawer, she wondered how old they would be when she unrolled it again.

Leilah pushed the door to her room open, and by the brief pause she took before entering, Elke knew that her daughter could smell her, the mustiness of her chemist perfume, the castor oil she'd smeared onto her cheeks like a shield. It was mid-afternoon; yellow light filtered into the room and softened the edges of Leilah's belongings. Elke stood up to draw the curtains, and the room darkened. Leilah stepped in and, without a word, picked up a surf magazine and sat on the floor at the base of her bed. For minutes they sat in the dark room saying nothing. The only noise was that of magazine pages turning, slicing through the air to reveal another man standing on a wave, or another woman in a bikini, smiling over her ice-cream. Mother and daughter sat transfixed by these images, staring at the pages without so much as a glance at one another, as if neither existed, as if they were strangers in a waiting room.

"Why are you here?" Leilah asked, now halfway through her magazine. She changed the fold of her legs but didn't look up. Elke stared at the ocean in Leilah's lap, a double-page spread of a big-wave surfer, his body entirely surrounded by blue.

"I thought it was time to come home," she said flatly, the tug of her emotions all gone now, her body emptied of its rage, the ringing in her ears replaced by the thud-thud of her slowing heartbeat. "Are you glad to see me?"

"*Glad*?" Leilah's tone was mocking, though not enough to make her sound alive. "No one says glad any more." She turned another page and let out a short sigh. "I don't understand why you came home. You sounded happy down there, in your hut." She was trying to smirk but she only looked sad, her face lopsided, its usual symmetry all gone.

"I was always going to come back, Leilah. I wouldn't leave you." Elke imagined nails growing out the soles of her old takkies and sinking into the carpet, forcing her to stay put.

"But," Leilah said. "You did leave me." She looked up now, scorn spilling from the bowls of her eyes, and then swivelled on her bum so that Elke could only see her back. The shoulders were still wide but Leilah's waist was narrower than Elke remembered and as she stared at the odd, shadowy shape, she felt a sudden fear for this half-woman in front of her, this thing she'd created that could squash her with a glance.

Elke folded her hands in her lap and squeezed until the ends of her fingers turned pink, reminding herself that she was there, in Leilah's room, in Durban. She felt she might cry, a sensation so unusual for Elke that she could only dismiss it and carry on, as she had practised.

"Sweetheart," she said, "I spoke to Frankie while I was away. I called her house." Leilah shifted but didn't turn around. Elke continued, planning each word she was about to say. "I called to check how you were doing, because I was worried about you, and because I know how much Frankie loves you."

"Frankie doesn't love me." Leilah stopped turning the pages of her magazine and was looking as far down as her chin would allow. Elke could see the fuzzy bits of hair at the nape of her neck.

"She loved you enough to tell me something important about you, something I should have known all along, except I wasn't looking hard enough, or maybe I didn't know what to look for." Elke heard the slip, her pivot from Leilah towards herself. She undid the fold of her hands and balled them into fists, sufficiently tight to leave nail marks in the fleshy valley between her thumb and forefinger. Reorientated, she continued. "Frankie told me about the secret you shared with her. About Otto and the things he did to you. Things he should never have done." Elke had thought for a long time on the bus what to call the abuse and had decided on *things* because it sounded so ordinary. Things happened to everyone. Things could be fixed.

Leilah stayed quiet, her breath so low that her shoulders didn't rise or fall, no part of her was moving.

"I want you to know that nothing is your fault." Elke had practised this line so many times that now it sounded hollow. Her heart sunk as she considered that there was nothing she could really say, nothing that would reach into Leilah's childhood and undo the knots that lay there.

Gingerly, as if approaching her daughter for the first time, Elke walked slowly over to where Leilah sat and stood behind her hunched back. She placed her hands onto each of her daughter's shoulders, and exerting some pressure, tiptoed her fingers gradually up Leilah's neck. Carefully, so as not to hurt her, Elke pulled Leilah's bun loose and let the thick hair fall around her face. She started scratching Leilah's scalp and as the stiff knit of her gelled hair eased apart, Leilah started whimpering. Elke imagined falling to her knees, scooping this wounded animal into her arms, and holding her until she wept it all out. But it was too soon for all that. All she could do now was keep rubbing the head between her hands, and hope that at some point it would turn to face her.

Leilah stirred and Elke untangled her fingers from her daughter's hair. Once separated, Leilah tilted her head to one side so that Elke could see the smooth cheek, the strong bridge of her nose, the shining corner of her eye. She kept sitting like that, half-cocked, spine collapsed, magazine crumpled in her lap, and in those suspended seconds, Leilah looked to Elke like a glass tower. Its walls were tall and transparent, but Elke could not see in, her daughter's contents too muddied by her own reflection.

Months later, Elke would look back on that afternoon and recognise that her life existed in two halves, one before Leilah and one after. She would spend hours and years wondering which half was better, or if both ached equally, marred by all the things she couldn't see, no matter how hard she looked.

Chapter 16

They took the bus back to the cottage on the hill. Elke and Dwight were forced to decide this course of action without any input from Leilah, who hadn't spoken since the mention of Otto's name. They decided to take Leilah out of school, where Elke was sure she'd be terrorized, a mute girl who could look no one in the eye. Dwight had done little to dissuade Elke from taking her back to Sedgefield, satisfied – it appeared to Elke – to leave his daughter in the hands of his wife, and to continue with his life as if nothing had happened. He'd been almost as silent as Leilah, communicating instead with slow nods of his head, and golden tumblers of whiskey. For the three weeks that Elke had stayed in Durban before taking Leilah on the bus, she'd slept in the spare room. When she got up in the mornings, she found Leilah at the foot of Dwight's bed instead of hers and it occurred to Elke that Leilah was more like her father than Elke wanted her to be, her thoughts happiest in her own head, where no one could see or unpick them. It maddened Elke that Leilah sought safety with Dwight instead of her, this actionless man who'd seen something and said nothing.

Elke could not have imagined that the bus ride back to Sedgefield would be longer than the one to Durban, but it was. Leilah stared out of the window so fixedly, that Elke worried she would try to jump out. She did anything to prevent Elke's advances at communication, ignoring her offerings of food, and climbing so warily over her when she went to the toilet that the two never touched. Elke never moved out of her way, not even her feet, so desperate for Leilah to make some kind of contact with her, that she was willing to trip her up.

The weather in Sedgefield was miserable when they finally arrived, black clouds hanging low, blocking out the usual brilliance of the forest sky. Rain prickled Elke's neck as they walked up the steep hill to her cottage, and instinctively she stretched out her arm so that Leilah would tuck under her pit and be protected. Leilah stepped away quickly, slipping in some mud and grunting as she restored her balance. It was the first sound she'd made in a long time.

The house was cold when they arrived, and the cat was gone. Dust had settled over the few pieces of furniture that filled the one-bedroom space, and Elke hurried to switch on a lamp she'd brought with her from Durban at the beginning of the course. She hoped the warm glow would attract Leilah to the space but when she looked back at her standing in the doorway, Elke saw nothing more than a hunched shadow in a raincoat, the wheels of her rollie bag covered in mud, her lips glued stubbornly shut.

"We'll have to share a bed," Elke said, wondering why she felt so embarrassed. For months this house had been her sanctuary but here this dark and silent creature stood, looking at it as if it was hideous. It maddened Elke, enough to slam down her bag and start yelling. "Listen, Leilah! If you need to blame me, go ahead and blame me, but you can't look at this place like it's nothing. You can't look at me like I'm nothing. I'm your mother. I'm your fucking mother!" She strode over to Leilah and shook her by the shoulders, so vigorously that Leilah's tight bun came loose atop her head. Leilah didn't brush her off. She stood limp while Elke shook and when – exhausted – Elke let go, Leilah pulled her muddy wheels across the wooden floor and once in the bedroom, pulled the door shut. As Elke listened to the springs of her bed squeal, she keeled over and started to cry, biting into her knee caps so as not to make a sound.

For five more days Leilah said nothing. Elke left each morning to go to class, Leilah still in bed, rolled into her blanket like a gloomy sausage roll facing the wall. Elke left breakfast and lunchboxes in the fridge and, had she not found them half eaten on return, she would not have known whether Leilah had risen at all. The clean towel she left on the corner of the bed remained folded, and Leilah never changed her clothes. By the third morning, the room smelt sour, the dank stench of Leilah's unwashed hair and dirty bus clothes having taken over Elke's personal scent.

There was a growing desperation in Elke's demeanour, a hurriedness that took over as soon as she stepped out of her house in the morning. Instead of walking through the forest, she ran, screaming all the way to the village road, making her feel okay again. This feeling of okay lasted until she got home, until she found Leilah as she had been when Elke left, rolled up and facing the wall, windows closed and curtains drawn, no light or breeze or sound from outside, only

Leilah's stink. And then the scream would start to build again, until the next morning when Elke could let it out amongst the stinkwood trees.

"This can't go on," she said on the fifth morning before she left. "If you haven't showered and washed your hair by the time I get home, I'll drag you in there and scrub you myself." Before leaving, she opened the windows as wide as they would go, tied the curtains open with double knots, and with a cable tie secured the front door hook to its eye on the wall. She cleared the fridge and cabinets of all food, placing everything into a bag and stashing it around the back of the house, in a black garbage bin so the stray dogs wouldn't smell it. She thought back to her father locking her in the basement as a girl and refusing her food, but assured herself that this was different. She was not locking Leilah away but trying to force her out, by starvation or any means necessary.

"You hid all the food?" Sam asked when Elke explained what she'd done.

"Don't sound so shocked. People go days without food." Elke's face was nuzzled into the massage hole so she could not see Sam's expression, but from the lameness of her usually strong hands on her back she assumed her friend must be disappointed in her. "Do you think I'm a bad mother?"

"You're asking the wrong person. I'd have no idea how to raise a child."

"Well then, stop judging me."

"You think I'm judging you?"

"Your hands feel like old banana peels being dragged

across my back, Sam. I know you're judging me." Elke turned over and looked Sam in the eye. "Tell me I'm wrong."

"You're wrong. If you want to starve your daughter, go ahead. I don't judge or condone your choices so stop expecting either from me. Now get up, my sloppy hands have had enough of you."

That afternoon, as she walked home, Elke alternated between watching her feet move, and directing her eyes towards the horizon – the sky, the trees, the Outeniqua Mountains in the distance. A strange sense was growing in her that none of this was real, the conversation with Frankie, the bus ride home, the afternoon with Leilah, the weeks of coaxing her to eat, the bus ride back. The silence. In this mushy place Elke felt herself being drawn back into her father's world of make-believe, one in which he was the saviour and she the naughty girl, deserving of regular spankings. She wanted to grab on to anything that she could touch, smell, or hear. Even the ringing in her ears had become a kind of cruel companion, a reminder that she was indeed there.

Elke crested the hill and saw Leilah sitting on the stoep brushing her hair. It was hanging all around her face, still half wet, the dry bits blowing in the afternoon wind and catching the last light. Elke stopped and watched. This was the first time she'd seen her daughter's hair loose in months. It had grown, the ends one or two shades lighter than the roots, still bleached from the sun they once knew, before rotting in the middle of her bun.

She took tiny steps towards Leilah, worried that this, too, was not real, that the scene would suddenly change. Were her eyes tricking her into seeing this lightness in her daughter, if nowhere else than in the tips of hair, which floated high above her head now, clean and free? She got to the edge of the stoep, careful not to stand in Leilah's sun, and sat down next to her, not so close that they were touching, but close enough to reach out and touch her. Leilah paused for a breath and then kept going, her movements careful, as if brushing the hair of a dying woman.

"Do you think I'll be able to have a baby, after what I did with Otto?" The question was so soft that it almost floated off with her hair, and for once Elke was grateful for Leilah's disappearing voice, for had the question been loud or sharp, it might have cut Elke open.

"Do you want to have a baby?" Elke asked, not ready to say *Otto* again, or any of the things that now accompanied his name.

"One day," Leilah said. "When I'm a grown-up."

Elke's face crumpled and she looked as far into the distance as she could, hoping Leilah wouldn't peek through the curtains of her hair to see the fallen face of her mother. She reached out and placed a warm hand on the top of Leilah's thigh, still moving slowly so as not to scare her off. It had been so long since they'd made physical contact that Elke wasn't sure how best to do it, or if touching was even allowed. She felt like she'd felt on her first day as a teacher, standing in front of a room of small strangers, waiting for them to bite her. Leilah had power over Elke, the power to shrink away from her again. But Leilah stayed put, and the two sat together for a while longer, until the crickets struck up their evening chorus and the sun sank behind the trees.

"Nothing he did could stop you from being a mom," Elke said once she felt she could speak without the muscles of her face tripping her up. "Nothing he did could stop you from doing anything." Leilah's thigh softened under Elke's hand. "You hungry?" she asked once the colours around them had changed from yellow to blue.

"Yes, I think so," Leilah said, and together they stood up and walked into the cottage, where Leilah had switched on the lamp.

Chapter 17

The next morning Leilah stayed in bed and said nothing, but that afternoon, when Elke returned from class, her daughter was on the stoep again, hair loose and knotted at the back, where her head had lain on the pillow. Without asking, Elke sat behind her, cushioning Leilah's torso between her legs. She took the brush that Leilah had placed beside her and began to comb out the knots, holding the roots firm so that they wouldn't pull at her scalp. When Elke looked up from what she was doing, she saw that Leilah had closed her eyes, and was tilting her face towards the sun. She pushed her knees further into her daughter's back, coaxing her to bend further backwards until her chin was leaning all the way up to the sky, her neck long and stretched, the fine veins of youth bulging ever so slightly beneath her skin. Elke dug in deeper with her knees, until Leilah's back was curved over her lap like a half moon, her elbows hooked around Elke's legs for support.

"Leilah," she said, though she knew it threatened this precious contact. "How would you feel about Dad and me going to see Otto?" Leilah jerked forward, so forcefully that Elke lost grip on the brush and she watched it dangle from a knot she hadn't yet managed to untangle. Leilah was running now, and Elke had to jump up to follow her, down the hill into the forest, faster and faster until the green of the leaves and the brown of the trunks were a blur. At the foot of the hill, just before the village road, Leilah stumbled over an exposed tree root and fell over. When she stood up and turned to face Elke, there was blood seeping from under her torn toenail and a wild fear in her eyes. Elke had to look away to stop herself from retching and when she looked back at her daughter, Leilah was staring darkly at her, seemingly trapped between a desire to keep running and her twitchy fear of the night. A family of birds took off from a tree somewhere above them, the flapping of their wings so loud that both Elke and Leilah looked up, caught for a second in the sound and motion of the natural world.

"I will never forgive you." Her resolution was so absolute that Elke had to take a step back, Leilah's scorn rising before her like a wall of flames. "If you tell him, if you tell Motheo, if you tell anyone, I will never forgive you."

Motheo. In the darkness since the call with Frankie, Elke had not even considered her son. When she would tell him, what she would tell him, how he would react - she hadn't considered any of it. For a brief second, Elke yearned for a time before her daughter, the years when it was just Motheo, Dwight and her, free from Leilah's needs and fears. "Otto has to be held accountable," Elke said, trying not to sound angry. "We have to make sure he doesn't do this to someone else. And at some point, we'll have to tell your brother. Otto was...*is* his best friend. Motheo still loves him."

"I still love him!" Leilah shrieked, sending more birds into the sky. Whatever softness had leaked into Elke over the last two days all but disappeared now, and the rage she'd been quelling returned.

"No, you don't. You're too young to love a man."

"I'm not that young, and he's not a man. He was the age I am now when we went to Swaziland." Leilah paused. When Elke's face dropped, she carried on. "You're just angry that I did something without you knowing. You don't care about me or Motheo, or anything except this stupid course. Why did you take us to Durban if you just planned to leave me there? I hate Durban and I hate you. You had no right to move me away from him. You had no right."

Otto's chubby face entered Elke's mind again, the long eyelashes that shuttered and opened so slowly, the shy fidgeting of his fingers around his mouth, the smile whenever he sat close to Leilah. Was it possible that they did love each other, that all of this pain was for nothing? If it started in Swaziland, then Otto *had* been just a boy, no older than fourteen. She looked at Leilah, her still-growing breasts, her pimpled forehead, and was struck again by a deep doubt in everything. To her surprise, it was the memory of her own father that brought Elke back to earth – his beating of her bare backside even as a teenager, the crooked feeling of his erect penis when she sat on his lap as a child, the funny way he looked at her when kissing her goodnight. No. Leilah had been the child and Otto the adult, she knew this more certainly than the ground beneath her feet and the sky above her head.

"I had every right," Elke said with renewed conviction, taking two big strides over to Leilah and grabbing her by the wrist. "I'm your mother, you're my child, and until you're eighteen, you have to listen to what I say. Now come, we're going home." Elke pushed

Leilah back up the hill, her bloody toe collecting dirt on the way up, her objections weakening from loud cries to pitiful sobs.

"Please Mom," Leilah said when they reached the top. "Please don't tell anyone. I don't know what I'll do if you tell anyone. I don't think I could carry on living." As someone who'd considered suicide on more than one occasion, who'd always held it in her back pocket for emergencies, Elke knew that Leilah, for all her hidden strength, did not have the fortitude it required to bleed oneself dry.

"One day my sweetheart, when you're my age, you will understand why I need to take control of your life now. You may still be angry, but you will understand, and you will forgive me."

Elke spent the next few days at the cottage, foregoing class and the relative peace it afforded her. She pulled Leilah from bed each morning and into a hot bath, scrubbing her back with a rough sponge, shampooing her hair and wiping the foam from her eyes. Tears had replaced Leilah's silence. She went to bed crying, and woke up crying. Bathing was the one time of day that her tears disappeared, lost in the warm water and soap suds, and dried away with a towel. Not wanting to leave Leilah alone, even for a few minutes, Elke stopped washing herself and as the days wore on, she noticed her hair matting increasingly to her forehead, soiled by sweat and the dust that played up with the evening wind. She was not only dirty but also hungry, too pre-occupied with ensuring that Leilah ate to think about food for herself. Elke made her three meals a day, each accompanied by sweet tea. Sam had taken to dropping off fresh milk each morning that Elke was absent from class. She seemed to have deduced what was going on from the few words Elke spoke of Leilah's suffering, and her response was to wheeze up the hill at the start of each day, her panting audible through the shaky door of the cottage, which stayed closed because Leilah didn't like the air outside. The milk was always warm, its raw cream settling at the top of the bottle in a gooey ring. It was the only sustenance Elke got, for when she saw Sam labouring back down the hill, she tiptoed outside and glugged down half the bottle. It filled the hole in Elke's stomach, which had less and less to do with hunger but which took a short leave of absence as the milk swirled and stuck to her insides.

Leilah only ate a few bites of each meal that Elke prepared, and it wasn't long before her sturdy collarbones and shoulder blades started to jut out. Elke did her best to ignore this physical shrinking, remembering how little she was able to eat when she learnt of her mother's passing, an ocean away, and too late for her to attend the funeral. She took to spoon-feeding Leilah, teaspoons of oats in the morning, forkfuls of rice in the evenings. Lunches went uneaten, left outside for the stray dogs to enjoy. Elke found comfort in collecting the empty plate from the back of the house in the cool mornings, licked clean and coated in fresh dew.

When, by the end of the second week in Sedgefield, Leilah still wouldn't lift her own fork, Elke knew she had to give up on her course. She had no reason to believe that her daughter was getting better – the crying hadn't stopped and any attempts to talk to her about Otto were fended off with even louder wailing – but she knew she was Leilah's only hope of smiling again, however long that would take.

"I'm going to come home with you," she said to Leilah one morning in the bath. "I'm going to stay home." Leilah didn't respond, but that day she ate half a sandwich for lunch, holding the bread herself.

"Here," Leilah said between nibbles. She pushed the uneaten triangle of cheese and salted tomato towards Elke, and for a brief moment caught her mother's green eyes. "This half is for you." Elke took small bites at first, the bread heavy on her tongue and sticky on her palette, but once the food touched her stomach, her mouth stretched wider to take bigger bites and as she finished, she wondered if any sandwich would taste that good again.

Dwight

Chapter 18

Dwight had only flown twice in his life, once from Cape Town to Johannesburg for his mother's funeral, and then from Cape Town to Durban to start his new job with Khalid Kassem. The funeral had been a day-long affair, a church ceremony followed by curries and fizzy drinks at his childhood home. His mother, who liked to be called Ma Pat by everyone, wanted an open casket. He hated her for this when he made the arduous walk from his pew to the front of the church, the congregation's eyes glued to him, waiting for a tear or some other sign that he loved his mother dearly. He did not cry – Ma Pat would not have wanted him to – but his stomach did churn when he saw her dead face, coated in white powder, her upside-down smile painted a lurid shade of orange. It was the same makeup she always wore, foundation too pale, lips too bright; with her eyes closed, and her chin set in the stiff style of death, she looked uglier than usual. Dwight wondered why she would choose to be seen like that, her final appearance before returning to ashes.

He was just as surprised that she wanted to be cremated, something he only discovered upon her death. His interest in Ma Pat's final wishes had never extended beyond whom she'd leave their home to. This had less to do with his disinterest in her generally, and more to do with his poor attention to anything administrative. His sister Millie had managed everything from the sorting of her things to the food dished at the after-service, excluding Dwight from the family affairs just as she had done since his marriage to Elke.

Elke was pregnant at the funeral, Motheo had just turned ten, and the three had flown together on an early-morning flight, their bags too many to fit into the overhead compartment, the white air hostess glaring at him each time she offered a drink. He'd drunk a lot on that flight, stashing the empty bottles in his blazer pocket for Motheo, who liked how small they were and was still too young to regard them with any scorn.

Now, en route to Cape Town to confront Otto and his family, Dwight asked one of the hostesses, again a white woman though she seemed less put off by him than the one from the funeral flight, for a Scotch on the rocks. He and Elke must have looked a miserable pair, taking advantage of the empty seat in their row to sit apart. Dwight had never been a talker, but hugging and kissing were acts that he loved, and this refusal by his wife to bring her skin anywhere close to his made Dwight feel empty.

"Why are we doing this?" Dwight asked, two doubles down and bold enough to ask. Elke knew how much he disliked confrontation, and until recently she'd accommodated this weakness in him. But since he'd told her about finding Otto in Leilah's bed, she treated Dwight's timidity as something to be smoked out, never missing an occasion to tell him how cowardly he was, and how dangerous that cowardice had turned out to be. He should have felt these jabs more acutely, but he never gave them a chance to land. There was always something else to think about while she railed at him – his work, Mr Kassem's satisfaction with his work, the generosity of Fatima's smile whenever he entered the office.

"How many times are you going to ask me that question?" Elke shot back, still gazing out of the window, fixated on the brown plains of the Karoo stretching boringly below them.

"Until you give me an answer," Dwight said, tipping the contents of a third miniature into his plastic cup. They'd left Leilah in Greta's care, who'd agreed to sleep in the main bedroom so that Leilah could still migrate to her mattress and not spend the night alone. Even so, he knew she was struggling with the separation, her feelings towards Greta less than friendly, and her need to be under Dwight and Elke's wing – albeit bitterly – growing increasingly desperate. They'd left her screaming in the driveway as they left for the airport. He still struggled to swallow his upset at Elke for dragging him along on this trip, away from Leilah and towards the man who lay at the root of her anguish.

"I told you the first time you asked, Dwight. But you never listen."

"You told me we had to, and that was it." Dwight strained to remember the first conversation they had when Elke returned from Sedgefield with Leilah. For the first time in the almost two hours they'd been flying, Elke looked at him. She seemed tired, and something in Dwight stirred. He took a chance and reached across the gap between them to stroke her shoulder. It was an awkward angle for his arm, but when Elke didn't pull away from him, Dwight held contact, ignoring the crick in his elbow.

"I have to know what he did to her. Exactly."

"Shouldn't we ask Leilah that?"

Elke shrugged him off and her lips tightened, revealing the fine lines around her mouth. "I can't ask her because she doesn't have the words to tell me. And I can't wait the years it will take for her to form the words. How are we supposed to fight something we can't see?"

Of all their differences, Dwight believed this to be their biggest. Elke needed to see everything as it was; he preferred to see things the way they could be. "Why would you want to know the details?" he asked, astonished that Elke would want full-formed images of Otto and Leilah implanted in her mind.

"I'd rather *know* than *guess*," she hissed, looking at Dwight like he didn't understand pain as well as she did. "Wouldn't you?"

Dwight returned to his drink and said nothing, saved by the crackling voice of the captain announcing the start of their descent. "Strap in," Dwight said, passing Elke the silver buckle of her seatbelt.

"That's for the middle seat," she retorted, pushing his hand away and reaching under her bum to find her own. "If you want to do me a favour, don't act like a statue at this meeting. I can't be the only one asking difficult questions. Do you hear me?"

"Yes," he said. "I heard you. What are we going to tell Motheo?" *Must everyone know everything all the time* was what he really wanted to say.

"The truth," Elke said. "We'll tell him the truth as soon as we know what that is."

"But—"

"But fucking nothing, Dwight. We're a family and families don't lie to each other." Elke wound up her chair so that her back was at a right angle to her legs, and with her big hands folded in her lap like a rock, it was she who looked like the statue. Dwight cocked his head back and finished his drink with a slurp, slouching into his chair so that the gold contents would have a better chance of reaching all his corners.

Dwight felt strange entering Ottery again, the neighbourhood where he and Elke had raised their children, and where Otto and his family still lived. It was spring,

Cape Town's most generous season, the mountain green, the summer winds still sleeping. But even so, Ottery looked brown and dusty, the road devoid of any greenery, the cars old and cheap, their owners poorly dressed. Dwight couldn't help but compare this place to Westville, whose high gates and tall trees smacked of money, something he'd come to like over the preceding year. Ottery looked common by comparison, and while Westvillians still regarded his brown skin as foreign, he did not belong in Ottery either. The working class was behind him, and he did not want to go back.

Elke was sitting in the passenger seat of their rental vehicle, wearing loose denim shorts and a t-shirt with faded flowers on it. She'd rethreaded her sandals with white shoe laces that didn't cut into her ankles as the leather strapping had done. The overall look was that of a woman who didn't care how seriously people took her. She was a serious person and that was enough. Dwight had packed a suit for the meeting but left the blazer at their hotel when he saw her worn clothes and ragtag footwear. They must have looked ridiculous that morning, two glum and mismatched people sitting in the breakfast lounge of the Holiday Inn, she saying things he could no longer remember, he alternating between his eggs and a Bloody Mary.

"It looks different, doesn't it?" Dwight asked, a need suddenly rising to distract from the task that lay before them. "Ottery – it looks different."

"How so?" Elke asked, rolling her window a little further down and waving her hand theatrically through the air in a gesture meant to deride his smoking.

"I don't know, just different." He didn't know how to explain his feeling that Ottery was their past and Westville was their future. He didn't think she'd agree with him, for

Cape Town was as precious to her as it was to Leilah. He knew by the eagerness with which she spoke Afrikaans to the hotel receptionist and the homeless men who stood at every traffic light. There was no Afrikaans in Westville.

"Is that it?" she asked. "*Just different.*"

"What more do you want me to say? It feels different, and I was just wondering if you felt it too."

"Jesus, Dwight. Your breadth of communication never ceases to amaze me."

"I'm scared," he said, the words falling out of his mouth like pebbles too quickly for him to pick up. She did something unusual then, taking a fresh cigarette from his pack and lighting it for him, before placing it tenderly between his lips. It had been over a decade since he'd seen her light a cigarette, and he enjoyed the look of smoke exiting her puckered lips, escaping through the open window in a neat whisp.

The Hendricks household was on the slightly fancier side of Ottery. The houses in their street were framed by concrete walls with barbed-wire trim, whereas their old home in Lea Road had nothing to separate it from the outside. Anyone could have entered their premises, and many did, asking for money or food, which Elke always gave them, despite Dwight's objections. Kids, too, wandered freely into their garden, swimming in their pool and picking the loquats off their tree before Dwight had a chance to sample them. His childhood home in Johannesburg had been like this, a shared space for all those who knew his parents – there were many – and so he grew up believing that there was no part of the world that belonged solely to him. Even his bedroom he shared with his sister, who spoke over him and teased when fluff started growing from his chin. He wasn't allowed to say anything about the changes he saw in her body – Ma Pat did not allow for such observations – and this discrepancy between what Millie could say and what he could say left him feeling out of place, a visitor to his home, no different from the steady stream of hungry friends and relatives who always joined his family at the dinner table.

If there was any similarity between Ma Pat and his wife, it was this peculiar need to invite people in. When Leilah was a little girl, Elke had allowed a homeless couple to erect a shack at the end of their driveway, a kindness that left Dwight feeling estranged, much as he had as a child. Back then he never objected to Esther and Jonathan crapping on their lawn or eating all their food, just as he never asked Ma Pat if they could, one Sunday, enjoy a meal without having to share it. Dwight couldn't express his feelings, and he'd long ago stopped trying.

Cole Hendricks, Otto's father, was a contractor, a successful one by Coloured standards and though he'd always treated Dwight kindly Dwight felt a certain resentment towards his old friend. It wasn't just Cole's financial success that he found irksome. Though he was no less Coloured than Dwight, Cole looked white, whiter than Leilah, and had Dwight been as pale as that, had he won the genetic lottery amongst brown people in South Africa as they had, he too could have been successful on his own terms. He wouldn't be crunching crooked numbers for Mr Kassem, or be treated always like a handlanger.

Dwight pulled over on the side of the road just before they reached the Hendricks driveway, and lit another cigarette. Elke's decision was so brutally quick that he'd had no time to digest everything, or to think of what he should say. The last time the Jacobs and the Hendricks had seen each other, they'd been friends, their sons were best friends. But none of this mattered to Elke, whose determination to unpack everything as quickly as possible felt like running too quickly down a hill, head too far forward. He had the distinct feeling that he was about to fall and cut his face wide open.

"Where do you think we'll sit?' he asked Elke.

"Why is that important?" she responded irritably and he felt silly for asking.

"I want to know where to walk when we get inside, in case I head in the wrong direction. It could be the kitchen counter, or the dining room, or the TV lounge. It's a lot of unknown."

"Let's just get in there, and get out, before you lose your nerve," she said, laying a cold hand unexpectedly over his, which was wrapped around the gearstick so tight, the veins down his arm were popping. He loosened his grip and flipped his palm to meet hers. They sat together like that until he'd finished his cigarette and flicked it out the window.

"Okay," he said. Her face looked older than it had when she'd first left for Sedgefield. "Let's go." They parked on the street and walked up to the Hendricks gate hand in hand, Elke leading and Dwight a half step behind. It was Beryl who answered the intercom, and she sounded the same as she always had, her greeting clipped but polite. Beryl was a *good Coloured woman,* Ma Pat would say, *never letting truth get in the way of her fine manners.* Dwight watched the ground as he walked up the narrow set of terracotta stairs to the front door, tripping up the final stair and landing against Elke's back. She turned around and put a firm grip on each of his forearms. Yesterday's drinks churned in Dwight's stomach and he had to swallow hard to stop bile from seeping into his mouth.

"You okay?" Elke asked, but it was too late for him to respond. The door was open, and there stood Beryl, her hair swept into a neat updo, small gold hoops hanging from her ears. She smiled and beckoned them in. The house smelt of roast chicken, and the tiles throughout the foyer were so clean, they looked wet. Dwight walked carefully, fearful that he might slip and fall. The bile sat stubbornly at the back of his throat, refusing to go down, no matter how many times or how hard he swallowed. He wondered if he'd be able to speak at all.

"Cole is just finishing up some work in his office," Beryl said. "Let's sit in the kitchen while we wait for him and then I'll call Otto. I've made a plate of snacks and the kettle is on for tea." Beryl flashed a sweet smile over her shoulder as she walked away.

Dwight noticed Elke's fingers splay and stiffen at her sides. She followed Beryl silently into the kitchen, her spine rigid. Dwight felt like a marshmallow by comparison, his body collapsing over itself as he trailed the two women, counting his steps to distract from the retch rising into his mouth. The kitchen was too warm, the smell of roast chicken too strong. Another day, another circumstance, and all this homeliness might have comforted Dwight, but now it felt overwhelming and he had to excuse himself to go the bathroom. When he returned, Elke was sitting at the counter, running her hands across the faux marble surface as she always did when considering what to say. Beryl had her back to them, fussing over a plate of sausage rolls.

"I think it's time to fetch Cole and Otto," Elke said as Dwight sat down. "We're not here for a catch-up. We told you over the phone, so please let's stop pretending that nothing has changed."

"I still don't understand why you needed to come here,"

Beryl said, her attention still glued to the plate of snacks. "Why this need to upset the apple cart when our families live so far apart?"

"Upset the apple cart?" Elke asked scornfully. "Your son is the upset here. How can you be so casual about the damage he's inflicted? My daughter is a shadow, Beryl, a fucking shadow!"

"As is my son," Beryl said, turning on her heel to face them. Her face had hardened but it looked vulnerable, like an ice block on the verge of melting. Her updo was coming undone, her hands fretted with the tie of her apron. "Otto hasn't been well since you called to arrange this ridiculous meeting," she continued. "And I won't stand by while you sicken him further."

Elke took in the woman's pleading stare, and Dwight thought she might back off, maybe even leave. But then Beryl started arranging her sausage rolls again, and she stiffened. "Your son was sick a long time ago, Beryl. If only you'd noticed. If only someone had noticed." Elke shot Dwight an accusing look. "I think it's time to call your family," Elke said, staring so unflinchingly at Beryl that Dwight had no doubt who was the stronger opponent. "Dwight, where would you like to sit?"

Dwight froze. All he wanted was to go home, to see and hug Leilah. This house – all its years of lies and Sunday roasts – was closing in on him. There was no room here in which he would ever feel comfortable or safe.

"We'll wait for you in the dining room," Elke said when Dwight remained mute. She walked off and Dwight followed, stepping carefully between the lines of grout, counting the tiles as he'd done before. Elke sat on the side of the table facing the door, and folded her hands on its transparent top. Dwight sat next to her and stared at his reflection in the polished glass, the indistinct image of a man who did not belong there. He redirected his attention to a clock on the wall so he wouldn't have to keep looking at himself. It was one of those clocks that could have been inherited from a wealthy aunt or purchased from a Joshua Doore. Only rich people would know the difference, he thought, realising that he did not. A bell went off as the clock struck 1pm and the thought of a drink crossed Dwight's mind. Another time and Cole might have offered him one. They would have sat together on the settee in the lounge while Beryl cooked and Elke stomached her gossip. Dwight suspected that Elke had never liked Beryl. She was the kind of woman Ma Pat had wanted him to marry, a good Coloured women who cooked every night and avoided confrontation. Instead, Dwight chose Elke, the very opposite of Beryl, the very opposite of him. He needed Elke to say all the things he couldn't. He needed his wife long before he loved her.

Otto shuffled into the room, ducking to clear the doorframe. He'd aged in the year since Dwight had seen him, his moustache thick and black, his chin poorly shaved and spotted with little cuts. There was no denying that he was a man, ten years Leilah's senior, a couple of years shy of a quarter century. For the first time since that grim afternoon when Elke returned unexpectedly from Sedgefield, anger sprouted in Dwight, the emotion he'd always done his best to avoid following an ugly explosion in his youth when he had torn Ma Pat's kitchen to pieces, snapping the handles off each of her teacups, breaking her plates across his knee, hurling her glasses against the wall and watching as the shards fell around her slippered feet. He left her alone to clean up the mess and following that day, they never spoke of it. Ma Pat – who only kissed him on his birthday and Christmas – never touched him again, and while Dwight had long ago forgotten what caused him to snap, he remembered the damage his rage could do. In his early days of fatherhood, when he married Elke and adopted six-year-old Motheo from her previous marriage, he'd struggled to keep his anger towards the young boy down. He took to slapping his new son when he ran around demanding too much, then hugging him straight afterwards in a silent apology. When Leilah was born, he stopped the hitting and turned his anger to drink instead, diluting his temper with whiskey and ice, and falling asleep before its glow wore off.

But there was no whiskey here and the hot spark he'd felt in Ma Pat's kitchen all those years ago returned, set off by Otto's moustache, his height, his fat spilling out of his chair. He imagined Leilah, four years old, sitting next to this giant man and when he compared the two creatures, the muscles of his jaw began so seize. He ran his tongue along his teeth, softening his jowls just long enough to greet Cole, who had followed Otto in, with Beryl coming in last. The two families sat opposite each other at the table, Otto snugly between his parents, Elke and Dwight an arm's length apart. Cole, too, seemed to have aged, and the smile lines around his chestnut eyes didn't stretch as far as they used to. He was nonetheless handsome, more handsome than Beryl was pretty – no fat around his midsection and a squareness to his shoulders that Dwight still envied, though he was now, surely, the bigger man. Father to the victim, not the perpetrator.

"How are you, old friend?" Cole asked, his smile warm despite the iciness that had settled in the room. Cole leaned across the table and took a sausage roll from the plate of pleasantries, placing it carefully on a paper napkin Beryl handed him without taking a bite.

"Ag, alright," Dwight managed to say. "Work's going well." He picked up a sausage roll, put the whole thing into his mouth and swallowed without chewing.

"I saw Khalid in the newspapers," Beryl said casually, a jab, Dwight thought, the first punch thrown. "Something to do with a less-than-savoury arms deal. Is it true that Zuma has him in his pocket?"

"I wouldn't believe everything you read," Dwight replied through pursed lips, half annoyed, half embarrassed that he might have pastry in his teeth. "Politics is a nasty business." He looked at Beryl, willing himself to challenge her glib confidence, peeved at the insinuation that she and her family were the more proper party. He knew his boss had connections to Zuma, but Khalid's dealings with the presidential hopeful were par for the course when it came to doing business in South Africa. He didn't judge the man who was funding his new life in Durban, a life away from the Hendricks family – and others like them.

"What the fuck are we actually talking about here?" Elke half shouted, her hands reaching across the table towards Otto, who hadn't said a word. Dwight didn't try to calm her. He needed Elke to lead the conversation, and though he'd agreed to back her up, he knew he wouldn't say much. Speaking seemed too hard a task without violence, not without breaking this contrived scene apart, the same way he had his mother's kitchen.

"Please don't swear," Beryl said, her tone falsely appeasing. "I don't see the need to jump so quickly into anything. You look hungry, Dwight. Should I fetch us something more substantial to eat? The chicken smells just about ready."

"If you step one foot out of this room, I will pull you

straight back by that pretty little bun," Elke said, loud but even-keeled. Beryl pulled her chair back in, lifting it a millimetre off the ground so as not to scrape the tiles. "When did it start?" Elke asked. "Leilah told us about Swaziland, about you fiddling with her in the pool. Is that right, is that when it started?" She was staring directly at Otto, her pupils so dilated that her eyes were no longer green but black.

"Elke," Cole said, rubbing his temples. "I don't think questions like that are going to get us anywhere."

"I'm speaking to Otto now," Elke said. "You'll get your chance to speak, to explain your vile parenting." There it was again, Dwight thought, deflected blame. It wasn't Cole and Beryl who had abused their daughter, but in Elke's eyes they were just as much at fault. They had raised a beast and let him off the leash. "So, I'll ask again. Did it start in Swaziland, and what – exactly – did you do to her?"

"Yes," Otto said, the fat around his eyes and mouth appearing to drop. Dwight had never seen someone look so wretched, not even his daughter.

"Yes, what?" Elke said.

"Yes Aunty, it started in Swaziland."

"And what did you do?"

"I touched her, under the water. She didn't squirm, so I carried on. I thought that maybe she liked it."

The bile that had been sitting in Dwight's throat rose into his mouth now, warm, sour goo that stung the insides of his cheeks. He squeezed his eyes shut and forced it down, holding onto the arms of his chair as anchorage.

"Four-year-olds don't understand what they like and dislike. All they know is trust and distrust, and she trusted you. We all did, you nasty prick." Elke's voice was a razor.

"She might very well have enjoyed it," Beryl said, her

voice somehow jolly, as if she'd been groomed for this conversation her whole life. "Leilah liked the attention. She was always walking around the pool naked, hugging Otto, kissing his face. What do you expect from a teenage boy? At that age there's no telling between good or evil, so who are you to judge my son? Only God can do that."

Elke didn't flinch. Dwight had never seen his wife so steadfast, nor so eerily beautiful. "When else? Our house, your house? How often?"

"Your house, when I slept over, I went into her room at night." Otto had not looked up since the meeting began.

"Did you have sex with her?" Elke's face remained deadpan while Dwight could feel his teeth starting to chatter. For the first time in his life, he thought he might cry.

"No, never," Otto said softly, bringing his hands up to his face to cup his face. The sleeves of his sagging jersey slipped down his forearms and Dwight saw red lines marking his wrists, crude cuts recently scabbed. Elke saw them too, her eyes darting to the scars before Otto had a chance to drop his hands back into his lap. Her pupils shrunk back for a second, and Dwight reached out to touch her arm. She pushed him off as her eyes once again darkened.

"Good," she said. "What else?"

Dwight's bile subsided as he let go of his breath. Elke's clipped sentences were holding him in place. Longer sentences – fuller pictures – would surely have made him retch, right there on the glass table.

"We..." Otto paused, and looked across to each of his parents. Beryl didn't return his gaze – she was obsessing over a spot of chicken grease on her blouse, trying to rub it clean – but Cole did. He reached out and put a hand on his son's shoulder, mouthing the words *it's okay*. "We did everything except sex Aunty."

Everyone was looking at Elke now, even Otto, and Dwight could see her face starting to wilt, its reassuring coldness falling away.

"Did it happen here too?" Dwight asked, the depth of his voice taking him by surprise. He sounded like a man, maybe even a father. "At your house?" He looked at Cole for what felt like a long time, before replanting his gaze firmly on Otto.

"Yes, sometimes, but not a lot. Mom used to check on me too often. She still does." Otto looked shy now, like a boy again, his fingers scratching at his shaving cuts and taking off dry bits of skin.

"Where?" Dwight asked, too scared to ask if *a lot* happened under his roof.

"My bathroom, the one in my bedroom." Otto kept looking at Dwight as he spoke, a pleading eye contact, one that robbed Dwight of his fire.

"Show me," Elke said. She'd regained herself, though Dwight could tell she was barely hanging on. Her body had gone limp, even if her face was standing its ground. "Show me where you hurt her. The rest of you can stay here."

"I don't know if that's appropriate," Beryl said, an urgency to her tone, denting her composure. "I don't think you should be alone. Please, would you take Dwight with you?"

Dwight felt a pang of shame. He was seen as the buffer between his wife and Otto. Elke looked at Beryl with a combination of pity and searing dislike. She was too big a woman to say what she thought.

Now you know how it feels.

Elke followed Otto into his en suite bathroom, and

Dwight followed Elke. He'd never been to this part of the Hendricks house, he had never considered that a child could have his own bathroom. The bathroom looked like a woman's, even though Otto still lived at home, and used it every day. Dwight realised it must look the exact same way it had when Otto had Leilah in there – the tissue box in a floral fabric cover, the heart-shaped soaps on the corner of the bath, the crisp pink hand towel folded neatly on a rail alongside the sink. Had Leilah noticed these feminine details while Otto moved his hands across and through her? Had she found some refuge in them? Dwight sat down on the closed toilet seat, which was covered in the same floral fabric as the tissue box, and dropped his face into his hands. Ever so quietly, he started to sob.

"I've seen enough," Elke said. She lifted Dwight up by the armpits and led him out of the pink room, leaving Otto behind, his shape filling the doorframe for a moment before he followed them.

"I have one more question," Elke said when they were all sitting back at the table. Beryl and Cole hadn't appeared to speak to each other while they were alone. "Have you done this to anyone else?"

"No," Otto said. "I only ever loved Leilah."

"Why?" Dwight heard his voice but it sounded like an echo. His heart thudded in his ears. "Why?"

"Because…" Otto paused. "Because she smelt nice."

Days later, when Dwight thought back on Otto's reply, he could still taste the rage in his mouth, fouler than the bile. He could still hear the sound of his teeth grinding, so vigorously it made his head hurt. He could still smell Leilah as a baby, a mix of cinnamon and freshly cut grass. More than anything, Dwight could recall the stabbing realisation that if he did not get up and leave, Otto would have died. Dwight would have moved too quickly for Beryl to stop him. He would have broken that boy's neck as easily as he'd broken Ma Pat's tea sets.

Chapter 19

"Why did you leave?" Elke asked when they were back in the car. The ignition was on but they were idling. Dwight was too dazed to differentiate between the accelerator and the brake. He took his hand off the gearstick and slid lower in his seat, trying to unjumble his thoughts. "I-I..." again he felt he might cry, confusion overwhelming him. "I just had to. Why did you follow me?"

Elke didn't answer. She was staring out the window. She looked like a shell, skin holding nothing together. "Did you see the cuts on his wrists?" she asked after a while.

"Yes," Dwight said.

"Do you think he's a bad person?" she asked again.

"Yes," Dwight hoped he sounded convincing. He couldn't say what bad looked like, but Elke – this newly unsure Elke – appeared to need some show of certainty, an assurance that up was up and down was down. For once, he thought, he'd tell a lie worth telling.

"I want to visit the old house," Elke said.

"Okay," Dwight said, shifting the car into first gear. "Let's go."

He wound his window down and lit a cigarette for the drive, watching the colours and shapes of his old neighbourhood blur by. Lea Rd was just as it had been, the lawns all bleeding straight into the street, scraggly dogs wandering around picking up scraps, though they all had owners. As they approached the cul de sac in which their old farmhouse sat, he recognised one of the Riley kids riding his bike. Liam or maybe Joshua, he'd always struggled to tell the two brothers apart, their hair shaved in the same way, two stripes cutting away from their temples in parallel lines. He thought Elke might stop to greet him – she'd always had an affection for the two boys, who played cops and robbers with Leilah without treating her like a girl – but she took no notice. They parked a few metres into their old driveway, hidden from anyone who might recognise them and expect to catch up, and climbed out of the car. Slowly they stepped onto the same gravel their shoes had crunched for twelve years before moving to Durban, from Elke's pregnancy through to Leilah's puberty.

"Doesn't look like the new owners are home," Dwight said, sheltering his eyes from the light. The fig tree was still there, fragrant fruit bulging under the spring sun, giant black and yellow beetles buzzing around, just as combative and intimidating as he remembered them.

"Let's walk to the front," Elke said, her back already turned to Dwight as she made her way warily down the drive. They passed the house with its tattered wraparound balcony; they passed the giant Ficus to which Leilah's rope swing was still attached; they stepped over the low wall that separated the back from the front. Elke led them past the pool, its odd shape reminding Dwight of the hosepipe Elke had used to outline the pool for the builders. They sat under the shade of a weeping poplar on the small hill that rose up behind the pool fence. It was the hill where they'd spent Sunday afternoons with the Hendricks family, congregating around a half-barrel braai, squashed together so that everyone could be in shade. Elke and Dwight sat down and looked up at the weavers' nests, which still hung heavy from the poplar's bowed arms, some old and empty, others brand new and home to hungry chicks.

"I'm glad they didn't cut down the poplar," Elke said.

"Why would anyone cut it down?" Dwight replied,

wondering why she thought so little of the new owners, who'd been nothing but accommodating during the transfer of the house.

"People are crap," she said.

"Am I crap?" he asked, shamefaced.

"You just sat there," she said quietly. "You promised me you wouldn't just sit there."

"I don't think I promised," Dwight said.

"You nodded. That's as close to a promise as I could ever expect from you."

"You're right," Dwight said, not because he was too tired to argue, which he was, but because she was right. Confronting Otto wasn't his idea, but he should not have left her so alone in there. Dwight bent over his knees, untying his dress shoes before lying on his back. Unexpectedly, Elke lay down next to him.

"I needed you to back me up," she said, laying an arm over her forehead and eyes. "But you barely said a word."

"I know," Dwight said. "I'm sorry."

"I don't need you to be sorry," Elke said. "I needed you to get angry with me, *for* me. Beryl treated me like I was nuts. Do you have any idea what it feels like to be blamed for the pain someone else inflicted? I was the scapegoat in there. Leilah was the scapegoat in there. How could you not be angry?"

"I am," Dwight said, as he lay his hands over his chest in an x and closed his eyes. The dappled light from the tree played across the insides of his eyelids and for a moment he was a young father again, sprawled on the hill with Leilah napping across his chest, her soft snore lulling him also to sleep. "But I don't trust my anger. I don't trust anything I feel."

"Can you tell me why?" Elke asked, rolling onto her side to face him.

"Something happened," Dwight said. "When I was a youngster. But it didn't really happen to me, it happened to someone else." He went quiet again.

"And?" Elke asked, shifting closer towards him. Her tone was blunt but not unkind, the razor edges were all gone. Dwight knew he had to carry on. This one time, his feelings had to make words.

"I had a cousin," he continued, eyes still closed. "Her name was Cass but we all called her Kitty. She had these big almond-shaped eyes, like a cat, and when she looked at you, no matter how bad your day had been, her eyes made everything okay. We were joined at the hip, Kitty and me. I got on better with her than I did with my sister because she never tried to boss me around like Millie did. She never treated me like I was weak." Dwight paused, and Elke reached her hand across the x on his chest. "One day," he continued hesitantly, "I walked into the bathroom at Ma Pat's house, I must have been eight or nine, and I found one of my dad's friends in there, sitting on the toilet with Kitty on his lap. He had his hands under her dress and moving around, and Kitty's eyes were squeezed shut, like she was pretending to sleep. Uncle Mick – my father's friend – looked up when I opened the door, and he grinned. And as he was grinning, his hands were still moving, and Kitty never opened her eyes. I wished she would, so I'd know that everything was okay. I kept holding the handle down while I pulled the door shut, so the lock wouldn't click too loudly when I let go, and went straight outside to sit in Ma Pat's quince tree, where I knew the adults wouldn't find me. I sat there for an hour maybe, trying to remember everything I saw, trying to understand if what Uncle Mick was doing was bad. I still wasn't sure when I went inside to tell my parents, but I thought I should tell them anyway, just in case."

"You were right," Elke said softly. "You were right to tell them."

"But I didn't. I've never told anyone, until now."

"Why?" Elke said, her hand slipping off his crossed arms.

"I wanted to but when I climbed out of the tree and went to the kitchen, Uncle Mick was sitting there with my dad, and some other friends, and when they saw me, they all started laughing. *Mick tells me you've been fooling around with your cousin* my father said. *It's okay my boy, but just remember, blood doesn't bugger around with blood.* They all started laughing again, Uncle Mick the loudest, and I thought I must be the bad one, the one lying or making up stories." Dwight took a breath and opened his eyes to let the dappled light fall in. "I think I've been making up stories ever since."

Chapter 20

Spring had bled into summer when the Scorpions raided their house. It was already humid when Dwight opened his eyes at 7am, and he lay still for a moment to find his bearings, wrapped in a blanket with one foot sticking out to cool. It wasn't his alarm that woke him, but a feeling that something in his home was amiss. His chest felt tighter than usual and the sound of a male voice hung in his memory, though it was quiet now and he wondered if he'd been dreaming. Dwight sat up and, with sleep still clogging his eyes, peered towards Leilah's mattress to see if she was there. It lay empty, although these days that wasn't unusual. In the month since they'd returned from Cape Town, she'd taken to waking up with the sunrise at 5am and returning to her own bed. Dwight took this as a good sign, an uptick in independence or at least an attempt to appear more independent. Elke didn't agree. She appeared hurt by Leilah's choice to keep migrating to the main bedroom instead of the spare – where Elke now slept – and Dwight wondered whether his wife would ever be able to separate her own suffering from that of their daughter.

The mattress was neatly made as usual – the pillows stacked, duvet rolled into a tight, unobstructive roll – but when Dwight walked to Leilah's room to check on her, he found it empty. He descended the stairs as quickly as he could, taking two at a time despite the sharp pain in his knees, and arrived at the front door wearing just his boxers. His curls were plastered messily to his forehead and he could feel the gum in the corners of his eyes, making it hard to blink normally. Leilah was standing dead still, hands hanging limply at her sides, and he saw how much weight she'd lost, the v's of her shoulder blades protruding through the worn fabric of her nightie.

In front of her stood a white man wearing a high visibility vest, so tall and looming that Dwight instinctually lay a protective hand over his exposed chest before stepping in front of Leilah and tucking her behind his back with a gentle scoop of his arm. The tall man's eyes followed Leilah until she was out of sight – hungry looking, Dwight thought – before presenting Dwight with an official-looking piece of paper.

"Mr Jacobs?" the man asked, though the question in it was barely audible.

"Yes," Dwight said, reluctantly taking his hand off his chest so that he could reach for the piece of paper.

"We have a warrant to search your home. Please step aside."

"Wait just a moment," Dwight said, pushing back with his voice, his stance unchanged. "Who are you?"

"We're from the Directorate of Special Operations, and we have a warrant to search this property. Now please, sir, step aside."

For the first time Dwight's eyeline broadened beyond the tall man to see a troop of twelve or so more men standing behind him, forming a bright orange-and-yellow snake down the driveway. Some were white, others black, no Coloureds.

"Please take a step back," Dwight said, holding the leader's eye as determinedly as he could. "I need time to read this." He felt Leilah stir behind him, and he squeezed her arm a little tighter, a sign to stay unseen, a sign that he was still there, between her and the head of the snake. Dwight closed the door on the tall man. Click, and then quiet.

"Who are those guys, Dad?" Leilah whispered, slipping alongside Dwight and leaving no space between them.

"They're just here to look through some things. I think they're investigating Mr Kassem, but it has nothing to do with me, and it has nothing to do with you. You've done nothing wrong, baby. Do me a favour, and go to your mom's room. I'll be right behind you." Leilah took a small step forward so that she could look at Dwight and he grew suddenly shy under her gaze, crossing both arms across the firm ball of his belly. "Go on," he said. "I'll be up in a minute."

Dwight read the piece of paper slowly, running his eye along each letter of his name, reading the date and taking a moment to make sure it was today. There was a circular stamp at the top of the warrant surrounding a stylised scorpion. Its pincers made sharp angles away from its body, its tail was erect and ready to sting. The Scorpions, he realised, aligning the organisational title the tall man had offered with the more colloquial term used by the press. They'd formed only recently – to investigate cases of corruption and other white-collar crimes – and it occurred to Dwight that he might really be in trouble. Khalid was Zuma's financial advisor, and Dwight was Khalid's. He was a link in a chain he hadn't wanted to see. He folded the piece of paper and slipped it into the pocket of his checked boxers. With as much confidence as any half-naked man could muster, he opened the door and invited them in.

They entered quickly, their boots striking the floor with force, and split into small groups, invading the house with unsmiling efficiency. *Justice In Action*, their stamp had read – bold capital letters surrounding the image of the scorpion – but watching these strangers Dwight felt a distinct sense of injustice, his presence barely acknowledged, his humanity unseen. Not even the leader spared him a second glance but began barking orders to his men, cutting the snake into pieces, each capable of bringing harm to Leilah and Elke.

"The middle room upstairs," Dwight said, grabbing the tall man by the arm so that he would pay attention. "My wife and daughter are in there. Please give us a chance to get dressed."

"Why isn't your daughter already in school uniform?" the man scoffed, as if Dwight's parenting were also under investigation.

"We home school her," Dwight replied, matter-of-fact, his nerves so tattered that he felt almost invincible. He had no shirt and no power, what more could they do to him. "She's ill, and needs to be home. So, I'll ask you again, give us time to get dressed, and we will do everything we can to accommodate you."

"Okay," the man said. "But hurry up. And if I catch you trying to destroy any evidence, I won't be so friendly." He called one of his men and instructed him to follow Dwight up the stairs. Dwight walked slowly, hoping that Leilah had had enough time to explain things to Elke, and to cover herself up. When they reached the upstairs corridor, Fritz started barking from inside Elke's room, and Dwight heard the swish of the man behind him reaching for his holster.

"Our dog is old, and lame," he said without looking back. "He won't bite. Thanks for walking me up. It's this room here. I'll be out in a moment."

"Step aside sir," the man who was his shadow said firmly, nudging Dwight out of the way and opening the spare room door after a single, unanswered knock. He peered inside, hand still firmly on his gun, before slinking back and gesturing for Dwight to enter, a sheepishness to his demeanour now, as if he'd seen something he shouldn't. Dwight nodded a form of thanks, and slipped into the room, opening the door just enough to accommodate his girth.

Elke and Leilah were sitting on the bed in silence, a blanket wrapped around both of them, and Dwight took a seat next to them, his weight upsetting the balance of the mattress so that his wife and daughter slid closer towards him. Elke's face was set in an expression that was neither fearful nor brave, her eyes fixed on Dwight in a plea for assurance that she'd never before made.

"It's okay," he said. "Leilah, put something of Mum's on." He kissed her on the forehead and held her hand as she stood up to look for a dressing gown. He turned to Elke. "We just have to sit tight while they do their work," he said. "They're an organisation investigating the link between Zuma and Mr Kassem, not us. They won't find anything that could get me into trouble." This was only half a lie. Dwight didn't know if he was in any legal trouble, but he did know the Scorpions wouldn't find anything work-related at his home, for he had never mixed the two. Elke knew nothing of what he did at the office, a sore point up until now when Dwight's fierce privacy around his work felt like a lifeline. Elke stayed quiet, resigned. "Do you have something that I can wear?" he asked, brushing a loose piece of hair off Elke's cheek.

"You can wear a pair of my shorts," Elke replied, an incomplete smile pushing at the corners of her mouth. "Your hips have always been narrower than mine." She got up and rustled through the small collection of clothes she'd transferred from the main bedroom to the spare. "This should fit," she said, holding up a clean pair of khakis. He took them, grateful she hadn't offered him her gardening shorts.

"And a shirt?" he asked.

"Here," she said, pulling out a t-shirt that Dwight recognised as one of his own. "I like sleeping in it, and I knew you wouldn't notice it missing." Another day, and he might have taken this as a criticism, but now he felt a surge of confidence as he slipped the t-shirt over his head, the smell of his wife's night cream in his nose. She smoothed his hair, and wiped a crusty piece of sleep from his eye, and together the three of them stepped out of the warm room, Dwight in front and Elke behind, Leilah between them like a delicate vase wrapped in newspaper. Fritz limped close behind.

Dwight expected Elke to come at him with a string of angry questions, but she didn't. She stayed quiet for much of the morning, watching the men from a distance as they emptied out all her cutlery and underwear drawers, as they dug through her pile of Pick 'n Pay receipts, as they lifted all her rugs and checked for hidden chambers. She kept Leilah at her side and nodded at Dwight whenever he looked in their direction. Dwight felt it was a show of faith, a sign that he was still the man of the house, and it buoyed him just enough to look these men straight in the eye whenever they asked him a demeaning question or stumbled upon something embarrassing. Like Motheo's dusty stack of Playboy mags, and Dwight's colonoscopy report, and Leilah's sanitary pads. They combed through every one of the Jacobs' possessions and Dwight's only defence was to follow the men through every room, to let them know he was there, watching them, just as they were watching him.

He thought of calling Mr Kassem, but there was always a man loitering around the home phone, and Dwight's cell was one of the first things to be seized, along with his personal computer and a pile of floppy discs older than Leilah. In any event, Mr Kassem's house was surely undergoing the same search and while he'd shown himself to be a generous employer, Dwight knew it wouldn't extend beyond his own good fortune. By now the Kassem's would be tapping into resources Dwight did not have, lawyers, publicists, family connections, and though Dwight might have liked the same network behind him, he felt a certain pride to be a man standing alone, the same man to whom Elke kept looking for assurance, her eyes as green as clovers.

"I want to go outside and sit with my family in the garden." Dwight said to the tall leader, craning his neck so that he could look at him. The physical discomfort was a nice distraction from the torture of holding another person's gaze, an act that usually made him feel like a bug being fried under a microscope.

"Fine," the man said. "But I'll need to pat you all down first."

"Is that really necessary?" Dwight asked. "You've been here for six hours and haven't found anything remotely incriminating."

"It's not for you to decide what's incriminating," the man said, already walking to the lounge where Elke and Leilah were sitting. "Stand up ma'am," he said. "I have to search you before you leave."

"Where are we going?" Elke asked. A hint of fear had crept into her voice.

"I thought it would be nice to sit in the garden while these men finish up," Dwight said, stepping once again between his family and the man. "Would you like that, Leilah?"

"Yes," she said, standing up. Elke's gown hung loosely off Leilah's hands and created a crumple of thick fabric around her feet.

"I have to search you first," the tall man said, trying to sidestep Dwight. Leilah stuck her arms out so that she looked like a T, and waited quietly for the man to pat her down.

"There should be a woman here to do this," Dwight said, stopping the leader from approaching his daughter.

"As you can see, Mr Jacobs," he said, "there are no women here." He was trying to push Dwight out of the way, who might have been shorter than him, but was at least a ruler length wider.

"Then I must insist that you leave her alone," Dwight said, blocking him off with a stiff arm. "You can check me, and then we're going to go."

"Open your gown, sweetie," the tall man said, looking over Dwight at Leilah. "I need to see if you're hiding anything under there."

Obediently, Leilah started untying the bow around her waist but Dwight stopped her, turning around to place his hand over her shaking fingers. "That isn't going to happen, sir," he said, forcing his back to straighten, and widening his shoulders as best he could. He pulled Leilah in towards his chest, and turned to face the tall man again. "You are not touching any one of us. And if you don't move out of our way right now, I will lay a complaint against you for inappropriate behaviour towards a minor." The tall man appeared to shrink, if only by a centimetre, and he made an exaggerated sweep of his arm, gesturing for Dwight and his family to leave the room.

The backyard of this most recent rental was Dwight's

favourite of the three houses they'd lived in since moving to Durban. It rose up behind the kitchen in a gentle slope, and the surrounding walls were lined with the banana trees that Elke had brought with her from Cape Town. From home to home those trees travelled, uprooted along with the family, and then re-rooted, the old brown leaves dropping with each shift, making space for new ones. There was a troop of monkeys that frequented the backyard, considered a pest by most Westvillians but a treat for Elke and Leilah, who would sit at the kitchen window to watch the troop play and pick fleas from each other's coats. That hour of the day – monkey hour – was the happiest Dwight had seen Leilah since the truth of Otto came out. Her eyes danced as she watched the baby vervets doing acrobatics across the lawn, and occasionally she even smiled.

Though it was earlier in the day than the monkeys usually visited, Dwight took them to the hill now. They could see two men in the kitchen sifting through Elke's gargantuan pile of mismatched Tupperware and years-old ice cream containers, as if they were the bullet that would take Zuma and Khalid down. It was hot out, and the grass felt dry and prickly under Dwight's feet. Elke lay out a blanket and told Leilah it was okay to take off her gown now if she liked but she wandered off towards the back of the garden still covered, her eyes searching the tallest banana trees, as if willing the monkeys to arrive and save her. Elke sat down and let out a great sigh, and Dwight plopped down next to her, his knees cracking as they bent. Quiet settled as they watched the two Tupperware men sweating. They both started to chuckle, the absurdity of the situation dawning on them, or perhaps the heartache of the past months needing some place to escape.

"What's so funny?" Leilah asked, appearing behind

them, her hips slipping into the gap between their shoulders.

"Ag," Dwight said, wiping a tear from his eye. "Sometimes things are so sad, they become funny. Do you know what I mean?"

"Not really," Leilah said, sitting down. "Dad, are you going to jail?"

Dwight put his arm around Leilah while he tried to think of a comforting answer. "No, my baby," he said after a long pause. "I'm not going anywhere."

"Is Otto going to jail?" Leilah was looking at him firmly now, her eyes reflecting the sky.

"Do you want him to go to jail?" Dwight asked.

"No. I've been telling you that the whole time – he didn't do anything wrong. But you guys never listen to me."

"Leilah," Elke said, her voice crisp and certain. "We do listen. We listen to the things you say, but also to all the things you don't say. What Otto did to you, he did in secret, and when things are done in secret, the things you can't hear are just as important as the things you can."

"That makes no sense," Leilah said, agitated. "You always tell me to speak my mind, but when I do, you don't believe me. So why speak at all if words mean nothing?"

"They don't mean nothing," Elke said. "What you say is what you think, and I always want to know what you think. Even if I think something else."

"So you think Otto should go to jail?" Leilah asked, her bottom lip jutting out in defiance, something Dwight hadn't seen in a while. Elke opened her mouth to answer but nothing came out. She looked lost, and for a moment Dwight felt the ground falling away below him. He took a deep breath and stepped in.

"I want to tell you something Leilah," he said. "Is that okay?"

"How do I know if it's okay before you've even told me?" she retorted, her renewed cheek giving Dwight some hope.

"Quite right," he said, a small smile to his lips that faded when he continued speaking. "What happened to you, with Otto, it happened to your mom too, and me, sort of."

"I don't believe you," Leilah said softly, her small flame extinguished. "We were the only ones who did what we did. No one else. That's why we didn't tell you, because we knew you wouldn't get it. He told me you wouldn't get it."

"But we do get it, baby," Dwight said, running his fingers through his daughter's curls. "Grown-ups did things to us when we were small, and we kept it secret because, just like you, we thought we were the only ones. I know you don't feel like a child, because you're brave and you notice things that even smart people don't, but Leilah, you are a child. Or at least you were one when Otto touched you." Dwight shivered at the word *touched*, and had to stop speaking to catch the tears in his nose. Out of nowhere the monkeys appeared on the lawn around them, the pink new-borns clinging to their mothers' teats while last year's batch made awkward leaps through the banana trees, trying to find their wings. Dwight hoped they would distract Leilah from what he'd said, but she barely seemed to notice them.

"Why are you telling me this?" Leilah asked, staring at the small mounds of her toes under her mother's gown.

"Because," Dwight paused. "Because I want you to know that – however much you hate us now – we are doing better than our parents did. And that is all we can do."

Leilah pried her eyes away from her feet and looked first at Elke, then at Dwight. For a moment he worried that he'd said too much, placed too great a burden on his daughter's already tired shoulders. But then he saw something that would grow familiar in the years to come, the look of a woman in Leilah's still-girlish face. "I don't hate you," she said, and in that moment the woman in her disappeared. "Do you think the babies will get scared if I go sit closer to them?" she asked.

"Maybe," Dwight said. "But you can still give it a bash."

Leilah stood, using the shoulders of both parents to lift herself up, and untied the sash of the gown she'd been drowning in since morning. "Okay, I'm going then," she said, taking a small step out of the pool of fabric at her feet. Leilah's skin looked browner than usual in the hard afternoon sun, and her chameleon eyes had shifted to green, just like her mother's.

To Dwight's relief, and some surprise, Mr Kassem's dealings did not land him in jail although Mr Kassem was not so lucky and was found guilty of corruption after a lengthy court battle, and a couple of years after his imprisonment, Zuma became president. Dwight leaned on this irony whenever Elke questioned his loyalty to Mr Kassem, the fact that one co-conspirator would be locked up while the other went on to lead South Africa's so-called freedom party. He hung desperately onto the reins of Sunrise Holdings while Khalid's legal fees bled the company dry, determined to believe that he hadn't been duped, and that success was something he could still attain. He worked and reworked the numbers, spending later and later nights at the office, defending Khalid's innocence, even once he'd gone to jail. Dwight visited him there a couple of times, sitting quietly in the visitor's area while his mentor and only Durban friend railed about the injustices of the South

African political system. Once Zuma came into power, Dwight was optimistic that Khalid would be pardoned, but the new president had some three hundred other pardon applications to sort through and Khalid's was far from the top of the pile.

"When will you give up on that silly man?' Elke asked him at dinner one night, in front of Leilah.

"When I know for certain he's guilty," he said, avoiding his wife's eye.

In truth Dwight had few options beyond Mr Kassem. There were no job offers on his table, and it was more natural for him to cling to a sinking ship than it was to start afresh. He renamed the company, and took on shares, hopeful that he could turn it into something of his own. It worked to some extent, a contract here, another there, enough to keep his family afloat, to keep Leilah in school, and his family in Westville, though he never made enough to buy them a house. They kept hopping from one rental home to another, taking along the banana trees, which multiplied year on year.

Frankie

Chapter 21

For the first two weeks of the final school term, Frankie waited for Leilah every morning at the pillar where they'd first met, blazer buttoned though spring was over and would soon become summer. Confident, leaned up against the concrete with an air of indifference, arms folded loosely across her chest as she surveyed the quad. Frankie had no problem staring down any boy or girl who looked at her doubtfully and on those days that they did get to her, she closed her eyes and pictured Leilah picking her way through the crowd, arms wrapped around herself like ribbon around a present. As she approached, Frankie would smile to say *where the fuck have you be*en and Leilah would blush to say *sorry*.

But Leilah didn't come and as the days wore on Frankie crept further and further around the column, until shadow hid her from view. She added a scarf to her armour of uniform, and bound it around her neck until there was no wool left hanging. It staved off the cold, and made a mask. Though her shoulders never hunched, Frankie's insides felt like they were losing their form and she began to wonder if her body might fold in on itself if she kept waiting in that sunless place.

Rose met her there some mornings, offering jellybeans and looks of pity. "Maybe Leilah changed schools," she said at the end of the second week. "Have you ever thought of that?"

"Don't be stupid Rose. Why would she change just before the end of primary school?"

"I don't know," Rose said, taking a small step back and offering Frankie another sweet. "A new school is all I can think of. It's not like her parents would let her stay home this long." Her hand was still lingering between them, a pink jellybean staining the soft middle of her palm. Frankie left her hanging.

"You don't know anything about Leilah or her family, so please keep your lame opinions to yourself."

"Jeesh, grumpy much?" Rose turned on her heel and disappeared into the crowd. Frankie waited until the second morning bell before running to class, knowing Miss Caxton would rap her across the knuckles for being late. She didn't mind that as much as she minded the idea of Leilah arriving and not seeing Frankie waiting for her. She'd let her knuckles go black and blue, if Leilah would just come, and be black and blue with her.

Frankie stood in the tuck shop line, hands buried deep in her pockets, trying to ignore the dull conversations going on around her. She found the girls at this school boring, the way they hiked their skirts up, showing off their knees to any boy who was interested. The boys were just as bad, standing in clusters, laughing at the air, trying to outtalk one another. None of it made sense to Frankie. If Leilah were there, she would have made a joke about the stupidity of teenagers and Leilah would have laughed into her hand, even though she wanted to be one of those girls who thought enough of her knees to show them off. Instead, Leilah wore her skirts as long as the prefects would allow, which did her no favours since her calves were like hourglasses, full at the center and nipped in below the knee. They needed to be seen as a whole to be appreciated, not cut in half.

"What can I get you Frankie?" Martha, the lady behind the tuck-shop counter asked. She was shaped like a teepee, a likeness reinforced by her love of long dresses.

"One packet of jellybeans, please. Not the sour ones, the regular kind."

"That's not your usual order," Martha said, reaching under the counter and pulling out the jellybeans.

"They're apology beans," Frankie said. It was rare that anyone took notice of what she liked. "I was rude to Rose, and she's got a soft spot for these things. Do you remember Rose?"

"The black girl?"

"Ja," Frankie said, pulling a five rand coin out of her breast pocket. "The black girl."

Rose was sitting at their usual lunch spot on the pavilion overlooking the girls' field, eating a sandwich with the crusts cut off. "I didn't mean to snap at you this morning," Frankie said. It was as close to an apology as she could get. "I'm mad at Leilah, not you. How does someone just drop off the face of the planet without saying goodbye?"

Rose slowly finished chewing, like she had nowhere to be, and laid the rest of her sandwich carefully into her pink and yellow lunchbox. "Maybe she's mad at *you* Frankie, did you ever think of that?"

"Ja, that's the first thing I thought. She is mad at me, but that's not an excuse to stop existing." Frankie sucked her cheeks in frustration. "You know what Leilah's problem is?"

"No, but I'm sure you're going to tell me."

"She doesn't know what she wants or what she's afraid of. She doesn't know anything about anything, not school, not herself, not the world. I tried to explain things to her, to make sense of it all for her, because, you know, I wanted to help her. I did everything for her and this is how she repays me, by acting like I don't exist."

"I thought you said she stopped existing"

"Shut it, Rose. You know what I mean."

"No actually, I don't know what you mean. You've been sulking for two whole weeks, waiting for someone who obviously isn't coming back."

Frankie collected loose spit at the back of her mouth, formed a tunnel with her tongue, and shot out a perfect ball, right in front of Rose's feet.

"That's disgusting," Rose said, scrunching her nose and scooching her feet to the side. "You're being childish." Frankie rubbed the spit out with her shoe and stared at the smear it made on the ground, half-heartedly trying to find some kind of shape in it. "If you ask me," Rose continued, "Leilah's not worth the effort. You know she never returned that yellow dress I lent her? I didn't bring it up because she looked so down after the school disco, but don't you think that's rude, taking someone's stuff and not giving it back? It's no different from stealing."

A fresh ball of phlegm formed at the back of Frankie's mouth as she remembered Leilah on the night of the dance, how pretty she'd looked in Rose's yellow velvet dress, and how ugly she'd turned after kissing Aarush. "Leilah Jacobs is the rudest girl I know," Frankie said, fishing the jellybeans out from her pocket and dropping them into Rose's lunchbox. "She can't see past her own nose - you know what I mean?"

"I know exactly what you mean," Rose said, smiling down at the sweets. "Leilah is a selfish person."

Frankie's face dropped. She didn't mean Leilah was selfish, just that she was too scared to look at the world. She pictured her lost friend's nose. It was broader than most noses, but paired with her chin – which stuck out like a windowsill – her face was balanced. Though her eyes were uncertain, and her lips trembled like jelly at the slightest sign of confrontation, the bones underneath were sturdy and definite, like a rockface Frankie could climb without falling.

"Want to come to my house this afternoon and listen to music?" Rose asked, giving Frankie a sideways glance.

"Ja, okay," Frankie said, though she felt awkward visiting Rose's house. The two-mom thing was baffling and she found Trudy intimidating. Her white hair looked like spider's kill and she used words that Frankie didn't understand. "About Leilah…about not seeing past her nose, I didn't mean that like you said it. She's not selfish, she just doesn't know that much about the world. She can't see it so well. That's what I meant."

"Okay," Rose said. "But I still think she's selfish."

"Did you get the *Spice Up Your Life* CD yet?"

"I got it last week," Rose said happily. "I know the words of every song already. We should dress up as our favourite Spice, and do a dance routine. That would be fun." Rose popped the last bit of her sandwich into her mouth, and Frankie watched her chew, bites so small she looked like a movie star, not that movie stars were black, but if they were, Rose could be one.

Trudy was at work when they arrived at Rose's house. Zenzile was leaning over the stove, frying onions. She kept tending to the pot as she greeted the two girls, a neat swivel of her long neck to the left while the rest of her body remained perfectly still. A cool trick, Frankie thought, being able to move one part without disturbing the rest. Zenzile was beautiful in the same way Rose was and looked nothing like the other maids Frankie had known. Frankie wondered why a woman like Zenzile would give her child to a crazy lady like Trudy. Sure she was black, which meant she was probably poor, but that was no reason to live like this.

Frankie didn't know much about those informal settlements on the outskirts of the city. She'd only seen clips of them on the news, rows and rows of corrugated iron houses no bigger than a garden shed, and, though she couldn't imagine Rose and Zenzile living there, it was strange seeing them here in this big fancy house with all-white neighbours. Surely there should be some place in between, a place where Zenzile could be Rose's whole mother, and Rose could speak Zulu and be a normal black girl. Frankie wondered if she was evil for having these thoughts – of blacks and whites being separate and happy – and a fresh wave of longing for Leilah crept in. Leilah didn't know much of the world, but she knew enough of Frankie to believe she wasn't evil.

"Sawubona, mama," Rose said, approaching her half-mom in long, even strides and leaning over the pot to take in the sweet smell.

"Sawunbona, Zenzile," Frankie echoed, embarrassed of her Afrikaans accent. It didn't match the roundness of the Zulu greeting. "Thanks for having me."

"Nothing to thank me for, Frankie. This is Rose's house more than it is mine. What do you girls want for lunch?"

"Nothing mama," Rose replied softly. Frankie noticed that she was looking at her feet and shifting awkwardly from one to the other, unusual acts of submission for her self-assured friend. "We'll be up in my room listening to music. Can I help you with anything before we go?"

"No," Zenzile said, her eyes glued to the sizzling contents of the pot. "Go and enjoy yourselves. The afternoon sermon is about to start – just switch on the radio and leave me to cook."

Frankie followed Rose out of the kitchen, more certain than ever that two moms wasn't normal. Trudy was the clear boss but Rose only dipped her head for Zenzile. And Zenzile just called this house Rose's house, so did that make Rose the boss? Frankie's head spun with questions she dared not ask and she swore that next time she'd have a good excuse not to come, not even for the Spice Girls.

Rose's room didn't look like a teenager's. The walls were beige, or *nude* according to Trudy, and the heavy curtains didn't have any patterns on them. There was a dressing table and a nightstand, things only old people used, and a tall lamp in the corner with a tasselled half-moon shade. A circular rug lay at the centre of the big room – with more circles inside it – and it sucked Frankie's eyes in, like Kaa from the Jungle Book. It was creepy. The only thing of Rose's she liked was a Titanic poster above her bed: Kate and Leo flying off the front of the ship, her eyes closed and dreaming of somewhere else, his focused solely on the curve of her neck.

"Did you decorate your room like this?" Frankie asked, placing her satchel down more carefully than she would at home.

"Kinda," Rose said absent-mindedly, "with lots of help from Trudy."

"I can see that," Frankie said. "It looks like Trudy's handywork."

"What's that supposed to mean?"

"It's very grownup is what I mean."

"Well, Trudy treats me like a grownup."

"Is that why you call her *Trudy*, and Zenzile *mama*?"

"No. I call Zenzile mama because she gave birth to me. And it would be confusing otherwise. How would they know who I was talking to if I called both of them mom?"

"Good point," Frankie said. She wanted Rose to keep talking, to unravel the confusing ball of string that was her family, but she knew that wouldn't happen. Rose could say she had two moms like it was no big deal, but no big deals are always big. "Should we start this dance routine or what? I'm gonna make a giant fool of myself, but if you want to do it, we can do it."

Rose perked up. "Let's choose what to wear, and then we can work out the steps." She bounced over to her wall of built-in cupboards and opened the doors wide. For a moment she stood like Jesus on the cross, her vast collection of hung-up clothes a line of colourful disciples. "Who do you wanna be?"

"Sporty Spice," Frankie answered quickly, dreading the thought of having to put on a dress. "And you?"

"Posh Spice, obviously."

"Why obviously?"

"Because she wears the best clothes, and she's dating David Beckham. He's so cute, I could die."

"You think David Beckham is cute?"

"Yesss!" Rose squealed. "Don't you?"

"No...I don't look at boys like that."

"Like what?"

"Like you do."

"That's weird," Rose said with a giggle. She gave Frankie a funny look, and turned her attention back to being Posh.

"Not as weird as you liking white guys," Frankie muttered.

"Did you say something?" Rose asked, pulling her pinafore over her head.

"Nothing important. Just get dressed so we can start this thing. I have to be home before five."

"I'm going as fast as I can." Rose was in her underwear, examining one dress, sliding the hanger across and examining another. She was thinner than Leilah, and because she never hunched, her spine curved in all the right places. It looked like a string of finely tied knots running from her coccyx into the nape of her neck. She couldn't deny that Rose was beautiful but she didn't make Frankie tingle, not the way Leilah's nose and chin or the shifting colour of her eyes did.

Frankie had a headache by the time she'd walked home. She'd felt ugly dancing next to Rose, who'd borrowed a strappy pair of heels from Trudy's cupboard to match the black strappy dress she'd chosen to be Posh. The routine had been basic – Frankie couldn't string more than four moves together without forgetting what came next – and when Trudy got home, she'd insisted on seeing them perform.

You'll get there Frankie, just loosen up.

Sunette was sitting at the kitchen table when she walked in, holding her head in both her hands. It was an unusual sight and as Frankie got closer, she noticed the bible on the table. Its two halves were held down by their salt and pepper shakers.

"Alles alright ma?" Frankie asked, being careful not to move or speak too loudly.

Sunette didn't look up; she was too preoccupied in what she was reading to notice Frankie's entrance. She pulled up a chair and sat down, and only then did Sunette's attention shift.

"Don't sneak up on me like that, Frankie. You almost gave me a heart attack."

"Jammer ma. I tried to greet you, but you didn't hear

me. Everything alright? You look sad."

"Sad? No, I was just..." She paused and looked at the pages again. "I was just doing my daily reading. I wish you would do yours." Sunette's attention was still on the pages, but she seemed somewhere else, her head not moving demonstratively from side to side as it usually did when she studied her bible. Frankie peeked down at the verse her mother was staring at.

Hebrews 13:4 - Give honour to marriage, and remain faithful to one another in marriage. God will surely judge people who are immoral and those who commit adultery.

Frankie strained to steady her breathing. She considered the passage, running the words over in her head a few times. *God will surely judge people who are immoral and those who commit adultery. God will surely judge. God. Judge. Adultery.* Sunette stirred in her seat, turned a finger-full of pages over, bookmarked her coverup, and closed the bible. The frayed edge of its red satin place keeper hung limply, not quite long enough to reach the kitchen table. Frankie bent down to unfold and refold her socks, frightened that her glimpse into Sunette's private thoughts would be discovered if she made eye contact.

"Please slice some onions for me, Frankie. I'll start the bolognaise after my bath." She put the bible under her arm and left the kitchen, her footsteps so small and light that they made no sound at all. Frankie only stopped fiddling with her socks when she heard the tap water running. Tiny black dots danced in front of her eyes when she stood up and she had to hold onto the table to steady herself. She didn't have to guess who the adulterer was. Though she'd been preoccupied with Leilah's absence, the recent changes in her mother hadn't gone unnoticed. The afternoon hours she'd been spending away from home, the shaking hand she placed on her father's shoulder once he'd sat for dinner, her complete silence while she stood and dished, as if her very existence would give her away.

Frankie tried to picture her mother with another man, sliding first her Christian coat off and then her pastel cardigan; unbuttoning her blouse, her trousers, her bra. Taking off her underwear. Was he tall or short, fat or thin, thick-haired or bald, green, blue or brown eyes, Godless or God-fearing? Frankie's head began spinning as the pain in her temples spread across her skull, throbbing now, out of sync with her heartbeat. *Ba-ba, ba-ba, ba-ba.* She wanted to cry, to let the pain seep out. But the tears wouldn't come, they enjoyed teasing her like Rose and the boys at school enjoyed teasing her.

That's weird. You're weird. Just put on a dress.

God. Judge. Adultery.

Ba-ba. Ba-ba. Ba-ba.

Frankie stumbled to the vegetable stand and grabbed an onion from the bottom basket. Pieces of its thin skin came off in her hand, and she started rubbing it vigorously, letting all the dry bits fall to the floor. She grabbed a knife from the drawer, and without a board, sliced the onion in half on the spot where her mother's bible had rested. Halves into quarter into eighths into chunks, until finally her spiteful tears flowed, hot and acrid.

Chapter 22

Frankie lay on her bed after eating and stared at the fine cracks in her ceiling, trying to trace where it had all gone wrong. She thought back to the phone call with Elke, how strange she'd sounded. Normally Leilah's mom sounded like a man, her voice deep and sure of itself, but that night it was pinched and pleading, as if someone had been strangling her on the other side of the line. *Some promises are meant to be broken, especially if it's to help someone we care about.* What choice did Frankie have then, except to tell Elke the truth? She wondered – not for the first time – if Leilah would have done the same, spilled the beans on someone she loved if she knew it was the right thing to do.

"Please Frankie, you can't tell my mom any of this," Leilah had said a week after the school dance. "Not about Jack, and especially not about my brother's friend. She won't get it and she'll try to fix everything. I'd hate that more than anything, my know-it-all mom treating me like a clock that's stopped ticking."

Frankie had nodded. She'd wanted to say *you have stopped ticking* but Leilah looked so frightened, making quick little shakes of her head, as if trying to expel something out of her ears. "Are you sure you don't want to tell the school about Jack? That disgusting pig should be expelled."

"You think I was the only one who got fingered that night? No one's gonna care that the most popular guy at school showed interest in a mongrel like me."

"Why do you call yourself that?"

"Because it's true. Even you told me to keep my dad a secret. Why would you have done that if I wasn't such a freak?" Leilah had looked crazed then. "You know I'm right. Most girls in our class would kill to have Jack do to them what he did to me."

Frankie hadn't wanted to picture Jack on top of Leilah, putting his hand up her dress and opening her up. But it was all she could do. Again and again the image ran through her head. She could see the scene playing across her ceiling now, just as clearly as if she'd been standing next to them, her feet buried in the ground, her mouth sewn shut. Leilah had been wrong about Jack. What he did to her was not normal teenage stuff. He was older than them by two years, and Leilah said she was pushed onto her stomach when it happened. If it were normal, he would have looked her in the eyes, to see the way they changed from blue to green and back to blue. He would have told her he found them pretty.

She'd wanted to tell Elke about Jack, but she couldn't bring herself to betray all of Leilah's trust. Her instinct was to choose the boy-man from Leilah's childhood; he seemed like the bigger monster, even though Jack was a total fucktard, and deserved to have his balls popped. A nutcracker would do the job nicely. His balls were definitely small enough to fit into one. Frankie daydreamed of cornering him at the end of a narrow corridor one day, and doing it, squashing his nuts. He was always naked in these dreams, shorter than Frankie and cowering under her shadow, his reckless, nasty, violent fingers plugged into each of his ears, trying to wish her away.

The day Leilah had told Frankie about Jack, they'd been sitting in the cul de sac where they liked to smoke after school, a short rollerblade away from Leilah's house; after walking sideways up the hill that led into Leilah's driveway, they'd smoke five cigarettes each and rollerblade down again, holding hands to go the same speed. Their eyes would weep with the passing air, hearts racing from love and nicotine.

That particular day there had been no hand holding. As much as Leilah wanted to pretend that what Jack did to her was nothing, it had done *something* to her, and it was Frankie's thing too now, passed from Jack to Leilah to her.

"I don't think you're a mongrel," Frankie had said limply, rollerblading in tight circles around Leilah, trying to spin a web that would stop her from floating any further away.

"Whatever. I'm sick of talking about Jack. Can we please just change the subject?"

"Okay." Frankie stopped circling, and lit another cigarette. The afternoon sun had begun to soften, filtering through the purple flowers of a nearby jacaranda tree and casting coloured light across Leilah's cheekbones. Frankie had watched her for a while, waiting for a signal. What did Leilah want to talk about? What could Leilah talk about without disappearing any further?

"Why did you kiss Aarush at the disco?" This was not the question Frankie had intended to ask but the kiss had been on her mind.

"You asked me that already," Leilah had answered flatly. "At the dance, remember?"

"Ja, I remember. You said you did it because you felt like it."

"How come you're asking me again then?"

"I dunno." Usually, Frankie had answers for things, but every time she replayed that kiss, her head felt fuzzy and her chest clammed up. "I guess because I still don't understand how you could just *feel like it*?"

"How's anyone supposed to know why they feel

anything?"

"You just know. I feel like an apple because I like apples. You felt like kissing Aarush, because...you like Aarush?" Frankie took too long a drag from her cigarette, and coughed up the smoke in messy clouds.

"I don't know what I like."

"Did his lips feel nice?"

"Ja, they felt quite nice, I guess. I don't have anyone to compare it to."

"What about your brother's friend?" Again, not a question she'd meant to ask but the sense that she was losing Leilah was making her irrational. Bit by bit, her friend was getting fainter, and if Frankie didn't colour her in again, she'd be nothing but an outline.

"That was different," Leilah said, so softly and sadly that Frankie had wondered if she missed him. "He was different."

"How was he different?"

"I was the one who kissed Aarush. Otto...Otto was always the one kissing me."

"Do you think it's okay that he did that, kiss you without you kissing him?"

"What's the difference between me kissing Aarush, and Otto kissing me? Someone's gotta do it." Leilah's sadness was gone and the flatness had returned. Like the dead-straight highway running through the Karoo, inviting tired drivers to fall asleep and die.

"The difference is, Aarush kissed you back. Did you kiss Otto back?"

"I didn't know how to." For a moment Leilah had seemed like she was going to cry, but it was just the light bouncing off her eyes, making them look wet. Frankie took another drag, and offered the remaining half of her cigarette to Leilah. "Thanks," she'd said, brushing fingers with Frankie as she took it. That was the first time they'd touched since the dance, and Frankie realised now, lying on her bed, the last time they would touch.

"Frankie," she said after taking a half-hearted drag. "Do you know what happiness feels like?"

The question had taken Frankie by surprise. Happiness wasn't something she'd wasted time thinking about, but in that moment an image of Leilah kissing her at the pool in Ifafa had sprung immediately to mind. "I'm happy when I'm with you," she'd replied, shy all of a sudden. Did Leilah see the same picture? Or was that kiss as meaningless as the one she'd given Aarush, something she'd done just because she felt like it? Frankie knew it was nothing like the kisses Leilah got from Otto. Their lips had only touched for a second but it was a real kiss *between* two people, not one on the other, or the other on one. Frankie had never forgotten the cold-sweetness of the peach liquor, the feeling of their noses touching or the goosebumps Frankie got when Leilah's fingers touched her skin, light as a moth landing.

Leilah cocked her head at Frankie's answer, but she hadn't smiled, or frowned, or even blushed. Frankie had started circling again, pushing off her rollerblades with as much power as she could muster, desperate for the thrill and blindness of rushing down a steep hill. Round and round and round, stumbling into the corners, and scraping her hand along the ground for balance. Only when she couldn't breathe anymore had she stopped, tilting her foot to activate the rubber brake pad at the rear of her blade. Her lungs ached from smoking too many cigarettes, her hands wouldn't stop shaking.

"Do you know what happiness feels like Leilah?" she'd asked, still gasping for air.

"No," she'd replied flatly. "That's why I asked you."

Frankie had left then, left Leilah alone in the cul de sac to stare at her feet and wonder about happiness. If she'd known that Leilah would soon disappear and never speak to her again, she might have stayed longer, tried harder.

A few days after that Elke had called.

Please Frankie, I need your help.

There's something wrong with Leilah.

I need you to tell me, word-for-word.

Some promises are meant to be broken.

The Night of Spilled Secrets had been Elke's fault, not Frankie's. She'd pretended to be her friend, spoken in a soft voice, nothing like the loud Elke she knew. What else could Frankie have done? Lying on her bed now, staring at the cracks in her ceiling, she thought again of her own mother, the liar and the cheat. All mothers were filthy liars; passing their shadows down the line of command only to tremble or scold when their kids feared the night.

How could she convince Leilah that she'd had no choice but to break their pact? Would she care that only half of her secrets were brought to light? Frankie hadn't said anything about Jack, even though Elke had pushed for more. Didn't that count for something? The pain behind Frankie's eyes started to build again, and she had no reason to slice open another onion. She slipped Alanis Morrisette into her Walkman. That's what she felt like now, a jagged little pill, ready to be swallowed if it meant she could also disappear.

Her mom wouldn't buy her the CD – she hadn't dared to ask – but Leilah had had no problem getting money from Elke to buy each of them one. Elke was cool like that, or at least she used to be cool, before she forced Frankie to share stuff she wasn't meant to share. At another time, in what seemed like another life, Elke had poked her head through the door whenever Leilah played the album, and asked her to turn it up. She learnt all the words of *Hand in my Pocket* and sang from the kitchen while making tuna-and-pineapple toasties. Frankie had hated those sandwiches, but she ate them, even the little bits of spiky peel that always made it onto the bread. She ate them because Elke treated her better than any adult had treated her. The only grownup Frankie liked had taken from her the one person she loved.

She slid her legs off the bed and forced her torso to straighten up. She couldn't look at the cracks anymore. All this backtracking had only made her headache worse. She could hear the Afrikaans news starting on the TV; her parents would be glued silently to the screen for the next thirty minutes. She tiptoed to the edge of her room, peeked down the corridor to make sure it was clear and slipped out and into her parents' bedroom. She headed to Sunette's side of the cupboard, opened the door slowly to stretch out its creak and took out one of her church dresses, pale blue with white embroidery around the neckline. She laid it gently over her arm and bent down to examine her mother's shoes. There were no high heels, this was nothing like Trudy's cupboard, but she did find a pair of sandals that looked more pretty than practical. She slipped her fingers into the heel straps, and tiptoed across to Sunette's dresser. One of her mother's most prized possessions was a jewellery box that opened to a spinning ballerina and a tinny rendition of some classical song that Frankie didn't know. She opened the box, hoping that the TV would drown out the music and the squeaking sound of the ballerina spinning. Inside she found a string of small pearls. She picked it up and let it slip down her arm, closed the box, and opened the top drawer of the dresser. There was her mother's bible again, glaring at her. She shut the drawer and opened the next one. There she found what she was looking for, a collection of lipsticks in various shades of pink and peach, a silver compact containing blush and a tube of mascara. Frankie grabbed all of it, knowing her mother might notice before she could return them. She didn't care. As Frankie closed the drawer, she caught a glimpse of herself in the dresser mirror and cringed. The handful of makeup, the pearls running down her arm, the shoes angling awkwardly to the ground, the dress bunching in the crook of her elbow. None of it looked like her. But that's what she wanted, to step into another skin. To be a girl, a normal girl.

Back in her room Frankie stripped off her uniform, and stood in front of her mirror. She examined her body, the absence of a waist and a bum, no rounded set of breasts. Everything about her was straight and flat, boring lines running from the crown of her head to the tips of her toes. She had none of Leilah's curves, none of Rose's delicacy. She was a two-dimensional creature, a paper cutout. Frankie ran her nails down the length of her skinny arms, her rectangular torso, her beanstalk legs, and watched the red lines form, some detail at least, something to break the uniformity of her shapeless body.

Gently she removed her mother's frock from its hanger and put it over her head. It fell to her feet without any help; there was no part of Frankie's body that stood in the fabric's way. It felt like a wave passing over her, and for that moment Frankie stood peacefully with her eyes closed, enjoying the sensation of soft dress on skin. She avoided the mirror as she re-opened her eyes, knowing how ugly she'd look, and knelt to put on the sandals. A new wave of soft fabric, sliding up her buttocks and back as she bent own. She remained crouching for a while, spreading the hem of the dress all around her. For a short while, she felt cocooned. She stood again and slipped the pearls around her neck, then applied a thick layer of lipstick without looking where the outline of her lips was. They were so thin anyway. She didn't need the mirror to remind her. She ran a finger across the lipstick like she'd seen her mother do, smoothing out the oily colour. Her finger was pink when she'd finished, and she rubbed it onto the balls of her cheeks, smiling like Rose had showed her. She imagined perfect circles forming on her face as she grinned. It's the best way to create a natural blush, Rose had said, which Frankie found strange since she'd never seen a black person blush.

Dressed and made up, Frankie returned to her place on the bed. She lay flat on her back with sandals dangling off the edge, arranged the pearls evenly across her collar bones, and placed her hands along her sides. Staring at the cracks in the ceiling, she wondered if she'd be this way in her coffin for family and church to see.

Chapter 23

Frankie avoided Rose after the Spice Girls embarrassment, spending her break time in the computer rooms playing Mario Brothers, or in the library reading. She'd never been a nerd but books had answers to things and their musty smell reminded her of Leilah's hair. One afternoon she found *A Dictionary of First Names* with a picture of an olden-day lady on the front holding a little girl on her lap and looking lovingly at a baby that lay in a crib next to them. The baby's face looked too old but Frankie understood that it was a boy and maybe that was the point. She went straight to the Ls to look up Leilah.

Leilah is a girl's name of Arabic origin. Translating to "night beauty," this name is often given to babies born around or after the midnight hour. Leilah's mysticism runs deep in Semitic and Iranian languages, with many variations in spelling sprouting from its roots.

Frankie moved to the encyclopaedia section to look up Semitic (subfamily of the Afro-Asiatic language family that includes Hebrew, Aramaic, Arabic, and Amharic) and Iranian (Iran, also called Persia, is a country in Western Asia). Searches for Hebrew, Aramaic, Arabic and Amharic led to another set of searches, and another and another. Feeling like a big wave was flooding her brain, she focused on "mysticism" (a fancy word for mysterious, she guessed, not wanting to go down another rabbit hole) and "night beauty". Leilah was night time beautiful, the kind you had to look at until your eyes adjusted. She might also come from Asia. She pictured Dwight, his big nose and high forehead, his reddish-brown skin, and long slender fingers. She didn't know much about Asians, except that they were brown, and also maybe Chinese. Leilah's eyes pulled slightly at the ends, like stretched almonds with blue-green filling. Maybe she had brown Asian *and* Chinese Asian in her. A tree started forming in Frankie's mind of all the people that came before her friend, blood lines spreading down from faraway lands, places Frankie would never see. She was overwhelmed by a sense of longing for the many threads that brought Leilah to South Africa, to Durban, to Westville, to this shitty school. To her.

It was an unusually cold day for Durban summer and Frankie wrapped her blazer around herself as she left the library. She thought back to her pool in Bloemfontein, how it froze over some winters and gave the impression of an ice rink. The first time she tested it, the thin surface layer hadn't held her weight. Though she was only five or six, she could still remember the crack of the ice, how pleasant it had sounded before the water took her breath away. Her mother saw it happen through the kitchen window and had pulled Frankie out before her lungs filled and froze. *Why did you do that?* Sunette had asked in a shrill voice, hugging Frankie as she spanked her bottom and cried through chattering teeth. Frankie hadn't understood the problem. She'd enjoyed those few seconds of being a frozen, unfeeling thing. It was getting out that hurt.

Frankie's fingers started to go numb and her bum started to sting as the memory played over in her mind. She could still feel her mother's cold embrace, the sound of her teeth hitting teeth, the pulse of her racing heart. She arrived home with Sunette still clinging to her.

"Frankie, you're home." Her mom was sitting at the kitchen table again, although she didn't have her bible this time. "How was school?"

"School was okay," Frankie said. "I miss Leilah." She looked sheepishly at her mother, expecting a scolding. But Sunette looked more sad than angry, as if Leilah had disappeared from her life too.

"I wasn't sure if I should tell you," her mom said softly, "but Elke called again last night, while you were showering. She wanted to speak to you."

Frankie stared. "What did she say, exactly?"

"She said she had something to tell you, that's all. You can call her back now, if you want." Her mother's sad expression had changed to one of resignation, as if she'd been tensing all the muscles in her body, and was finally letting them go. Frankie nodded. "My dogter," Sunette said, when Frankie's back was to her. It had been long time since she'd called her daughter. "Be careful, okay?"

"Careful of what?" Frankie didn't turn around, afraid that Sunette would look at her and not want to be her mother anymore.

"Be careful of who you love." Frankie walked out, tears gathering in the corners of her eyes.

"Elke, its Frankie."

"Frankie, thank you for calling me back. I wasn't sure your mom would pass on the message."

"She's not all bad," Frankie said, bothered that Elke thought so little of her mother.

"No, of course she isn't," Elke responded quickly, but Frankie didn't believe her. Elke would never see the side of Sunette that Frankie had just seen, the side that makes mistakes and feels sad about it. "How are you doing Frankie? I miss you. Leilah too."

"If Leilah missed me, she would want to see me. That's

how missing works." Frankie didn't like this sweet-talking Elke.

Elke sighed, and Frankie could hear her switching the receiver from one ear to the other. Her earrings made a soft crackle into the line, the same ones she always wore, old South African pennies punched and hung onto silver hooks. "Leilah's not herself at the moment Frankie. You shouldn't take it personally."

"Tell me something I don't know. And please don't tell me not to take it personally. What a stupid thing to tell anyone."

"You've always been smarter than most kids, Frankie." Elke's deep voice was back, not trying to cajole or comfort. Frankie relaxed a little. "I wanted to call to say thank you."

"Thank you for what?"

"For telling me about Otto. I know that was difficult for you."

"You forced me to break Leilah's trust, Elke. And now she won't speak to me. Why isn't she at school anymore?"

"Because she's too sick to come to school."

"Sick like the flu?"

"No Frankie, not like the flu. She's sick in her heart. She's sick because of what Otto did to her, and because she kept it a secret for so long."

"But Leilah said it was normal, the kissing and stuff. She said Otto was like her boyfriend."

"Do you think that's true, Frankie, that a boy who's turning into a man can be a little girl's boyfriend?" Frankie's legs felt tired, her feet too small to hold her up. She'd never felt this exhausted. "Frankie? Are you still there?"

"I'm still here." Frankie slid down the wall, stretching the tight curl of the phone wire into a straight line. She hugged the receiver between her ear and shoulder, wrapped her arms around her legs and let her kneecaps fill her eye-sockets. "One of the choir boys at my church in Bloemfontein kissed me once. Down there. I wasn't as small as Leilah was, but I was small enough to hide under my bed when we got home. I remember the dust under there made my nose itchy. That's how my mom found me. I couldn't stop sneezing." The line went quiet long enough for Frankie to think Elke was upset with her. Her father had been upset when she told her parents about the choir boy. He'd said she shouldn't make up stories to get attention. Her mother had just looked at her feet and said nothing. That was the same day Frankie fell into the ice-pool, when Sunette had hugged her so tightly. Hugged and spanked. Spanked and hugged.

"Frankie," Elke said finally. Her voice was whispery again, but this time Frankie didn't mind. She let the soft sound of her name sit there. It felt like Elke was holding her. "I'm so, so sorry. That boy should never have touched you. He's sick, my darling. And you...Frankie, you're perfect." Frankie started to weep. *Sick* ran through her.

"But you said Leilah was sick," she said through loud sobs. "If Leilah's sick, then I must be sick too. I'm just as sick as that boy, and so is Leilah." She was crying so hard now that she had to put her fist in her mouth to quieten down. If her father found her like this, he'd never let her see Elke or Leilah again.

"Frankie," Elke said, her voice as steady as she'd ever heard it. "I want you to listen to me carefully now sweetheart. You and Leilah aren't sick. You're healing and often that looks the same as sick. Like a fever. You know a fever is your body fighting the germs so that you can get better?"

"No," Frankie said, her sobs getting shorter and quieter. "I thought the fever was the sickness."

"No. You feel bad, and look quite bad, but actually something good is happening. Your body's fighting for you to get better, just like Leilah's mind is fighting for her to get better right now. You telling me what happened got her mind to stand up and fight. Does that make sense?"

Frankie stopped crying. "I think so. Is my mind fighting too?"

"I think your mind started fighting a long time ago, Frankie. I wasn't just being nice earlier. You are smarter than the rest of them. Your mind's been working all along."

"Why do I still feel so sad then?"

"Oh sweetheart, you see things others don't, and the more you see the more you hurt. But, Frankie..."

"Yes?"

"You're perfect."

Over the next two months Elke picked Frankie up from school every Tuesday and Thursday and they went for milkshakes in Pinelands, a scrappy suburb with a road for panel beaters, a road for appliances, and a road for fast-food. There were fewer trees than in Westville and a lot more Citi Golfs. It wasn't the kind of place Sunette would go shopping, and Elke didn't seem to mind lying to Leilah to spend this time with Frankie. She said some lies were okay. She asked Frankie to tell her more about the choir boy. She listened, even when Frankie said very little, and hugged her when she started to cry. Elke didn't mind her t-shirts getting snotty, and the only sound she made while Frankie wept was a low humming noise on every exhale. The soft circle of fat that surrounded Elke's waist felt like a cushion that Frankie could melt into, and she did, until one day the crying stopped, and Frankie could just drink her milkshake and talk to Elke about anything she wanted.

Sinning didn't seem like such a big deal in Elke's world, even her mother's affair, which Elke found very funny. "There's life in her yet!" She'd exclaimed when Frankie told her, which Frankie didn't really understand but the smile on Elke's face was all she needed to forgive Sunette. That afternoon when her mother got home from wherever she'd been, Frankie hugged her narrow waist and copied the humming sound that Elke always made. "What's gotten into you?" Sunette wanted to know as she shook Frankie off, but later they drank tea together and watched soapies on the couch, hip to hip without silencing the kissing scenes.

The next morning, when Frankie saw her mom hunched over a pot of oats, she approached her quietly and put her hand on the small of Sunette's back. She got close enough to hear small sobs coming from her mother. Frankie wished she could speak to her like she spoke to Elke. She wanted her mother to cry on her shoulder, as she'd been allowed to do on Elke's. She wanted Sunette to forgive herself for the man, because why should anyone believe in God if forgiveness is off the table. But Frankie knew none of this was possible. "You're standing too close," Sunette said, as if reading Frankie's thoughts. "Sit down before your dad comes down. I'll have your oats ready in a minute."

When her dad came down, he said how relieved he was that Frankie wasn't spending so much time with Leilah anymore. He said marriages like her parents' should never have been decriminalised. It was the first time Frankie had heard the word decriminalised but she knew what criminals were, and she asked Christo what stealing and killing had to do with the Jacobs. "Back in the day, before

Africans took hold of our country, whites married whites. Anything else was against the law, South African law and God's law." He spoke slowly, blowing on a hot spoon of porridge between words. They spent the rest of breakfast in silence.

"How come you and Mr Jacobs were allowed to get married?" Frankie asked Elke a few days later. "I thought..." Frankie didn't know what to call Mr Jacobs. For some reason *Coloured* seemed rude. "I thought whites and non-whites weren't supposed to get married, during Apartheid I mean."

"You're right, they weren't. It was a criminal act for Dwight and me to get hitched. The government wanted to protect the purity of the white race." Elke didn't look offended or mad. She looked like she was talking about other people. "But that law was done away with in 1985, so we got married the following year."

"Oh," Frankie said, scrambling to make sense of what she'd heard. Leilah was born the same year as her –1985 – so that meant she was a bastard, or bastard*ess*? She'd only heard men being called bastards in the movies. "So does that mean Leilah was illegal?"

"If Leilah is illegal, then so are you. That law was as stupid as it was cruel. There's no such thing as a pure blood."

"Not even me? Look how white I am."

"Even you, Frankie."

"I don't think that's right, Elke. My parents are both white, and their parents were all white, and their parents' parents were all white. I'm not like Leilah." She's special, she wanted to add, but shyness prevented her.

"Have you ever heard of homo sapiens?" Frankie hadn't,

although she had heard her dad speaking about homosexuals. Boys loving boys. Girls loving girls. Also against God's law, he said.

"No, I haven't. What are those?"

"They were the very first humans, and guess where they came from."

"How should I know? They don't teach us this stuff at school."

"They don't teach you a lot of stuff at school. Homo sapiens came from Africa, eastern and Southern Africa actually, so not too far from where we're sitting now."

"What's your point?"

"My point is, you might look white, your granny and great-granny might look white, but their great-great-great-great-*great* grannies were African long before they were Dutch." Elke made a big circle with her hands on the final great. Frankie pictured Leilah and Dwight's web of family lines, reaching out of their heads all the way to Asia. Did she have those lines too, or was she just a tight ball of Bloemfontein whiteness?

"It's hard to imagine," she said, confused by the endlessness of time, and how she fitted in.

"None of us are pure, Frankie. And none of us are meant to be."

The sky was darkening when Frankie found herself walking in a direction different to home. School had just finished and fat clouds were gathered low in the sky. The air was so thick with moisture she felt like she was walking through honey. Beads of sweat gathered all around her hairline and her toes, heat-swollen and sticky, rubbed uncomfortably against themselves in her shoes. The skies would open soon and if she didn't get home she'd be caught in the thunderstorm, but Frankie kept walking, away from her house and towards Leilah's. Frankie knew Leilah wasn't ready to speak to her yet, Elke had told her so, but she needed to go there, to see the house still standing, to walk down the driveway where they used to hold hands, and to catch a glimpse of the pool where Leilah had told her about Otto. It would be full of summer rain now. Leilah had cussed at her mom for not using the hosepipe like *normal people*, but Elke had insisted on leaving the pool empty through the dry winter and letting it fill naturally in summer. Water from the gods, she'd called it.

As she walked, Frankie thought about the choir boy again. She hadn't meant to keep it from Leilah that day in the pool, but she'd already told the bed-wetting thing and it seemed unfair to share two secrets when Leilah had only shared one. But why then hadn't she said something about it when Leilah told her about Jack? Before Leilah, she'd never had this many questions. Some of them books could answer (girls can also be bastards). Others were impossible to alphabetise which made encyclopaedias and dictionaries useless (Do minds break the same as hearts break?)

There was a loud crack above Frankie's head, and the first drops of rain started to fall. She considered running, but these summer storms were inescapable. One or twenty minutes made no difference, she'd be soaked through either way. Frankie took off her blazer and shoved it into her rucksack. With arms bare, she turned her face to the falling rain and closed her eyes so that she wouldn't be blinded. She stood like this on the side of the road until the roots of her hair were wet and the thin blue fabric of her pinafore stuck to her body. Then she tucked her thumbs into the straps of her satchel and started moving forward, her pace as quick as her heartbeat.

When she arrived at the top of Leilah's driveway, a river of rainwater was rushing down the steep line of crosshatched bricks. She stepped into it, and let the river run through her shoes. She started walking, keeping her eyes glued to her feet so that she couldn't make out how far she'd gone. She wondered if the dog would hear her and bark, and realised that part of her wanted to be noticed, while the other wanted to go unseen. She left it up to chance and kept walking. When she reached the bottom of the driveway, she saw Elke's car parked, surrounded by a wet blanket of fiddle-fig leaves. It was Leilah's jobs to rake the leaves into piles and deposit them in the compost, but now they were everywhere. Leilah hated the job of raking the leaves; they attracted rain spiders and made her arms itch. Before the Night of Spilled Secrets, Frankie had helped with the creepy chore every afternoon that she visited. They'd throw handfuls of leaves at each other and shout "spider bomb!" until Elke came outside and told them to stop buggering around because lunch was almost ready.

Frankie bent down and hobbled awkwardly to Elke's car. She peeked over the hood, into the TV lounge where she'd watched soap operas and Power Rangers and plaited Leilah's hair. There she was, lying curled up on the couch and wrapped in her favourite blue blanket. She was staring into the television screen, barely blinking, and through the rain her eyes looked grey. Frankie dipped behind the car again, worried that Leilah had seen her, but everything stayed quiet. All Frankie could hear was the rain falling on metal, and the voice in her head telling her to go home. Frankie scooted further around the car so that she wasn't in Leilah's eyeline and looked again. Elke was there too, in an armchair that faced the driveway. She had her reading glasses on and appeared so settled in her spot next to Leilah that Frankie felt jealous. She kept staring at Elke, sure now that she wanted to be seen, standing in her wet clothes, begging for forgiveness. She stood to full height and the movement caught Elke's eye. They looked straight at each other, a clear recognition, but Elke's attention shifted quickly to Leilah, whose dry, blanket-wrapped body hadn't budged. Elke turned to Frankie again and smiled the smallest of smiles before adjusting her glasses and going back to her book.

Frankie felt like an intruder then, peering through the rain and glass at a family that wasn't hers. She thought back to her first image of Leilah, hiding behind the pillar at the start of the school year, her eyes full of fear. Had they changed places now, Frankie wondered, or had she been just as lonely as Leilah that day? Frankie crawled to the foot of the driveway before she got up and started running, faster and faster until the ache in her heart disappeared, forced out by breathlessness and physical fatigue.

She got home to find her mother gone, stripped off her wet clothes, and lay in the empty bath shivering. She switched the hot tap on full, the cold one just a bit, and slowly-slowly the scorching water rose around her. Feet and bum, calves and elbows, neck and chin. She wanted to be swallowed, but the escape hole wouldn't let her. It slurped and sucked until Frankie switched off the taps and lay like a crocodile, hungry and unseen.

Leilah

Chapter 24

"How are you feeling about starting high school Leilah?"

Elke was dropping her off at the entrance to Kingston Girls' High. The new building was only a couple of hundred metres from the primary school yet to Leilah it felt like an entirely different world, not least because it was all-girls so the chances of running into Jack Bertram were slim. The boys' high school was on the other side of Westville but Leilah still checked all the mirrors when her mom pulled up to the gates, searching for Jack's sure and slouchy way of walking. It's what she remembered most about him, the way he moved, like he had nowhere to be and no one to run from.

"I feel fine, Mom," Leilah replied, her eyes still darting from left to right, checking and rechecking her blind spots as if testing for her driver's licence. "And even if I wasn't, I'd still have to go. No offence but you're not that great at home-schooling."

"Hah!" her mom said in her unaffected way. "Let's see you teach geometry and then tell me how lousy I am." She grinned. "Last touch." Elke gave her a little pinch on the elbow as Leilah was getting out. She did that often these days, now that Leilah no longer wished to be hugged or kissed. Small touches here and there, contact that her mom seemed to need and which Leilah could allow. Tickling was out of the question, as was stroking her head and brushing her hair. *The space around me is my space*, she'd said one night at the dinner table, and for once her mom hadn't argued.

"I have that appointment after school," Leilah said

reluctantly through the car window. "With Andrea."

"Yes, I know," Elke said. "I'll be here at three to pick you up. Try not to think about it too much. Enjoy your first day of school."

Her mother drove off and for the first time in five months Leilah stood alone, without her parents nearby. It was mid-January, the heat thick as honey, but she kept her jersey and blazer on, along with her new black stockings. She'd been happy to discover that stockings were part of the high school uniform, but as she got out the car and saw other students pouring into the gates, she realised she was the only one wearing them. Clearly it was a winter thing. She shrugged, still happy to have her calves covered. She liked this uniform much more than the primary school one – navy skirt and white shirt with maroon trim, her name pinned to her pocket in clean, capital letters. Elke still insisted on buying her uniforms second hand, but at least she'd allowed Leilah a new blazer. She stuck her hands deep into the pockets now, hoping to look unfussed, but her hopes were dashed as she entered the school gates and a cluster of girls started laughing.

"Hey eighth grader," one of them shouted. "You know it's summer, right?"

Leilah pushed on, walking so quickly past them that her pits began to sweat. She'd been so busy worrying about finding her class, meeting her new teacher, and what she'd do if she bumped into Frankie, that she'd forgotten about the new hierarchy. Eighth grade meant four long years before she'd be at the top of the pile. At least she had her blazer. She sunk her hands even deeper into her pockets, determined to blend in with the effortless cool these girls seemed to ooze, maybe because there were no boys to see them.

Leilah had missed orientation, telling her parents that she wasn't ready to see the school without the structure of a timetable, without a desk that was hers. That was partly true, but she also wasn't ready to walk these grounds with both her parents by her side. It would have been impossible to hide the fact that Dwight was her father, and she did not want to start high school with everyone knowing she was a halfie. She was peculiar enough as it was and as she ascended the stairs that fed into the central courtyard of her new school, she realised her black stockings weren't helping. She saw a few fat girls standing towards the edges of the quad and, after a quick calculation, decided it would be better to wear socks, even if they broke her calves in half and made them look thicker.

Disoriented, Leilah pulled the map of Kingston Girls' High from her blazer's inner pocket, and pinpointed her homeroom class, which she'd circled in yellow highlighter. The two-dimensional map looked nothing like the maze of concrete buildings and stares, swimming pool, tennis and netball courts, hockey field, climbing wall, art studios and science labs that stretched out like a spiderweb around her. Her chest started to tighten as she made small circles on the spot, trying to angle the map so that it would align to the three-dimensional world around her. The first bell rang, and girls started scattering, some as short and young as her, others tall and big-breasted. Just as Leilah thought she might lose all her breath, there was a light tap on her shoulder and she swung around to see a frizzy-haired Indian girl with pockmarked cheeks and a giant smile.

"You lost?" she asked, rearranging the bag on her back, which was so heavily loaded that it hung almost as low as her skirt.

"Um, yes," Leilah replied apologetically. "I'm in Grade 8B."

"Oh, that was my class back in eighth grade," the girl said happily. "Not quite the A class, but who wants to be right at the top anyway. They're all such goodie-goodies." The girl grinned, and Leilah got the sense that she too was a goodie-goodie, or at the very least a goodie. "I'm Sumaya," she continued. "Head Girl, and still in the B class. Trust me, that's where all the fun happens."

"I'm Leilah, I'm new."

"Just like all the other eighth graders," Sumaya said with a wink. "Come on, I'll show you to class. There's only five minutes between bells, and we've already used two of them." Sumaya navigated the school maze as if it were her own home, shooting off greetings to a dozen people along the way, carrying her backpack of bricks with extraordinary ease. Leilah found herself smiling as she ran to keep up, thrilled that this frizzy-haired brown girl, *Head* Girl, was so well liked, and still taking time to light Leilah's way.

"I'll leave you here," Sumaya said, somehow guessing that Leilah wouldn't want to be escorted to the very end. "Your classroom is three doors down on the left, you'll see the label on the door. Good luck, Leilah. And enjoy it. The years go faster if you enjoy it." She turned and disappeared as naturally as she'd come, humming the tune to *Hit Me Baby One More Time* loud enough for others to hear. It was the second time that morning Leilah had been told to "enjoy it". Joy was not something she thought of much, or even aimed for. She would far rather feel comfortable than joyful, and if she could get through this day not feeling too big or too odd or too brown she could easily forget about joy.

The classroom was almost full, and Leilah was relieved to see that none of her old classmates were there. She felt a twinge of guilt for having called her mom a bad teacher since Elke's lessons got her through the Grade 7 exams with a B average. Grade 8B was three classes up from "mixed ability", which is where she'd been placed last year, and where Frankie would no doubt still be. Leilah scanned the room for an empty chair, and noticed how many Indian girls there were, along with one who looked Chinese, and two black girls. Still no Coloureds but Leilah had grown used to that. Indians were Durban's brown people, and she'd come to feel safe amongst them, sometimes trying to copy their accent because it made her dad laugh, a sound she liked even though she still couldn't be seen with him. The only free spot was right at the front, and she slipped into it reluctantly, fearful that Miss Caxton might return out of nowhere and make a fool of her again.

Much like the start of last year, everyone in this class seemed to have a friend or friends, and she wondered if Frankie and Rose were still sharing a desk, swapping summer stories and gossiping about Leilah's absence. There was a hot lump of anger permanently behind her eyes now, and it pushed away any happy memories of Frankie, leaving only the belief that her friend had betrayed her. She'd come to like the anger, which damned up her river of tears and made it possible to get up in the mornings and wash her own face. She'd cried enough in Sedgefield, and in the weeks that followed, and found it now to be quite boring, the salty exhaustion and puffy eyes, the pointless stream of sadness.

A pretty woman wearing flared blue jeans and a striped blouse entered the room, and Leilah assumed she must be lost. She was too young to be a teacher and she walked the way regular people do, no ruler in hand or pile of exam papers tucked nobly under one arm. She wasn't carrying anything except a small leather bag with tassels hanging off the bottom, and a copy of the Oxford Dictionary with a rainbow of page markers sticking out the side. Leilah sat transfixed, absorbing every detail of the woman's body, face and movements, committing it all to memory.

"Hello class," the woman said, putting her curiously small pile of possessions on the table. "My name is Mia Foley and I will be your homeroom and English teacher this year. I'd prefer you to call me Mia, but the bigwigs at this school keep telling me that's a no-no, so Miss Foley it is. Now, let me get a good look at all of you." She surveyed the room, her blue eyes resting patiently on each face, not searching for flaws or misfits like Miss Caxton had done, but with interest and maybe even pleasure, as if Grade 8B were a meal to be savoured. "It'll take me a while to know all your names, but let me start with you." Miss Foley landed her gaze on Leilah.

Leilah's legs began to itch under the hot black stockings, and she wished she'd taken off her blazer, which felt too formal in Miss Foley's presence. "I'm Leilah," she said, fiddling with the zip of her pencil case. "Leilah Jacobs."

"It's very nice to meet you, Leilah Jacobs. Tell me, what is your favourite word?"

"I don't know." Words weren't something Leilah used a lot. She thought about things, but put on the spot like this, she couldn't work out if her thoughts happened in words. And if they did, which thoughts could she possibly tell this class that wouldn't embarrass her?

"Okay, let me rephrase," Miss Foley said. "What are the words you say most often?"

"Say most often or think most often?" Leilah asked, trying to sort through the jumble in her head.

"Good question," Miss Foley said. "Let's start with the words you say."

"Mom and dad, I guess." Leilah regretted how childish she sounded.

"Very good," Miss Foley said, and Leilah couldn't work out if she was teasing or encouraging her; she seemed like a woman who could do both simultaneously. "Mom and dad are important words aren't they. Does anyone know why?" The class stayed dead quiet and Leilah felt even more idiotic, silencing her classmates with such a poor example. "They're important because they're familiar," Miss Foley continued, "and words become familiar when they make sense to us. Familiar words, if used with confidence, are our best chance of getting our thoughts across to others, which is the whole point of a shared language, isn't it?"

The class was still silent, though Leilah was sure she could hear everyone thinking, like she was. Her brain still felt jumbled.

"English," Miss Foley said, breaking and continuing Leilah's thought, "requires me to teach you lots of different words, often for the same thing. Just think of 'smile', 'giggle', 'chortle', 'snigger', 'smirk'. These are all words to describe the curling of one's lips but each one means something different, in the dictionary, and also in the minds of people. One pair of lips, a hundred ways to move them, and a hundred more ways for that movement to be understood. Your job is to choose the right word for the right thing for the right reader – or listener – and to accept that even if you choose what you believe to be the best one, it might still be interpreted as something that you didn't intend. That's the magic of language – it's shared but different to each of us and we, as learners of language, get to jump that gap between the shared and the singular, again, and again, and again. Make sense?"

None of it made sense to Leilah – not in a way she'd be able to recite or summarise – but she nodded profusely.

"Leilah," Miss Foley carried on, "if 'mom' is most familiar to you, what other words could you use to describe her that would make her familiar to other people?"

Leilah puzzled for a moment. "Mother," she said, pained by how simple she still sounded.

"Good," said Miss Foley. "What else?"

"Um, 'cook', 'gardener', 'driver'," Leilah continued, grasping at those things she could picture Elke doing. "Maybe 'teacher'."

"Great," Miss Foley said, apparently not as appalled by Leilah's simplicity as she was. "What about *monster*?" She clawed at the air and made a growling sound as she said it.

"Definitely monster!" Leilah blurted out too loudly, but when Miss Foley started laughing and the rest of the class followed, Leilah felt lifted. "'Witch', 'weirdo', 'nag', 'embarrassment'," she carried on, overcome by a warm sense of excitement.

"Yes, yes, yes!" Miss Foley responded gleefully. "What else – anything good to say about your poor mom?"

Leilah blushed and looked down to think. "She looks after me and my dad, so maybe she's a 'carer'?"

"I think she'd be happy to hear you say that," Miss Foley said, closing her eyes a second longer than a blink. "Maybe even your 'protector'?"

"Maybe," Leilah said, remembering the way her mom had starved her out of her room, and followed her home to Durban instead of staying in Sedgefield to become a 'masseuse'.

"Okay," Miss Foley said, shifting her attention off

Leilah and writing something on the board. "For your homework this week, I want you to think of one or two of your most familiar words, and tell me a story about them. You can write whatever you want, just be ready to hand it in next Monday and please write neatly. If I can't read what you give me, I'll have no choice but to fail you. Deal?"

"Deal," the whole class said in unison, all except Leilah, whose mind had disappeared into thoughts of her parents, and how she would write about them without breaking her trapped dam of tears.

Chapter 25

The drive to Childline was long and hot, Elke still refusing to use the car's air-conditioning.

"Why do you insist on making my life more difficult than it has to be?" Leilah grumbled.

"What are you complaining about now?" Elke asked. She looked amused.

"The only time you've ever used the AC was when Frankie was in the car. What about me, don't you think I like cool air too? I can't stop sweating."

"Then take off those ridiculous stockings and for God's sake lose the blazer. It's almost forty degrees today." Elke was tapping the steering wheel merrily as she drove, though the radio was off.

"Fine," Leilah said, a piece of spittle flying out of her mouth and landing on the dashboard. She yanked her blazer off dramatically, and after kicking off her shoes, started pulling off her stockings, so angrily they tore.

"Don't expect me to replace those," Elke said, still tapping.

"Don't worry," Leilah said. "I don't."

Elke pulled over into the shade of a large bougainvillea tree that had shed its flowers into a pink blanket on the road. Most of the flowers were squashed and bruised from cars driving over them, but there were a handful of fresh ones that Leilah stooped down to pick up once she was out of the car.

"Are those for me?" Elke asked, leaning clumsily through the passenger window.

"No," Leilah said firmly. "They're for Andrea."

"I thought you hated therapy?"

"I do," Leilah snapped, "but at least Andrea listens to me."

"Love you sweetheart," Elke said cheerfully, as if words rolled off her back like beads. "I'll be waiting here when you get out. Nice to see you barefoot."

Leilah looked down, and realised she'd left her stockings and shoes in a crumple at the foot of the car. She was about to grab them through the window, but Elke was too quick driving off, and Leilah was left there with nothing beneath her feet but the bruised bougainvillea blanket. It softened the tar and lightened her spirits, though Leilah would never say so to Elke, whose opinions she made a point of dismissing.

Andrea was everything Elke wasn't. The way she spoke reminded Leilah of her recorder lessons at Rudolf Steiner, when the whole class had to take turns blowing on a candle, enough to make the flame dance but not enough to extinguish it. That was how gently you had to blow so the recorder wouldn't squeak, and that is how gently Andrea spoke. She had hair that was half way between brown and blonde and it fell around her shoulders in soft waves. Andrea's clothes were never tight. She wore flowing pants and floaty tops; skirts that touched the ground but not enough to pick up dirt; dresses that swept across her collarbones without clinging to them. Her eyes were honey-coloured and her mouth was never puckered.

"Last week we started speaking about the dark," Andrea said when they were sitting on the floor of her purple office, fiddling with the same puzzle they'd been working on for three weeks, a five-hundred-piece image of a pine forest. Leilah wondered how many other puzzles Andrea must have, and where she kept all the unfinished ones. Hers was always waiting on the floor when she arrived, the trees and sky staring back at Leilah, inviting her to make them whole. "Do you want to talk some more about the dark today?" Andrea carried on, interrupting Leilah's thought.

"What do you want to know?" Leilah asked, fiddling with a piece of cloud.

"Maybe you could tell me what you see when you're in the dark?" Andrea replied, her eyes moving across the forest scene, looking for a place to fit her piece.

"I don't see anything," Leilah said, "that's why it's scary."

"But even though your eyes don't see anything, is there a picture you see in your mind, something you imagine?"

"I thought imagination meant making stuff up. Do you think my mind is making stuff up?" Leilah felt restless, trying to think of things her mind could see that her eyes couldn't.

"I think our minds are making up stuff all the time. When you remember something you did a long time ago, your mind is making up that memory isn't it? You don't actually see the pool you swam in on holiday, or the cake your mom made you for your birthday, but you can still picture it, you can still imagine it."

"Did my mom tell you about the pool in Swaziland?" Leilah asked, hurt.

"She did," Andrea said, "but I wasn't talking about that pool. I was talking about any pool. It was just an example."

"Oh," Leilah said, the hairs on her neck sitting back down. "Well, I guess then I do see stuff, even when it's dark."

"And what kind of stuff do you see?" Andrea asked, smiling as she found the home to her puzzle piece.

"Shapes," Leilah said. "They move quickly, and I never know if they're going to hit me or go straight through me, and take my insides with them."

"And what do you do to get away from the shapes?" Andrea asked, reaching for a fresh piece of tree trunk.

"First I stay very still. I can hear everything when I lie still like that. My mom and dad snoring down the hall, the clock ticking downstairs, the leaves moving outside."

"The leaves moving? Your ears must be very good at their job."

"Really?" Leilah asked. "I hate hearing everything. It makes my skin feel like it's burning."

"That must be painful for you," Andrea said, looking at Leilah now. "Did you know, your ears are designed to protect you?"

"No. What do you mean?"

"Well, if your ears are waking you up at night, maybe they're telling you something is wrong, and that you should do something to escape. They're like two little guardian angels on either side of your head."

"But there's never anyone there when I wake up," Leilah retorted, unconvinced by the image of two flapping fairies attached to her head. "Sometimes I think I can hear someone there, breathing on me, but when I switch on the light, my room is empty. I'd be happier if my ears just let me sleep through the night. If I could do that, I wouldn't have to move to my parents' room. I wouldn't feel like such a baby."

"Is that how you feel?" Andrea asked. "Like a baby?"

"Yes. No one my age sleeps in their parents' room. It's embarrassing."

"You might like to know that a lot of girls your age still sleep with their parents."

"Like who?"

"Girls who've been through the same thing you have."

"What have I been through?" Leilah asked, her indignation rising though she didn't like to get angry in front of Andrea. She didn't want to speak to Andrea the same way she spoke to Elke, but she was tired of grown-ups telling her what she'd *been through*.

"Why don't you tell me?" Andrea asked, as if reading her thoughts.

Leilah kept quiet.

"When I was little," Andrea said after a long pause, "we had a big fire in our house that started in the middle of the night. My parents got my sister and me out just in time, but it was still very scary, waking up and seeing all those flames, not being able to breathe properly. I still wake up during the night sometimes, and I can hear things – the sound of a match lighting, or a curtain burning, or my sister coughing. My ears still remember the fire, and they still wake me up, even though I'm old now." Andrea smiled. "Did your ears ever wake you up when Otto came to visit you at night?"

Leilah didn't want to answer. She didn't like that Andrea knew things she'd never told her. It was Elke's fault – telling stories that belonged only to Leilah and Otto. Anyway, it wasn't Otto her ears needed to protect her from. It was Jack Bertram. Except they hadn't. They hadn't heard him walking up behind her. They hadn't warned her to run and find Frankie. When it came down to it, her ears had been useless. She started sifting urgently through loose puzzle pieces, trying to find one with a straight edge, something to contain the incomplete forest.

"It's okay," Andrea said. "We don't have to talk about him yet. Keep telling me about the dark. After you wake up, and listen to the leaves, what do you do then?"

"I told you," Leilah said miserably. "I switch on the light to see if anyone is there and no one ever is."

"And then what do you do?"

"I close my eyes and try to fall asleep. I want so badly to fall asleep but when I close my eyes, there's always someone there. I can't see their face, I don't know what they look like, but they're there. I can feel them..." Leilah paused. "I can feel them sticking stuff into me." She looked up, past Andrea, to the wall behind her desk. There were drawings of young girls and boys, with big circles around their bodies and smaller circles around their private parts, like halos. Leilah envied them. Her halos must have gotten lost somewhere.

"Leilah, I want to tell you something really important," Andrea said, shifting off her haunches and destroying a corner of the puzzle. "No one, absolutely no one, is allowed to get inside your body. Not until you're big enough to invite them in. Do you believe me when I tell you that?"

"Is that what those circles are for?" Leilah asked, pointing at the drawings on the wall. "To keep people out."

"Yes," Andrea said. "That's exactly right."

"But those are just drawings. Drawings aren't real."

"No, they're not, but they show us what could be real, and when we know what *could be*, we don't settle for anything less. Do you want to have a circle like that around you?"

"Yes," Leilah said, picturing herself in a glowing yellow orb.

"Good," Andrea said. "You're going to get your circle, and I'm going to help you build it."

"Can we paint the circle rather?" Leilah asked. "I'm good at painting."

"Sure, we can," Andrea said. "Should I have my watercolours out for you next time, instead of the puzzle?"

"That would be better," Leilah said, stretching out her legs to kick at the pine forest, and watching the pieces come apart.

Chapter 26

"I have to write an essay about you guys," Leilah said to her mother and father. They were sitting at the beachfront Wimpy. Dwight was leaning back in his plastic chair with one hand over his belly, the other one holding a cigarette. Elke was squinting at the menu through her reading glasses.

"What a horrifying thought," Elke said, peeking over her menu at Leilah and lifting her eyebrows up and down like dumbbells.

"Tell me about it," Leilah huffed.

"Why are you writing about us, baby?" Dwight asked, smoke coming out his mouth along with the question. He looked like an unhappy dragon when he smoked and talked at the same time.

"Our English teacher, Miss Foley, told us to pick one or two words that we use most often and write a story about them."

"And you picked us?" Elke asked, her eyes back on her menu even though she always ordered the same thing: two runny eggs, brown unbuttered toast, extra tomato, Wimpy Mega Coffee.

"I didn't mean to," Leilah grumbled. "Miss Foley put me on the spot and I couldn't think of anything better. She said we have to write about what's familiar to us in a way that makes it familiar to other people."

"Do you know," Elke said, removing her glasses and putting on her teacher's voice, "the word 'familiar' is rooted in 'familia' or 'family', so you actually chose well Leilah, even though I'm terrified to see what you write about us." Elke put her glasses back on, visibly unterrified, and returned to her menu.

"I don't care about all that," Leilah lied. She actually liked knowing the lives of words, but she hated her mom thinking she was smarter than everyone else. "I wish I'd chosen something different."

"Like what?"

"I don't know. Like 'school' or 'Durban' or 'monkeys'; it wouldn't be difficult to write about those things."

"Are we difficult, baby?" Dwight asked, smiling at her as he lit another smoke.

"Mom is," Leilah said and Elke burst out laughing. Dwight joined in, his tummy rippling under the hand that wasn't smoking. "I hate it when you make fun of me," Leilah said, crossing her arms over her chest and jutting out her chin so they would know she was being serious.

"I'm sorry, baby," Dwight said. "Are we allowed to read this piece when it's finished?"

"Certainly not!" Elke blurted out loudly, and Leilah ducked her head instinctively, still afraid that someone from school would be there and notice them. "She won't be honest if she thinks we're going to read it," Elke carried on. "Write whatever you want to write, Leilah, and maybe one day – when you no longer think I'm difficult – we can read it."

"That'll never happen," Leilah said and again her parents started laughing, as if the wall she was so busy building between herself and them was a big joke. She took some comfort imagining Elke and Dwight trying to climb the wall, sweating and cursing and losing their grip. She smiled sweetly back at them, smug that they couldn't read her thoughts, which she wrapped up even tighter whenever Elke tried to steal them from her.

Their waiter arrived, the same one who always worked the outside section, the one whose bum cheeks moved independently when she walked. "What can I get you today?" she asked, looking at Leilah's little mismatched family as if they were nothing new.

Elke barked off her usual order, while Dwight ummed and ahhed between scrambled and fried. "Just order the scrambled," Elke said when the waiter started tapping her pen against her notepad. "You do this every time and you always end up getting the scrambled."

"Ja, but do I want scrambled *today*?" Dwight asked, scratching his beard.

"Yes," Elke said, handing the waiter her menu. "Leilah, what do you want?"

"I'll just have toast and jam," Leilah said, putting her hands around her waist and squeezing to see if her fingers could touch. "No butter." The waiter took their menus, and started speaking to one of her colleagues in Zulu as she walked off. Leilah wished she could do that too, flick a switch and become someone different.

"Why aren't you having eggs, baby?"

"I don't want eggs, I want jam on toast," Leilah said, enjoying the rumble in her stomach. It was a trick she'd become good at, replacing frightened-empty with food-empty.

"Let's go for a walk on the beach after breakfast," Elke said.

"That's a nice idea," Dwight replied, lighting his third cigarette.

Leilah slid lower in her chair, the churn in her tummy shifting from hunger to worry. She sensed Jack Bertram everywhere, in the reflection of the glass that encompassed Wimpy's outside section, in the distant laughter of teenagers in the skate park, in the sour taste of her breath whenever she thought of him. "Can we go to the amusement park at the end of the beach?" she asked. "I want to ride the Sky Way." Leilah figured that if Jack Bertram was on the beach, he wouldn't see her in the sky.

"Of course, we can," Dwight said, watching as Leilah rearranged the table sauces so the labels all faced the same way. "Will be nice to see the old flat again."

The same lady who'd served her a year ago was still at the ticket stand, not that she recognised Leilah, one face out of thousands. "You old enough to go on that ride?" she asked when Leilah approached the kiosk and asked for three swing chair passes.

"Yes," Leilah replied as confidently as she could. "And anyway, my parents are with me. They're over there." She turned and pointed at Elke and Dwight, who were leaning against the railing of the circling tea-cups, Elke saying something about something, Dwight staring into the distance as if he were standing alone.

"Those are your parents?" the white lady asked.

"Yes," Leilah said, irritated by this crumpled woman whose office was the size of a Portaloo. "Now, can I get my tickets?" Leilah made a false smile, her teeth clenched and exposed, and she realised this was the first time she'd been rude to a stranger.

"Off with you," the lady said flatly once she'd printed off three pink tickets from her little ticket-spitting machine.

"Where's my change?" Leilah asked, her confidence growing. "I gave you a twenty, the tickets are only six Rand each."

"You think you're a smart little thing, don't you?" the lady said spitefully, pushing a dirty two-rand coin through the narrow slot under her plastic shield.

"I am smart," Leilah declared, turning on her heel and

walking off as slowly as she could. Her cheeks were warm and her feet wanted to run, but she felt that she was better than the ugly old woman in the cage, and, believing that, Leilah forgot her own shadow.

The Sky Way was almost empty so Leilah stepped straight up to the ticket collector and handed him their three stubs. "Only two per chair," the guy said absently, as if he had a million better things to do.

"No problem," Leilah chirped, relieved to be given a free pass. "I'll go alone."

"No," Elke said firmly. "My daughter's only half size, surely it's okay if we go together?"

The guy looked down at Leilah and she felt him counting her centimetres one by one. "Can't one of you go with the girl, and the other go alone?"

"No," Elke said again. "We want to go together."

"Go on then," he said, no match for Elke. "But no rocking, these things aren't meant to carry more than 250kg." He looked at Dwight now, surveying his big tummy and rolling his eyes. Dwight looked down and tightened his belt a notch, his cheeks sagging with embarrassment.

"Come on," Leilah said, eager to get her dad into the sky, where his tummy wouldn't feel so heavy. She stepped between the two sets of feet painted onto the ground, and sucked in her ribs to make herself smaller. "Our chair is almost here, hurry up."

Dwight took one set of painted feet and Elke took the other, her face doing something Leilah didn't recognise. If she didn't know better, she'd have thought her mom was scared. Their chair lifted them off their feet and a small peep escaped Elke's lips as it swung backwards and forwards in the air to find its equilibrium. Leilah held onto the safety bar excitedly and peered over the edge at her feet dangling between those of her parents. Her dad was wearing his usual loafers, which closed around his heels and were in no danger of falling off. Leilah had taken off her slipslops so they wouldn't drop but Elke had forgotten to take off hers. Her mom's toes had clenched into balls, as if hanging onto her cheap shoes were like hanging onto life itself. As they lifted higher into the air, Elke's hands on the bar tightened, so much so that her knuckles lost their blood. Leilah leaned back and looked at her. Her mother's eyes were squeezed shut and she was taking short breaths, like Leilah did when she could hear the leaves moving.

"You okay, Mom?"

"She's scared," Dwight said when Elke didn't answer. "Mum doesn't like heights."

"Oh," Leilah said, her excitement dwindling. "I didn't know that."

"Ja," Dwight said, half chuckling. "Once she tried to take Motheo down the steepest slide at the waterpark – the Kamikaze I think it was called – and when it was their turn to go, she froze. The official had to pry her fingers loose one by one before he could move her out of the way." Leilah looked at her mom again, expecting her to laugh or at least give Dwight the side-eye. But her body was still rigid, her knuckles still white. A tear was running down her left cheek, so strange and lonely that at first Leilah thought it was sweat.

"It's okay to cry," Leilah said. "By the time you're finished, we'll be on the ground again. It's only a five-minute ride."

Elke let out a loud wail at the mention of five minutes, and another tear appeared on her cheek, followed by another and another and another. Leilah worried that if her mom didn't open her eyes soon, the tears would drown her brain, but she didn't want to say anything and sat as quietly as she could, wondering why Elke agreed to join them on the highest ride in the park. A seagull glided past, but they didn't notice. Her mom was still crying with her eyes closed, and her dad was doing his best to reach around Leilah and lay an arm on Elke's shoulder without rocking the chair. Elke's body stiffened next to Leilah when Dwight's hand reached her, but softened again, along with the squeeze of her eyelids. When the chair had completed its loop and the three of them were standing, Leilah ran off to find one of the shoes that Elke's toes hadn't managed to hang onto. She found it between the popcorn and candyfloss stands, and after apologising to the owners of both, headed back to the swing chairs. There on the bench, where everyone could see them, Leilah saw something she'd never seen in public, or maybe even at home – Dwight kissing Elke on the lips, and Elke kissing him back.

Chapter 27

<u>*Mom*</u>

My mom told me she swore when I was born, so loud that the other moms complained and the nurse had to tell her to zip it. She says it's the most pain she'd ever been in, and when the pain stopped, it was the best she'd ever felt. It took thirty-six hours for me to come out. I think that's because I was scared to be alone, or maybe my mom was scared to have me.

Elke (that's my mom's name) is different to how I imagine other moms to be. She burps all the time, even when there are people around, and she doesn't know how to plait my hair. Last year she left me alone for three months. It was supposed to be six, but I guess she felt guilty and came home. I'm glad she came home. I don't really like my mom, but when she's not there I feel like I'm walking through the deep end of the pool.

My mom's German, and in Germany they eat this dark bread called Pumpernickel. It's sour and dense and when my mom leaves the bag open and the crust goes dry, it cuts my gums and makes them blead. She always leaves the bag open, even though I keep reminding her to seal it. She must like stale bread more than she likes fresh bread. I just wish she wouldn't use it to make my sandwiches.

I don't think my mom wants me to be German because she never taught me how to speak it. She says she tried but

I kept asking her to speak to me in English. I don't believe that because if she really wanted me to speak her language, she would have taught me as a baby, before I could talk back. My mom doesn't lie but when she thinks she knows something, she tells stories that fit into what she thinks she knows. This must be the best part about being a grown-up – telling stories that everyone believes.

We've changed houses three times since we moved to Durban at the beginning of last year. My mom's very good at moving. She packed and unpacked everything while my dad was at work and I was at school, and it never took more than three days for all our furniture to be in the right place and our posters all to be hung. We don't have any photos up (my mom says she doesn't like looking at herself every day) but we've got good posters. My mom laminated them so they wouldn't tear when we moved. The posters have followed us everywhere, and her banana trees too, all the way from Cape Town, and from house to house in Durban. I don't know where she kept the trees when we lived in a flat on the beach last year, but after a week of living in our first house in Westville, they were planted and looked almost as green as they had in Cape Town.

One of our banana trees she stole from a place called Transkei, before I was even born. She told me Transkei is on the same side of South Africa as Durban, and it's got steep cliffs that end in the ocean. She wrapped the tree (it was still small then) in a blanket and when she and my dad were stopped on the road by the cops, she held the wrapped tree in her lap and pretended to feed it with a bottle. That's how they got the tree back down to Cape Town, and I think it's also why the cops let them go, because they thought she had a baby. My mom tells that story almost as much as she tells the story of swearing in the hospital. Elke's good at telling stories, just as good as she is at gardening.

<u>Dad</u>

People say my dad and I don't look the same, but we are the same. I can tell my mom wants me to be more like her, someone who screams when they're hurting, but I prefer to keep quiet, just like my dad. My dad taught me to think before I speak, and to say nothing at all if I really don't feel like it. In Westville, being quiet doesn't make you popular but in Cape Town, I thought I was being a good girl for thinking instead of talking. Thinking doesn't hurt people.

This year I'm going to try and talk more. Maybe if I learn more words for things, I'll get better at saying cool stuff and make some friends. My dad doesn't have any friends in Westville either. He only has the people at work, and they never come over to visit him. When my mom went away, my dad and I were friends. Dwight (my dad) taught me how to play chess, which is a good game for people who don't talk much, and we watched TV together, mostly cricket. My dad explained all the rules to me so now I understand cricket better than most girls do, not that I know much about most girls.

While my mom was swearing and I was being born, my dad was studying for his accounting exam. He's the first person in his family to be something other than a cleaner or a teacher, so I understand why he needed to study. But my mom tells that part of the story like my dad did something wrong. I don't know what else she expected him to do for thirty-six hours. That's a long time to sit in another room and listen to someone screaming.

I had a friend once called Frankie who said I looked like a white girl with a tan. I think she meant I don't look like my dad, who's darker than all the other dads in Westville. But when I look in the mirror, all I see is my dad. We have the same wide nose and wide nostrils. We both have big hands. His fingers are longer than mine but that's because I'm still growing. We both have curly hair that goes even curlier when we swim. My first proper memory of my dad has a pool in it. We went for a family holiday in Swaziland, and there was a pool at the place where we were staying. I wanted to put my toes in the water because I'd never seen a pool before and my mom asked my dad to go with me. I got to the shallow end and started walking down the stairs, and suddenly there were no stairs left and my head was under the water. My eyes were open and it was so blue, I didn't notice I'd stopped breathing. I'd never seen so much of one colour all at once. Suddenly my dad was behind me, in all of his clothes, dragging me out. He couldn't swim either so it must have been scary for him to help me. When we built our own pool in Cape Town, he bought me inflatable arm bands and on weekends he'd sit at the shallow end with me, hanging onto the wall and kicking his feet behind him to practice. He's still not very good at swimming but at least he can make it to the deep end now, without having to use a boogie board.

The only thing I do that my dad doesn't do is talk back to my mom. I think he loves her more than she loves him. I *don't think there's anything wrong with that but I do wish Elke would hug my dad more. He loves to be hugged.*

Chapter 28

Leilah was getting comfortable with high school. She could walk easily between her different classes and she knew three toilets she could use at different ends of the school. Most importantly, she'd found a shaded spot on a stairwell where no one really went. She ate her lunch there and spent the rest of break in the library. Now that she had her places to go, Leilah actually liked the spiderweb of her new school; with so many nooks and crannies, she'd managed to avoid Frankie completely. She'd caught a safe glimpse of her in assembly one time, a couple of rows ahead. Frankie was sitting cross-legged on the floor like all the grade eights did, but her head sat a few centimetres taller than everyone else's. Leilah had spent the morning hymns looking at those parts of her lost friend that she could see, the blonde crown of her head, the sharp angles of her knees, the cleft in her chin when she turned to look left or right. Leilah wondered if she was looking for her, hoped that she was. As angry as she was at Frankie, she couldn't help but daydream about her, her thin lips and sharp tongue, the way she made Leilah feel like she belonged to someone.

It was the Monday that Miss Foley would return their essays and Leilah approached her homeroom class with cloudy thoughts of failure and embarrassment. She walked head-down to her desk and sat down quietly, immediately leaning into her bag and taking out books and pens she could look busy with. Something caught her eye as she came back up, new names scratched into the lid of her desk, the cuts in the dirty wood still fresh and pale.

Leilah+Frankie1998.

She didn't recognise the names at first. When Leilah imagined she and Frankie side by side, it was always Frankie who came first, so it took a moment to understand that it was *her* carved there, visible to anyone that passed. Leilah looked around to see if anyone was watching her but the few students who got there as early as she did were nerds, buried in their books or repacking their Space Cases. Leilah ran her fingers along the two names, thankfully not too big, and up in the left-hand corner so that Leilah would still see them when her work books were open. She hated and missed Frankie for doing it like that.

Leilah opened her desk and there in the centre was a badly folded note. Leilah grabbed it and instinctively excused herself to go to the bathroom. No one heard so she got up and walked slowly out the classroom, picking up her pace as soon as she hit the corridor. The closest bathroom was at the entrance to the Matric quad and she usually avoided that area if she could; the seventeen- and eighteen-year-olds looked like creatures from another planet. But she went there now, only vaguely aware of the tall and confident figures that lingered around the quad, sharing weekend stories and laughing like the world was something they could have.

The toilet had one empty stall and Leilah slipped in and sat on the loo without closing the lid. The note had "Leilah Jacobs" written on the front, smudged. Frankie must have touched her name before the ink dried. Leilah opened it carefully, and smoothed the fold lines before she started reading. *Meet me at the high school recycling bins after school. They're behind the petrol station. Come alone.* There was a badly drawn smiley face at the bottom of the page that hardened Leilah's giddiness into anger. She tore the note up into little pieces and, cursing Frankie for once again forcing her hand, sulked back to class.

Leilah had all but forgotten about the essay when Miss Foley approached her desk and lay it down with a wink. "Your parents are all right," she said before walking off to hand out the rest of the class's. Leilah flipped to the last of her stapled-together pages, and landed her eyes on the *B* written in red ink. *Good start*, Miss Foley had commented below the grade and Leilah might have felt good reading it, had she not been thinking about Frankie and her demanding note. The rest of the day dragged. Leilah kept trying to imagine what could happen behind the petrol station, but never got further than seeing Frankie in her new uniform, standing tall like she was the boss. In the end it was Frankie's bossiness that convinced Leilah to go. The same bossiness she'd followed into class a year earlier, that stubborn crown on Frankie's head.

The petrol station was full of moms filling their tanks, and she had to weave through them, looking for the shadows like a thief. All the hot air stank like petrol, and Leilah thought she might faint. She almost wanted to. Ambulances coming to rescue her would make Frankie feel as bad as she deserved to feel. There was a big empty chamber behind the station, unlit except for the sun that reached weakly into the entrance and lost its way just before the bins. Frankie was standing between the light and the dark, her nose and the tips of her shoes letting Leilah know she was there.

"You came," Frankie said, stepping forward enough for Leilah to see her properly.

"Ja, I came," Leilah said, keeping a good distance between them. "What else was I supposed to do?"

"Not come," Frankie said smiling. "You stopped coming to school, didn't you?"

"Because of you," Leilah retorted, her anger refreshed.

"Because of that boy in the pool," Frankie said back, unwavering in her guiltlessness. "You got skinny," she continued, taking another step forward and surveying Leilah from top to bottom. "Don't they feed you at homeschool?"

"How'd you know I've been home-schooling?" Leilah asked, hooking her fingers into the straps of her backpack to steady herself.

"Your mom phoned to tell me," Frankie said, kicking a rusty Coke can with her foot. "She said I shouldn't worry about you disappearing because you'd come back. So, are you back?"

"Back where?" Leilah asked, daring Frankie to explain things Leilah knew she couldn't. She was mad at Elke for calling Frankie without her permission.

"Just *back*," Frankie replied, her foot searching for something else to kick. "You know what I mean." Leilah started rocking from one foot to the other, full of things she wanted to say but unsure of how to speak and growing increasingly uneasy in the dark room of rubbish. "I'm sorry," Frankie said, just as Leilah wanted to run. It was the first time Frankie had ever apologised to her and it sounded good. Leilah wondered if those who never apologise are actually the best at it.

"You should be sorry," Leilah spat back, not ready to give Frankie the upper hand. "You broke the one rule of being a best friend and told my secret. *My* secret. So, fuck you, Frankie. You had no right to do that." She'd never sworn at someone so directly; she wanted Frankie to wilt under the hard sound. But Frankie didn't wilt. *Fuck you* bounced off her like a raindrop. "My parents were sleeping in separate beds until just the other day," Leilah carried on, determined to make a dent. "My brother said he'd fly back from Germany and kill Otto when my parents told him about us, and every week I have to spill my guts to a stranger. She's a nice lady, but still." Leilah had to stop talking. Her head felt too heavy on her neck and her new bra was making it hard to breath.

"So, your mom and dad are back in the same bed now?" Frankie asked.

"Yes."

"And your brother hasn't murdered anyone yet?"

"No."

"And you get to spill your guts to a nice lady every week?"

"Yes... Frankie, what's your point?"

"My point is I'm not sorry about telling your mom what I told her. But I am sorry for telling you to keep your dad a secret. I shouldn't have done that."

"Why do you feel bad about that but not bad about telling my biggest secret? How would you feel if I told yours?"

"Who would you tell?" Frankie asked, taking another step forward. She was only an arm's length from Leilah now.

"Your mom. The school. You'd be the laughing stock of Kingston Girls' High."

"I don't think anyone at this school cares that I pee my bed," Frankie said. "And I know my mom wouldn't care. She'd just hate you for telling her."

Leilah couldn't name the smile Frankie was trying to pull but she looked less plain than usual, her small eyes and narrow jaw full of what Leilah abruptly recognised as sadness. "I'm sure someone would care," Leilah said limply.

"Maybe in your family, Leilah, but not in mine. Some parents are better when they know stuff. My parents aren't those parents." Frankie was looking at the ground like Leilah usually did; her blonde crown dulled in the weak light.

"And you think my parents are better now that they know?' Leilah asked. "My mom's even crazier than usual."

"Maybe she is crazy," Frankie said, looking up. "But at least she thinks you're interesting."

"That's just a nice way of saying she's nosy," Leilah said, running out of steam. She didn't want Frankie to get away with her betrayal but if this was a game of out-talking the other person, Frankie would definitely win.

"Want to share a cigarette?" Frankie asked, drinking from Leilah's weariness, like she'd always known how to do. "I've gone back to Stuyvesant's."

"Okay," Leilah said, too tired and hungry to argue. "But only if they're Stuyvie Blues."

"Obviously," Frankie said. "Let's go behind the bins. We'll get into trouble if a prefect sees us in uniform."

"Since when do you worry about getting into trouble?" Leilah asked the back of Frankie's head, following her closely into the darkness.

"Since now," Frankie replied. It was even damper and darker behind the bins, and Leilah began to shake.

"Don't worry," Frankie said, striking a match. "This will brighten things up." She kept the match burning but didn't light a cigarette, looking at Leilah through the amber glow instead, as if waiting for her to say something.

"Why do you feel bad about that stuff with my dad?" Leilah asked, the flame giving her some confidence.

"I don't know," Frankie said. "I just do. If I could go back and say something different, I would."

"Like what?"

"Like, *that's why you're prettier than the rest of these dorks.*"

The match went out before Frankie could see Leilah blush. "Do you know I hate the dark?" Leilah asked, stalling so her cheeks could cool.

"I know. But sometimes the dark is the best place to be. No one can see you."

"Maybe, but could you please light another match, and also one of those cigarettes you promised me?"

"Got somewhere to be?" Frankie asked, and Leilah could picture her smirking in the dark.

"Yes, if you must know. My mom's going to be here any minute to pick me up. And I have homework to do. Some of us actually care about school, and getting good grades."

Frankie went quiet, a sure sign of her hurt, and Leilah had to hold back from apologising. Poking at Frankie's insecurities was not nearly as satisfactory as she'd hoped. "How is school going for you?" she asked, replacing guilt with interest.

"Ag, the same. I'll never be as smart as you. But that's okay. I've got my personality to go on."

Leilah smiled, grabbing the moment of darkness before Frankie struck a new match. There was a cigarette dangling from her thin lips, which she lit before passing it to Leilah. It had been a while since Leilah had smoked, not since she last time she saw Frankie; she wondered if she could still pull it off and look like a cool girl. She drew on the filter and watched as the cigarette's tip flared up, and with slight trepidation sucked the smoke into her lungs. It went down smoothly, meeting a need in Leilah that she didn't know she had, and she exhaled with all the sophistication she could muster.

"It suits you," Frankie said, still holding the lit match and watching Leilah carefully.

"I know," Leilah said, taking another drag.

The match reached its end, and everything blackened.

"Want me to light another one?" Frankie asked, close enough so that Leilah could smell her breath.

"It's okay," Leilah said. "Not seeing isn't so bad." Leilah felt Frankie's long fingers reaching for hers through the dark, and for a moment or two, she let her take them.

Glass Tower

Acknowledgements

I would like to thank the following people for their help with this book: Robert Peett, my publisher, for his guidance, patience, and belief in the story I wanted to write. Karen Jennings, creator of the Island Prize for Debut Fiction from Africa. If not for the prize and her unwavering support, this book might never have seen the light of day. My editors Susan Mann and Martha Evans for cheering me on while offering invaluable critique. Annette Greene, my agent, for encouraging me to give Frankie her own part. My dear friend Simone Schultze for conceptualising the cover with me and bringing it to life. Oliver my husband for braving the many highs and lows that accompanied the writing of this book, and still liking me at the end.